DISCARD

A
Second
Life

A Second Life

Bob Williams

Another Quality Book Published By:

LEGACY BOOK PUBLISHING

1883 Lee Road, Winter Park, FL 32789

www.LEGACYBOOKPUBLISHING.com

A Second Life

Published by:
LEGACY Book Publishing
1883 Lee Road
Winter Park, Florida 32789
www.LegacyBookPublishing.com

2017© Bob Williams
Printed in the United States
ISBN: 978-1-937952-99-0

Cover Design by Gabriel H. Vaughn

Dedication

In memory of my father, Bob, and mother, Georgia, who exemplified "The Greatest Generation."

.

Acknowledgements

On two occasions I have had an idea pop into my head that caused me to lose sleep. The ideas grew, resulting in more lost sleep. It was my good friend, Steve Leggett, who encouraged me to put my thoughts on paper. He reminded me on several occasions that writing is more about process, and he was right. Steve has always been my first reader and has provided important feedback concerning the storyline.

I would like to thank my wife, Linda, for reading drafts and for providing me encouragement, particularly when I lost patience. I am very grateful that Bev Cox, Sandy Glaize, and Penny Leggett accepted my request to be readers. They provided invaluable feedback and editing skills. They helped broaden my perspective of characters and events in the story.

There are times when I cannot read my own writing. I am, therefore, thankful that Missi Feyer is still willing to type the various drafts of my manuscripts. I also enjoy the feedback I receive when talking with Missi about the book.

I appreciate the assistance I received from the Holocaust Memorial Resource and Education Center located in Maitland, Florida. The Center was invaluable in my research concerning the Dachau Concentration Camp. I never sensationalized any part of the story regarding characters who were imprisoned in Dachau. The descriptions and activities of the camp were taken from actual accounts shared by survivors. On a few occasions, however, I took the liberty to use my own judgment when describing certain aspects of daily life.

A special thanks goes to Legacy Book Publishing. I would especially like to thank Gabriel Vaughn and Tayler Woelcke for their collaboration in publishing my book.

CHAPTER ONE

Part I

Cambridgeshire, England, 1944

It is often said that you only have one life to live. But maybe, just maybe, some people have a second life.

I had spent the last two months in Jedburgh, Scotland, receiving extensive training in preparation for a secret mission in which a group of us would be dropped behind enemy lines. The drop would take place prior to the major land assault that was being planned by the American and British generals.

Reality was beginning to set in for the first time. I would soon be placed in combat and could possibly lose my life. After a night of drinking in a local English pub, I questioned if my life was even worth saving. For me, enlisting in the army at the age of seventeen was the ultimate escape from a life I found unbearable.

During training, all of the men in camp expressed excitement over the prospect of being dropped behind enemy lines. We were going to be the frontline troops who would meet face-to-face with the evil Nazi regime.

I did well in training and was often singled out for my accomplishments. I was not particularly happy when I was told to become an expert on the use of the Type B Mark II radio. Qualifying as an expert on the rifle range, I couldn't imagine why I was chosen to carry a radio.

*

Toward the end of my training, I met with a group of officers who asked several questions about my training, and my commitment to defeat the enemy. Although it became apparent I was being interviewed, I couldn't understand the purpose. Three days later, I was again taken into a small room with three high ranking officers. I learned of the existence of the Office of Strategic Service. The office was part of the U.S. Intelligence Agency. The mission of the Office of Strategic Service (OSS) was to link up and coordinate the resistance groups in sabotage and guerilla warfare against the German occupying forces prior to and during the invasion. A key member of the special three-member teams would be a paratrooper who could operate the B2 radio.

I eagerly agreed to become a member of OSS and left for training in Jedburgh, Scotland. The training was intense and physically demanding. Many times I doubted I was the right person for this type of mission. The physical training, however, became easier as I got in better shape. Many hours were spent jumping out of planes and studying maps. I received six weeks of intense instruction in French. I carried a long list of French words and phrases in my pocket, and practiced them constantly. I also continued my radio training and learned code language designed to confuse the enemy.

Halfway through training three-person teams were assigned, consisting of an American, a British and a French soldier. Two were officers and the other member was an enlisted man. Being a Private First Class, I occupied the enlisted slot. The Brit was a tall, red-haired man in his early thirties, who knew his stuff and enjoyed teasing the rest of us about our accents and appearance. I took a liking to him immediately. The Frenchman had escaped to England and couldn't wait to return to his home country and wreak havoc on the Germans. He was short, muscular and generally had a cigarette hanging from his lips. While in Scotland, all of the teams that were formed were referred to as Jedburghs. The term stuck, and became a sense of pride for all of us. After Jedburgh, all 280 of us were transported to Milton Hall in Cambridgeshire, England, to continue our training. This time, however, the training was specific to our mission. For the first time, I began to feel a combination of excitement and anxiety. We had trained for so long that we couldn't wait to put our skills to work. The realization that we were going to be dropped behind enemy lines began to sink in.

My team knew its stuff. We practiced and rehearsed every part for a week, since we weren't sure when the actual drop day would occur. Many factors needed to be considered before making that decision. One big factor was weather. Another component involved was contact with the French resistance fighters in France.

Colonel Hardaway, an American attached to OSS, called for a meeting at 0900 with the three teams that had been practicing together. We all squeezed in the small room adjacent to his temporary office and sat on folding chairs in three rows, facing the one chair where the Colonel sat.

The Colonel overflowed his chair. He was a big man with a permanent five o'clock shadow. Putting out his cigarette, he turned the page of a large flip chart located behind him.

He stood, placed both hands on his belt, and said, "I know that all nine of you are familiar with your mission. The mission will take place tomorrow so I'll go over the details one more time to make sure there are no questions."

This was the first time we had been given an actual date. We turned and looked at each other. Nobody yelled or made a comment. Everything we had done for the last two months had become real.

"As you know, the Germans have a prison near the town of Amiens. Most of the people being held in the prison are captured resistance fighters. These fighters have created hell for the Germans. The intelligence we have received suggests time may be running out for them. We have reports of executions, with the likelihood of more to come. I want to bust these people out. We are a few months away from our major assault in France. If you are successful, these resistance fighters can create all kinds of chaos for those fucking Germans. Their disruption can distract the Germans, which will help when our major assault takes place. Do you understand the importance of this mission?"

"Yes Sir," we all responded.

"All of our teams have one radio man. I'm changing this: PFC Thomas will be the only one with a radio."

This was a major change. In all of our training, each team had a radio man.

"The reason for only one radio man is explosives. The French resistance fighters told us they have limited explosives to blow up the prison walls. The other radio people will be dropped with explosives in their backpacks. You will be dropped at night. At this point the weather looks good. There will be some easterly winds so you may encounter some drift from the drop zone. There will be resistance fighters there to meet you, and they will insure that you make it to safety. We have been in constant radio communication with them.

"Up to this point, the Germans have been content with sitting on their asses. The fighters report that there have been limited patrols in the drop zone. Once you meet up with the fighters, you will coordinate efforts to blow up the prison walls and free as many prisoners as possible. I do expect to have casualties. The more prisoners we can free, the better. All of you are familiar with the pickup area. You all know how to signal the pilot when you want him to land. If for some reason Thomas' radio is not working, you can still go to the pickup zone every night for three days. We will be running reconnaissance every night looking for your pickup signals. If something goes wrong, go to the pickup zone. We are not positive how many Germans may be in the area. You will need to rely on the resistance fighters. I want to see all of you return from this mission. It is dangerous but the reward is great. If possible, return all of the wounded. If not, bring back identification. You will muster tomorrow at 1300 at the airstrip. Do you have any questions?"

Nobody said a word. All of us stood and made our way back to our temporary quarters, an old boarding house near the airstrip.

The officers on our teams went to their respective rooms. I shared a small room with the British soldier who would be packing explosives on our drop. I went to my duffel bag to pull out some paper. The British soldier, known as Wilson, was sitting at a small desk in our room, "Are you going to write a letter to your girlfriend?" he asked.

I flopped on my bunk, placed the paper on my lap and responded, "I'm actually going to write a letter to my wife."

Acting surprised he commented, "I didn't know you were married."

"I haven't been married long," I acknowledged, "I don't wear a wedding band because we have been in training." Suddenly feelings of guilt and the uncertainties of my marriage started to overcome me, I hoped Wilson's questions would end soon.

"I'm going to write my girlfriend too," Wilson added, as he tapped his pen on the desk. "I'm planning on marrying her when the war is over. We've known each other for years."

"She writes me faithfully every day. I haven't opened all the letters because I haven't had time."

I leaned back on my pillow as I pulled out the letter I had received two weeks ago from Diane. The letter was short. It was primarily an update on what she had been doing. The last sentence read, "I miss you." It was signed Diane. Although we were married, neither one of us had said, "I love you." Our circumstances were complicated. Still, I was hoping she would have said something more in her letter. I had only received three letters and they all basically sounded the same.

I grasped the paper as I began to write her. I couldn't say anything about the mission, which would take place tomorrow. I did say that soon all of my training would be put to use. I told her that I thought about her, and that I had dream about the river last week. I hoped this would bring a smile to her face. When I finished, I wasn't sure how I wanted to sign it. I sat there, staring at what I had written. Finally, I picked up my pen and wrote, "Love you, John." Then I walked across the base to drop the letter into the temporary mailbox.

Back in my room, I cleaned my rifle and packed my backpack. I also checked out the radio. Although I knew I wouldn't sleep, I needed to close my eyes and try to rest. The mission would be dangerous, and there was a chance some of us might not be coming back. I tried to think about other things, but that thought kept creeping into my mind. I had confidence in the mission because I knew that our training had prepared us to carry it out. After tossing and turning in bed for hours, I pulled out my French words and phrases list and silently practiced.

The next morning, the nine of us headed to the mess hall for breakfast. Unlike other mornings, there was no joking and teasing. It was a cool morning, with a pleasant breeze blowing through the mess hall. A few of our fellow Jedburghs joined our table. Although none of us talked about the upcoming mission, I was positive the other Jedburghs realized something was up.

The base was always a place of constant activity and today was no different. Everyone knew there would come a day when soldiers would be assaulting the beaches to push toward Berlin. I assumed we were a few months away from an actual invasion. I never dreamed I would be behind enemy lines on March 11th.

At 1300 hours, our mission team was waiting in the hangar next to the runway. In typical military fashion, we hurried to the hangar only to wait. The Colonel conducted yet another review. Although we would encounter a stiff wind, there was no change of plans. He emphasized that if we got separated, it was important to quickly get to our designated meeting place.

The drop area was a large field adjacent to a farm. The intelligence from the French resistance fighters indicated it was relatively safe. Men would meet us and then lead us to a barn where we would develop our prison escape plan. We would wear our respective military uniforms, which meant we were truly part of a joint military action.

At sunset, chow was delivered to us. I drank so much coffee that I kept heading to the latrine every fifteen minutes. I wasn't the only one; all nine of us were pacing back and forth, making side trips to relieve ourselves.

The Colonel called us together when it was time to load up. We gathered up our gear and made our way to the B-24. Before boarding, each man applied blackout to his face. When I saw the other two enlisted men carrying their backpacks full of explosives, I was glad to have the radio on my back. Within minutes, we were crossing the English Channel and heading to Amiens. Although there were no reports of German aircraft in the area, we all knew that could change in a heartbeat. None of us spoke. The Frenchman lit up a cigarette and began humming a song that sounded like a hymn. I tried to keep my mind blank, but the more I tried to keep my mind free of thoughts, the more I thought of my father. What would he think? In his eyes, I never did anything right. I was not a real man like my older brother. To keep these thoughts at bay, I started rehearsing my French.

When a light came on, we were close to the drop zone. I wished I had gone to the bathroom but it was too late now. We stood and attached our lines. The captain gave a thumbs up sign and we all did the same. I was next to last to exit the plane. As soon as my chute opened, I began to drift to the right. It was a full moon and visibility was good.

I could see the other parachutes to my left. I continued, however, to drift further to the right. I could see the outline of a barn further to the left. At least I could see where we were to meet up. As I slowly drifted further right, I saw flashes lighting up the ground to my left. At first I didn't know what was happening, but then I realized there was a fire-fight taking place on the ground. Suddenly a truck's headlights came on, and I could see Germans firing at the men on the field. The fire was returned as the men fell to the ground. More troops jumped out of the truck and began running toward the field. Then a flare went up, revealing a sky full of parachutes descending toward the ground. I was horrified when I saw German soldiers running toward the parachutes and firing at them. Within seconds there was a loud explosion, causing a fireball to fall to the ground. This was one of the men carrying explosives. I could see that a few of the men had made it to the ground. I also witnessed two men shot in midair. Although I was further right, I could see a soldier running towards me. The flare had been extinguished, but the full moon had allowed the soldier to keep track of me. I could see him stop to lift his rifle. I then felt a burning sensation on my back. The radio was struck and the heat from the round and the radio burned my back. I tried to get my pistol out of the holster, and in the process it fell to the earth. The German was underneath me, waiting for me to hit the ground.

I then saw another man come out of the tree line and shoot at the German. The German stumbled backwards but managed to lift up his rifle to return fire, striking the man in the face. As I hit the ground, my parachute drifted over the German and covered him. He was struggling to free himself from the parachute. I detached the chute and threw the pack off my back. I grabbed my rifle, which was attached to my pack, and fired into the parachute. The German, hidden by the parachute, fell.

I could hear more rifles being fired in the distance. I also saw Germans forming in front of the truck. I ran over to check on the man who had saved my life. He no longer had a face. He was wearing clothes that a farmer might wear, and I assumed he was one of the French resistance fighters. I looked at my surroundings, and I wasn't sure what to do. The mission was fucked. I knew I just needed to get away. Without another thought, I began to strip the clothes off my body, including my underwear with my name stamped on it. I put my clothes on the Frenchman and his clothes on me. Luckily, we were nearly the same size. His shoes were a little tight but everything else fit. There was blood on his shirt, with pieces of flesh embedded in the fabric. I grabbed his rifle and glanced back at the dead body that was now me. A cloud hiding the full moon gave me a few moments of darkness. In the distance, I could hear Germans running. I started to run but stopped. I wasn't sure what to do with my dog tag, and I could hear the Germans approaching. I hurriedly took off my dog tag and placed it around what was left of the Frenchman's neck. I then sprinted toward the tree line. As I reached the trees, I spotted a road about fifty yards away. I stumbled through the woods, tripping twice on tree roots. When I got to the road, I wasn't sure which direction to go in. I remembered the maps of Amiens and the surrounding countryside. My best guess was that the town was to the left, so I turned right and ran as fast as I could. When I grew tired, I would walk about twenty yards before starting to run again.

I saw headlights in the distance; I dove into a small ditch next to the road. The truck that passed was transporting German soldiers. I thought to myself that the person who reported that this area was safe was full of shit.

I reached a crossroad, and decided to take the smaller gravel road. The road had several large holes that had been formed by the rain. I knew that I was deep in farmland; I could see crops in the fields and cows grazing in a pasture. I figured I had covered over two miles. I spotted a small farmhouse that had an old truck parked in front. As I got closer to the house, I saw that a light of some sort was on, but I wasn't sure what to do next. The French would probably welcome an American, but I also knew that I would likely scare someone if I just knocked on the door. I waited out by the truck a few minutes, trying to decide what to do.

A dog appeared and started to bark. I tried my best to calm the dog by saying "good boy." The dog started barking louder, and I then heard a second dog begin to bark. I almost started running when the front door opened. A small woman with dark hair that fell across her eye was standing in the doorway. She kept saying, "Joseph." I walked toward the door and she again said, "Joseph."

As I got closer, she screamed and ran inside. She grabbed a small boy who looked about two years old, and ran to the back of the house, falling to her knees. She clutched the boy and began screaming, "Les vetements." She kept screaming that phrase over and over again. Then she started screaming something else; I wasn't sure what it was. She started pointing at me and screaming, "Le mari." I was trying to make sense out of her hysteria. Although my French was limited, it hit me what she was saying. I was wearing her husband's clothes.

CHAPTER TWO

Allentown, Pennsylvania, March 15, 1943
One year earlier —

I couldn't wait to attend Allentown High School. My older brother, James Thomas, was the ladies' man at school. I naturally thought this would reap certain rewards for me. James was good looking and knew it. He always knew what to say around girls and I was amazed by how silly girls could be when they were around him.

It didn't take long to see that his popularity with the ladies did not translate to his teachers. When they took roll and called my name, John Thomas, they often followed up with a comment about my brother's lackluster academics and expressed hope that I would do better. Most would say something like, "I hope you are a better student." James was more interested in girls, did very little homework, and frequently disrupted the class to the point that he was a regular visitor at the principal's office.

When my brother finally graduated from high school, I was glad for several reasons. During my junior year, I no longer had to contend with his reputation. After graduation, James had enhanced his reputation as the "wild one" through bar fights and time spent in jail. When the war broke out, it was suggested by the judge that he enlist. Two months later, James headed to Paris Island, South Carolina.

I was just glad that I no longer had to share a room with him.

Although James would stand up for me if anyone gave me trouble, it bothered me that he had a need to torment me. He loved to rough house at home. He was bigger, stronger and he wanted me to know it. I had the cuts and bruises to show for it. While my mother often yelled at James, my father would say, "Let them be."

My father admired everything about James, who he considered to be a man's man. My father would actually brag to the other men at Bethlehem Steel, because he saw a lot of himself in James.

My father teased me for studying and wanting to do well in school. He encouraged me to be more like James.

During the Depression, my father was laid off for a few months and his drinking got worse. He was an alcoholic who got mean when he drank. In the past, when he got angry with my mother he would hit her. Once James struck him, but it never happened again. My mother tried to keep the peace, but was quick to give up. She always seemed tired and sad.

In my junior year of high school, things were better. James was in the Marine Corps. Since my father came home from work exhausted, drinking a six-pack of beer sent him to bed early, and I was no longer hassled about doing schoolwork. My room became a refuge for quiet and calm.

I enjoyed my English class at school. Mrs. Turner had all of us write a poem about a character we were to create from Canterbury Tales. Most students complained about the assignment, but I immediately went home and created a Merry Minstrel character. The following week, Mrs. Turner decided to read my poem in class, causing me great embarrassment. A few students gave me the "brown nose" signal. After class, Diane Clark walked up to me and commented,

"I really liked your poem. How long did it take you to write it?"

I turned and responded with confidence, gloating that she had even asked me. "A couple of hours," I said.

"I spent three days on mine," she followed, "even copying a few lines from another poem."

I had known Diane Clark since the fourth grade. She was the quiet girl who stood back and let others do the talking. In high school, she came out of her shell. She was five-four with long wavy brown hair. She never wore makeup and wouldn't be caught dead wearing a tight skirt. Her dad was a Baptist minister, which explained the natural look and loose dresses. She never attended dances and avoided the popular diner.

As we walked toward our lockers, I offered to help her with her writing. "Just let me know; I'm available when you are."

She smiled and said, "That would be wonderful. I don't like English class. Why do we have to read all that stuff? I have absolutely no interest in any of it."

"Some of it is really good," I interjected. "You just have to be in the right mood."

Diane shrugged her shoulders as she opened her locker. "I guess I'm never in that kind of mood," she murmured.

As we got our books from the locker, I turned to walk down the hall when Diane asked if I wanted to walk her home.

Gasping for breath, I said, "Sure. I don't have to work today."

"I could use your help with my books," she said with a smile.

When she started to hand me a few books, I took all of them from her. I had never walked a girl home from school before. Most days after school I was usually in a hurry to get to work at my neighbor's grocery store located near my house.

I had no clue where Diane lived. We walked in the opposite direction of my house and turned down several streets. I had to shift the books to my other arm. Diane did not offer conversation, but when I asked her a question, she would answer. She did ask about my notorious brother. We talked about summer plans and the events surrounding the war. She was not aware that James had enlisted in the Marine Corps and said her older brother had failed his physical.

She stopped in front of a house with a white picket fence around it and took her books.

She touched my shoulder gently and thanked me for walking her home. "This is the most we have ever talked," she said.

"You're right. We've had the same classes but just never sat near each other."

Why had I made such a dumb remark? I thought to myself. *We had many opportunities to talk with each other over the years. We were just kids with other things on our mind.*

I heard the screen door bang open and saw Reverend Clark walking by the porch rail. He looked unhappy.

I said, "Good afternoon, Reverend Clark." He didn't acknowledge me.

Loudly he said, "Diane, get inside! I don't want to see you with this boy. Do you understand?"

Diane looked pensively at her father and replied, "Yes, sir."

"Reverend Clark, I was just walking Diane home from school."

Angrily he shouted, "I told you, I don't want to see you at my house!"

As I turned to walk home, I heard him say to Diane, "I don't want you around that no count Thomas family!"

CHAPTER THREE

Amiens, France, March 16, 1944

All night long, I could hear the French woman crying. She took her son in the bedroom and locked the door. I wasn't sure what I should do. It would be dangerous to get back out on the road. I was tired, confused, and unable to make a decision. I collapsed on the floor next to an old couch. With the couch supporting my back, I bent at the waist and placed my head on my knees, feeling paralyzed over what to do next. Between sobs, the French woman yelled, "Lavie." I wasn't familiar with what the word meant but I figured it had something to do with her life. I speculated she was not only traumatized about her husband's probable death but also distraught about what action to take.

Later in the night, I nodded off, after lying down on the couch. Just before daybreak, a noise in the kitchen awakened me when I sat up I noticed a blanket had been placed over me.

The small farmhouse consisted of a kitchen and a sitting area with the couch where I had slept. It had one bedroom and a loft area, there was also electricity, but I didn't see a toilet. I assumed they used an outhouse. The woman was putting wood in an old wood-burning stove. I could smell bread baking and coffee percolating.

I stood up and walked toward the table. She motioned for me to sit down. She placed warm bread, cheese and a cup of coffee in front of me. Then she left to attend to the boy who was just waking up. When she re-entered the room, she sat down across from me. Her eyes were red and her hair was sticking to her face from all the tears. She was wearing the same clothes she had been wearing when I had arrived. She started speaking in French. I shook my head and ask if she spoke English.

She said, "Non." It seemed my French skills would be put to the test.

I spoke mainly in French with some English tossed in. I acted out a scene and gestured with my hands. Occasionally, she shook her head and acknowledged that she understood. I continued to speak broken French and acted out a shooting scene. Based upon her expression and head nodding, I realized she was aware that I was an American soldier, and that her husband had saved my life. I wasn't sure if she totally understood why I had changed into his clothes. She gestured the milking of a cow, and I understood she needed help with farm duties. I nodded and said, "Oui."

Suddenly her facial expression changed and she appeared both worried and excited. She kept repeating the same sentence. When I didn't understand, she stood up and acted like she was burying something. She wanted me to bury her husband. I said, "Allemand," which I thought was the word for German, she understood. She went to the bedroom and returned with a clean shirt and keys that I assumed were for the truck parked in front of the farmhouse.

I stared at her; she looked so young. She was probably my age, but could easily pass for fourteen. The sad and troubled look remained on her face. I put on the clean shirt and took the keys from her hand.

Before going to the truck, I made a stop at the outhouse. When I returned to the truck, the woman and boy were standing out front. Bypassing the truck, I walked toward them, pointing at her I said, "What is your name?"

She said, "Camille Bernhardt."

I then pointed toward the boy, "Joshua."

She pointed at me and I said, "John Thomas."

I turned away, but she grabbed my arm and signaled for me to wait. She ran into the house, and returned with an old blanket that had holes in it. She handed me the blanket and went back inside. In the back of the truck I saw empty milk containers and some old crates. I placed the blanket in the back and got in the cab. The truck was old but well cared for and it started immediately.

When the sun came up, everything looked different. I had no difficulty finding the main road and turned toward town. I recalled there were trees near an open pasture about three miles from the farmhouse, but I wasn't certain. The truck bounced on the old dirt and gravel road. I was worried I had gone too far and was contemplating turning around when I spotted the heavy wooded area. I parked on the side of the road and grabbed the old blanket.

The woods looked familiar. The trees were so close together it was a wonder I didn't run into one when I sprinted through them. Halfway through the wooded area, I stopped and turned my head to see if I could hear anything. After hearing only a few birds chirping, I moved toward the open field.

Emerging from the tree line, I saw my parachute directly in front of me. Walking closer, I saw the body of the man who had saved my life. He was wearing my uniform, including my boots, but in my haste I had put the pants on backwards. I pulled the parachute off the dead German, and saw that my bullet had struck him in the back of his head.

I returned to the body of the Frenchman and placed the blanket over him. I bent down to pick up the body and stopped. Suddenly I realized my dog tags were missing; I looked to see if they had fallen inside the shirt. I looked under the body and rolled it over, but my tags were nowhere to be found. I looked out over the field to see if I could see any bodies. I had drifted farther away from the others, but I thought I could see something lying in the field. Although it was still early in the day, the German soldiers would be returning. I needed to check the bodies for dog tags.

I took off in a sprint, covering a distance of over 500 yards. The first body was French and there were two dead Germans. A parachute was still attached to a British soldier; his body had no identification. I came upon the body of the American who was carrying explosives. The bag containing explosives had been removed as well as the dog tags. More bodies lay in the distance; the body of the other man carrying explosives would never be found.

I was getting anxious. I had spent too much time looking for bodies. I hoped that some of the men from our mission had made it back to the pickup area. I assumed they had removed the dog tags from the dead bodies. There were several French resistance fighters lying dead in the field. There were also dead Germans, somebody would be coming back to retrieve them.

I hurried back to the body of the man who saved my life. I placed the body over my right shoulder and walked awkwardly back to the truck. I placed the body in the back of the truck and concealed it with the milk containers and crates. I took some straw lying next to the road and sprinkled it around the bed of the truck.

I did not drive slowly this time. Getting back to the farmhouse quickly was imperative. A truck approached from the opposite direction, but it was too late to turn around. I slowed down and looked straight ahead. As the truck got closer, I saw two German soldiers in the cab of the truck. I kept thinking to myself, "I'm a French farmer."

The truck pulled directly in front of me, leaving me with no choice but to stop. The soldier on the passenger side got out and approached my truck; he spoke German. I shook my head indicating I didn't understand him, and I prayed he didn't understand French. I started speaking in French as if I could really speak the language. I did use the word "le lait" which I thought meant milk. The soldier walked to the bed of the truck and glanced at the milk containers. He then waved at the driver and got back in the truck. As they drove off, my heart was racing wildly. That had almost been disastrous.

When I pulled up in front of the farmhouse, Camille and Joshua were waiting for me, she went straight to the truck bed. I got out and stopped her before she saw the body. I shook my head and said, "Non."

After my repeated head shaking, she seemed to understand it was better not to see her husband. Tears rolled down her cheeks. Joshua was unsure what was happening, and he held tightly to his mother's leg.

Camille turned and walked away. At first, I thought she was going into the house, when I didn't follow, she motioned for me to come. She walked behind the house and kept walking until she reached an area behind the barn that was close to a huge shade tree. She then pointed to the ground indicating she wanted her husband buried here.

I drove the truck around to the burial spot. Camille and Joshua went back into the house while I located a shovel. I had difficulty penetrating the ground with the shovel. I stopped to rest on three occasions. Finally, I felt the hole was deep enough for a body. I wrapped the body tightly in the blanket with some canvas from the barn, I lowered it in the ground and filled the hole with dirt. When I was through, Camille and Joshua came over to the burial spot. She walked close to me and said, "Merci."

I just nodded. I asked her the name of her husband.

"Joseph Bernhardt," she responded.

We stood there looking at the grave. Finally, Camille bowed her head and repeated a verse that sounded like a prayer. She looked up at me with sad eyes and touched my arm, she then took Joshua's hand and walked back toward the house.

I had just buried Joseph Bernhardt, the man who had saved my life. As it would turn out, I had also just buried John Thomas.

CHAPTER FOUR

Allentown, Pennsylvania, May 13, 1943

As the school year was coming to an end, the talk around school was about the war. The senior boys were enlisting so they could leave for boot camp immediately following graduation. I was sometimes envious of the guys who would be finished with school and heading off to fight.

The disaster of walking Diane Clark home was in the past. Each day she would meet me at our lockers and talk as if nothing had happened. She may have been embarrassed, but I assumed that was her way of handling it. It seemed easier to talk with her, because she was now actually contributing to the conversation. She would always ask about my brother. I told her he was heading to the South Pacific.

I continued to work at the grocery store after school. My father would always cash my paycheck, and give me only a few dollars for spending money. No matter how much I worked, I would always get the same amount every time. My father was adamant that I should start paying my way. That same rule, however, didn't apply to my brother. When my brother was broke, he'd just asked for more. The good thing about working was that I could sometimes borrow the family car.

On Thursday, I usually didn't have to work. I hurried home, threw my books on the kitchen table and headed to my room. Being the last week of school, I had very little homework. I turned on the radio and closed my eyes.

I was startled awake when I heard my father walk into the house, I had slept for two hours. When I walked downstairs, my father was in the living room drinking the first beer of his six-pack. When mother called us to dinner, my father grabbed his beer and came to the table.

After dinner, as I helped clear the table, the phone rang. My mother answered it and said it was for me. As I walked to the phone, she said, "It's a girl."

I spoke softly so my father could not hear me. After I hung up, I asked my father if I could use the car. I told him I was going to help a girl in my class with her homework assignment.

"Your brother would do a lot more than help a girl with homework," he grunted as he gave me the keys.

Diane was spending the night with her friend, Mary Freeman. She wouldn't have been crazy enough to invite me to her own house. I always enjoyed driving the car, sometimes I just wanted to keep driving and never look back. It gave me a sense of freedom, even if only for a short time.

When I arrived in front of Mary's house, both girls were standing in the front yard. They were both wearing shorts and colorful blouses. I had never seen Diane in shorts because she always wore dresses that came down to her ankles. Maybe the shorts belonged to Mary; they were both about the same size.

We spent the next hour sitting on the front porch talking about friends and school. As it started to get dark, Mary got up and walked inside the house. Diane then motioned for me to sit on the swing with her. She scooted close to me and crossed her legs, she had great legs.

After sitting for a while, I told her I needed to get back home. She walked me to the car and got in the passenger's seat. I thought she wanted to talk some more so I asked her a question about her church. She didn't answer.

Instead she said, "Would you like to kiss me?"

After a short pause I answered, "Absolutely."

She reached over put her arms around my neck and moved her face close to mine. The kiss was not a simple peck on the lips. I think we were both surprised with our response, we both eventually needed to come up for air. Following a few moments of silence, she told me she would see me at school. She opened the car door and ran up the steps to Mary's house.

During the last week of school, I saw Diane every day at the lockers. When we talked, she stood so close that we almost touched. She told me that she was spending the night at Mary's house on Thursday and asked if I wanted to come over. I wasn't sure if I could get the car, but I told her I would try.

On Thursday when I got to Mary's house, Diane was sitting on the front porch by herself. When she saw me, she jumped up and ran toward the car. This time, in addition to shorts, she was wearing one of the new midriff blouses, revealing more of her skin. The clothes had to belong to Mary. Diane's father would kill her if he saw her dressed like this. I had no doubt Diane's family would not approve of Diane being at Mary's house if they knew what she was doing. Mary and her family went to the Baptist Church also, but they must have had a different interpretation of church rules. Mary said her father was always traveling, so this could explain part of her newfound freedom.

Diane got in the car with a huge smile on her face. "How do you like my outfit?" she teased.

"I think it's great. But I'm not sure your father would agree."

With folded arms she replied, "He doesn't have to know everything I do. Let's go to the river."

The river was a popular place with high school kids. There were secluded places along the bank that everyone knew about, but I could tell that Diane had never been there. Her questions let me know this was a new experience.

Since it was a school night, there were very few cars at the favorite spots. I drove until I found a secluded stretch of riverbank, pulled the car over, and turned off the engine. Diane scooted over. We wasted little time talking, the kissing was passionate and we both had to pause for breath.

Diane found her composure and said, "Let's go swimming."

"Right now?"

"Sure."

She jumped out of the car and headed toward the river. Unsure of what to do, I slowly walked behind her. When she got to the riverbank, she took off her clothes until she was wearing only a bra and panties. She immersed herself in the water, I stripped down to my boxers and dove after her. We both splashed around and dove under water. I swam over toward her; she placed her arms around my neck. I immediately knew that more than my blood pressure was rising. She had to know the effect she was having.

After the kiss, she told me it was getting late. We put our clothes on and returned to Mary's house. During the next week, every waking moment took my mind back to Diane in her bra and panties.

The next week, Mary and Diane came to the grocery store where I worked. We talked for a few minutes while I stocked shelves. Diane let me know she would again be at Mary's house on Thursday. I told her I was sure I could get the car.

We followed the same routine. This time the midriff was replaced with another colorful blouse. As she got in the car, I did notice something different; she was wearing makeup and had gone a little overboard with the eye shadow.

I drove back to the same place on the river where we had been last week. The kissing in the car went up a few notches. I could hear her moans and both of us were sweating. As we stopped to cool off I asked, "Do you want to go swimming?"

"I can't." She replied.

"What do you mean?"

"My period."

I suggested that we sit on the hood of the car and look out at the river. The sun was just beginning to set and it was a beautiful summer night. We had our backs against the windshield and our legs crossed.

Diane reached up to my shirt pocket and pointed.

"Do you smoke?" she asked.

I pulled out the pack of Lucky Strikes.

"Sometimes at work I have a cigarette during break. I don't smoke all the time like some people."

"Can I have one?" she asked, as she scooted closer to me.

I was surprised with her request.

"You want a cigarette? Have you ever smoked?" I rebounded, as if I was protesting her request.

"No. I just want to try it."

I pulled out my lighter, lit a cigarette and handed it to her. She reluctantly took a few puffs and started to cough. I laughed and reached to take back the cigarette; instead of giving it back, she just held it in her hand like a movie star.

I lit a second cigarette, "Why does your dad let you go to Mary's house?"

"What do you mean?"

"I think he would kill you if he knew you were wearing Mary's clothes and leaving with me."

Diane seemed agitated with my question and responded, "Mary's dad is a deacon at my dad's church so it's OK. Mary's dad is always gone."

"What about her mother?"

Diane raised her arms in the air and said, "She's always drunk. She doesn't know what Mary does."

"Why do you spend the night on Thursdays?"

"I go to choir practice with her on Thursday. My dad likes to prepare his sermon that day so he's glad to have me out of the house."

Diane took a long drag on the cigarette, blowing smoke up over her head. I think I was becoming part of her master plan to rebel.

CHAPTER FIVE

Amiens, France, March 17, 1944

After the burial of Joseph Bernhardt, we returned to the house and Camille fixed dinner. I knew she was grieving, but I was amazed at how she found strength to carry on. She had me follow her to the bedroom where she showed me the clothes that had belonged to Joseph. I thanked her and returned to the couch. Little Joshua came to me carrying a picture book. Without hesitation, he climbed in my lap and handed me the book. I began to point to the pictures, attempting to pronounce the names in French. When I finished the book, he turned to the front of the book and started over. Pronouncing the words was actually good practice. I needed to improve my French and fast. I could communicate with Camille but most of the time I found myself acting out or gesturing instead of talking. When I started going through the book for a third time, I looked up and saw tears running down Camille's face. When she realized I was looking, she quickly wiped her tears and returned to the stove.

Tomorrow would be a big workday, the small farm had five milk cows that needed to be milked. There was also wood that needed to be chopped for the wood stove. Camille kept saying something about a William. I wasn't sure exactly what she was trying to say, but I think William was another farmer who would be coming to the house tomorrow.

After dinner Camille cleaned up and got Joshua ready for bed. She brought me a blanket and returned to the bedroom. I could hear her crying during the night. I kept thinking I needed to help her, and I then decided what to do next.

The day started early; before daybreak Camille was up and fixing something to eat. After breakfast and a trip to the outhouse, I met her and Joshua at the barn. She put hay in the troughs and retrieved two pails. She demonstrated how to milk the cow, and then got off the short stool and gestured for me to sit. I began to tug on the udder, making the cow jerk. She again sat on the stool and showed me how to squeeze. I tried again with the same results. I think she said something about pulling on the tit, which caused me to smile. When she saw me smile, she smiled back. The third time was the charm. The milk actually squirted into the pail. Camille moved on to another cow. We poured the milk into large containers; it took a lot longer than I would have expected. When we finished, she walked over to a churn. I recognized it because I remembered seeing them on farms back in Pennsylvania. She poured in the milk and demonstrated how to push up and down. I took over and after a few minutes stopped. When I stopped, she motioned for me to keep going. Camille was a hard worker and she knew what needed to get done.

After churning to the point that my arms were numb, I stopped. She scooped out the soft butter. I then took the cows out to pasture and returned to chop wood. I felt like I had already put in a day's work, but the sun had only been out a few hours.

I used the pump to draw water from the well to clean up. I went back to the house and got a shirt from the drawer, it was one of Joseph's.

Camille seemed pleased with the work that had been done, she thanked me by patting me on the back. This totally surprised me. When I turned around, she gave me a smile. She was still wearing her work clothes and had dirt on one side of her face. I still couldn't get over how young she looked.

I walked to the front door when I heard a truck coming down the gravel and dirt road. Camille touched my arm and said, "William, le fermier." William had to be the farmer coming to get milk. William got out of his truck and walked toward the porch. He was short, wide, with gray hair on the sides of his head. He looked to be in his sixties but could have been younger. Camille introduced me as Jean, a cousin of Joseph. She said something about Joseph being out of town. William stared at me for a few seconds and then motioned for me to help load the milk containers in his truck. As we were loading, he said, "Parlez Anglais?"

"Yes."

"Good. I can speak English very well. Where did you learn English?"

I wasn't sure how to respond. I hesitated for a moment and then replied, "I worked in England for a while."

"Interesting," he said, as he nodded his head.

After we loaded everything, I wasn't sure what to do next. William got in the driver's seat and said, "Let's go."

I got in on the passenger side. After William grinded a few gears, we took off in his old truck.

Before I had a chance to say anything, William spoke, "We're going to Amiens to trade goods. The bloody Germans will be everywhere. Let me do all the talking."

"Why are we trading goods?"

"The Germans take everything from the farmers, especially the bigger farms. What we have left, we trade to survive. Money comes in handy but it is more important to get things you can eat. We both have milk and butter, which we can trade for flour and some vegetables that will keep. I know that Joshua needs shoes. I'm going to see what we can do about that. Next time, you should bring eggs, I can sometimes get money for eggs."

"How did you meet Joseph?" I asked.

"I helped him get his farm started. He got most of his help from old man Bellamy. I just showed him how to do stuff. When the Germans came, we decided to go to town together."

As we drove toward town, we passed the tree line that was close to the drop zone. I was surprised how close we were to town. William was a smooth salesman, he knew everyone by name and was quick to ask about their families. He would go into his bargaining mode and before I knew it, we had accumulated a lot of important staples to take back home. I was introduced as Joseph's cousin and nobody said a word. As we were loading vegetables and fruit into the back of his truck, two Germans soldiers walked by and grabbed the only two apples we had.

When they left, William mumbled, "Filthy German pigs."

I learned a lot from William; he and the other people I met were just trying to get by. People stayed away from the German soldiers and tried not to make eye contact. Sometimes a trade did not seem to be fair. Most everyone, however, seemed to understand that a trade might go better the next time.

As we headed out of town, William seemed to be thinking about something. He made no comments about the bloody Germans. As we turned on the road that led to the farmhouse, he pulled over and shut off the engine, he turned and faced me.

"Are you an American?"

I paused and said nothing.

Finally William continued, "Were you part of the drop the other night?"

"Yes. I'm an American paratrooper."

I was delighted when he exclaimed, "This is good news. Maybe the Americans will soon be here."

"Yes. They are coming soon," I said. "How did you know?"

William turned in his seat and looked directly at me. "I knew that Joseph volunteered to help the French fighters," he continued. "He had never done anything like that. He was angry and wanted to help. What happened to him?"

"He was killed."

William lowered his head and replied, "That is too bad. His family will pay a price."

I quickly responded, "I'm trying to help his family."

"Why are you doing that?" William asked.

"He saved my life."

In a gruff tone William said, "I see. That still doesn't mean you have to help."

"I want to help Camille put the pieces back together," I said.

"You don't know what that entails," William remarked.

As William started to turn away I grabbed his arm and asked, "What do you mean?"

"Camille is in serious trouble," he added.

"Why?"

"She's a Jew."

"She's Jewish?" I repeated.

With a surprised look on his face William responded, "You didn't know?"

"No, I didn't."

"For a long time the Jews were rounded up. Then things died down. Joseph escaped because everyone kept quiet. I think that is about to change."

"Why?"

"The Germans have a new commander in this region. He has a renewed interest in rounding up Jews. I think it has something to do with the anticipated landing by the Americans and the British. The new commander is ruthless. He threatens people and has killed farmers for lying. It is only a matter of time before he learns that Camille is a Jew. He will also want to know what happened to Joseph. The paratrooper drop did not go well for the French fighters. I think someone told the Germans. They knew about everything."

Sounding desperate I asked, "What should Camille do?"

"She needs to leave," remarked William. "It is not safe here. Maybe she can hide until the Americans come."

"Did Joseph know this?"

"Yes. He was a stubborn man. He felt they would just ride it out."

"How did Joseph and Camille end up in Amiens?"

"I'm not sure of the details. I know Joseph felt like things were getting bad for Jews in Lille. He purchased the farm from someone in Lille and moved. I guess he thought it would be safer. For a while it was safe but things have changed. Old man Bellamy and I helped him get started on the farm. He really didn't know anything about farming. When the baby came, he was determined to call the farm his home."

I asked, "Does Camille know about the danger?"

"I'm not sure. I can't help but think she has to know there is danger. The Germans have come to the farm before and asked a lot of questions. They took food and threatened Joseph on more than one occasion."

We sat for a minute in silence before I continued my conversation with William. "How do you know so much?" I asked.

"I have helped the French resistance," admitted William. "I know a lot of people. I speak good English, French, and some German. I have even managed to buddy up with some Germans. That's how I know about the renewed interest in locating Jews."

"How did you learn English?"

"My father was Welsh and my mother French. I lived in Wales as a child. My name is William Williams but here people just call me William."

"Are things really that bad for the Jews?"

Looking surprised at my question, William responded. "It is worse than you can imagine. I know that many have been sent to death camps."

"I thought they were work camps," I said. "That's what we were told."

"They are death camps. That's why Camille needs to get out of here. Since people think you are Joseph's cousin, you aren't safe either. You can trust me; I will say nothing. Someone, however, will tell. When Joseph and Camille came here, they did not hide that they were Jews. When the Germans started rounding people up, they kept a low profile but with this new commander that will be impossible. This new commander is obsessed with finding Jews who are hiding."

When William started the truck I asked, "Will you be going to town next week?"

"Yes," he responded.

"I will talk with Camille. My French is not always good but I will do my best to let her know of the danger."

When we got back to the farm, Camille and Joshua were waiting on us. She helped bring in the goods and seemed pleased with the things we had brought back. She said something to William about shoes. He just shook his head no.

As Camille stored items, she made a comment in a low voice that I wasn't sure was meant for me. As she placed certain food items on the table, I realized she was preparing for Shabbat.

CHAPTER SIX

Allentown, Pennsylvania, Summer 1943

I was out of school for the summer and my hours increased at the grocery store; I didn't mind since it beat hanging around the house. My father, grudgingly, had decided to give me an extra ten dollars of spending money.

Thursday was no longer a guaranteed day off and getting the car was problematic, depending on how many beers my father drank.

I thought of Diane often. On two occasions, she dropped by the store to talk. She hadn't been spending time at Mary's house because her mother had things for her to do at home. In the third week of June, she came by the store and let me know she would again be at Mary's. In my mind, I had just gotten the green light. Now, getting the car was paramount.

My father had not been feeling well so he went to bed immediately following dinner. For once, my mother didn't say "Ask your father." All she said was "Don't be late."

I hustled over to Mary's and found the girls sitting on the porch swing. It had rained earlier and cooled things off. I noticed Diane was going with the heavy makeup look. Her hair was in a ponytail and she was wearing the midriff top. We talked for a while about our summer and shared names of people we knew who had enlisted in the military. Both of the girls were giggly and I suspected they might have been talking about me.

Mary got up and went inside. Diane stood up and we walked to the car. To my delight, she snuggled up next to me.

At the river, a man was fishing at our usual spot. I kept driving until the road became more like a path. We were bumping up and down, sometimes hitting our heads on the ceiling of the car. Finally, I found a good place to park that had a view of the river. It was a great location, more isolated than before.

After we parked, Diane reached over to put her arms around my neck. I immediately noticed the strong smell of perfume. As we kissed, I could feel the pressure of her chest rubbing against me. We were beginning to steam up the windows. Diane raised her head and again asked if I wanted to go swimming. Without saying anything, I opened the car door and she followed. When we got to the bank, we both started taking off our clothes. As Diane took off her blouse, she asked, "Do you want to skinny dip?"

Without hesitation, I said "Sure."

Out of the corner of my eye, I watched Diane take off her clothes. I had never seen a girl nude. I thought she looked perfect. I could immediately feel an erection coming. I quickly took off my shorts and jumped into the river. We both swam around, but managed to only expose our heads.

I swam under water and came to the surface close to Diane. It was a little awkward, for a moment, we just looked at each other. When I got closer, our bodies touched. I felt my body tingling and every touch of her skin felt like silk running against me.

Diane reached under the water and touched me. I raised my hand and touched her right breast. She then abruptly turned her back to me and said, "Take me home."

I kept saying sorry, but I wasn't sure why. We hurriedly put our clothes on over our wet bodies. On the drive home, Diane had tears on her cheeks. I was at a loss for words. At Mary's she leaped out of the car and ran up the steps.

On the drive home, I tried to analyze what had taken place at the river. Maybe there was something I should have done differently. It looked like Thursday trips to the river were over. Well, at least I still had the memory of our bodies touching.

CHAPTER SEVEN

Allentown, Pennsylvania, Summer 1943

Though I didn't expect to hear from Diane, I was hopeful she would come by the store. I kept busy with work and helping my mother with chores. She was tired most of the time. My dad never helped, all he wanted was more beer.

One afternoon I came home from work to find my mother sitting in a chair with her head on the kitchen table. My father was nowhere in sight.

I put my hand on her back and asked, "Mom, are you okay?"

"I'm not feeling well. I have a terrible pain in my back."

"Why don't you go lie on the couch?"

With a strained look on her face she said, "You've got to help me."

I took my mother by her left arm and helped her stand. Crying out in pain, she immediately sat back down.

I could tell she needed emergency care. "You need to go to the hospital, Mom. I'll pull the car around to the front and get Dad."

"Forget him. Just get his wallet," she moaned.

I helped my mother get in the front seat. She groaned as she attempted to get comfortable by shifting in her seat. At the emergency room, they immediately put her in a wheel chair and took her to one of the back rooms. I stayed in the lobby area. I gave the people at the desk my Dad's union card that contained medical coverage information.

Eventually, they admitted Mother and took her to a room. The doctor said she had an acute kidney infection, which would require her to be in the hospital for several days.

I stayed with my mother most of the night but returned early in the morning so my father would have a car for work. When I explained to my father what had happened, he complained about having to fix his own lunch for work.

As he walked to the refrigerator, I mumbled, "You ungrateful piece of shit."

He turned and said, "What did you say?"

"I didn't say anything."

With a look of rage on his face he responded, "I don't want any of your crap. You have dinner fixed when I get home."

"I'll need the car to visit Mom," I asserted.

"Your mother will be fine. You have dinner fixed and then go."

That afternoon I made spaghetti for the two of us and then went to the hospital. My mother looked better because she wasn't in pain. The doctors told her she would probably go home in two days. I pulled up a chair so I could sit next to my mother's bed.

She gave me a smile and I said, "Mom, how have you put up with him all these years?"

She patted my hand and replied, "He wasn't always like this."

"You could have fooled me," I said, "He thinks the world revolves around him."

"It's the drinking," she said, offering an excuse for his behavior.

"The drinking makes him worse," I said angrily, "He's always been an asshole."

"You shouldn't talk about your father like that," she responded. "He has always provided for us."

"Yeah, but he treats you so badly," I asserted.

"I just ignore him," she added, her voice beginning to reflect sadness.

"He's going to drive you to an early grave," I said in disgust.

"Don't worry about me," she said. "You need to take care of yourself."

"What can I do?" I pleaded.

"You can get out," she said.

I stood and walked over to the window. "You mean leave," I asked.

"Yes," she said. "After you graduate, leave home."

"Mom, I want to go to college. Dad would never pay for that."

"Join the service, then go to college," she said, trying to give me advice. "You can get the GI Bill."

I returned to my chair next to the bed and said, "Mom, what did you see in Dad? Why did you get married?"

"We had to get married," she answered.

I stood in silence, this had never been mentioned before. Suddenly I felt numb and overcome with uncertainty.

My mother came home two days later. My father never visited her at the hospital. When I walked in the door holding my mother's arm, he met us at the door. He was home early and I could tell he had wasted no time consuming his six-pack. He kissed my mother and said, "What's for dinner?"

As the blood rushed to my face, I yelled, "You asshole! Is that all you can think about?"

He responded, "I don't want any of your shit anymore."

I shouted back, "Get off your ass and fix your own dinner."

My father rushed toward me, throwing a punch at me. I easily stepped to the side. He fell on the coffee table, smashing it into pieces.

He jumped up and yelled, "Get out of my house!"

I bolted out the door and jogged to my friend's house. I grew up with Jonas Williams. I knew his family would let me stay with them; they didn't ask any questions. Every one of my friends knew my father was a nasty drunk.

The next day when I went home, everyone acted as if nothing had happened. This had happened too many times before. Besides, my father would not want to miss the paycheck I would receive on Friday.

CHAPTER EIGHT

Allentown Pennsylvania, Summer 1943

The next few weeks passed quickly. With my family I was never sure what "normal" meant, but whatever it was, we were back in our regular routine. My mother was feeling much better, which meant she would have meals on the table when my father returned from work. He came home each night with his usual six-pack. He seldom spoke to me, but for some reason he gave me more money from my paycheck, perhaps that was his attempt at reconciliation.

I did not hear anything from Diane but thought of her often. One Thursday, I took the car and drove by Mary's, hoping they would be sitting on the front porch swing, but I saw no one.

The next day at the store I was cleaning floors when Shannon O'Leary walked in the door. Shannon lived down the street; we had been friends since first grade. She was tall and slender, with pretty long red hair. Although we had seen each other at school every day for years, our friendship was centered on living in the same neighborhood. I remember the times she played baseball with the boys on our street. I also played dolls with her when we were children, but that stayed strictly between us. Shannon was bubbly, full of energy, positive, and fun to be around. I had seen her mother every week at the grocery store but hadn't seen Shannon since school was out.

She went directly to the shelf to pick up a small package of sugar. Then she walked over to me.

"I never see you here," I blurted.

"My mother's baking and she needed sugar," she said. "I'm bored to death so I told her I would get it."

"Why are you bored? We just got out of school."

"Yeah. Well, you know me; I can't sit still and do nothing. I've done some reading, I've also been writing to my father; he enlisted in the Navy. I really do miss him. What have you been doing?" she asked.

"Just working. My mother was in the hospital."

"Is she okay?"

"She's doing a lot better; she had a bad kidney infection."

I was startled with the quick change in topics when Shannon asked, "Have you been to the river?"

I paused for a few seconds, then said, "No."

She quickly jumped to another topic and asked, "Have you seen 'Casablanca'?"

"No, I don't get enough time off to travel that far," I said sarcastically.

Shannon just rolled her eyes and laughed.

"It's been out for a while but just now came to Allentown. Would you like to see it?"

"Yeah; I guess so."

As I continued to mop the floor, Shannon tapped me on the back and said, "That's wonderful, we can go together. Can you go tonight?"

"I think so. I'll have to ask my dad for the car."

With excitement Shannon replied, "I'll drive. Just come over to my house at six."

As Shannon turned, her long red hair brushed against my face.

"Remember. Six o'clock," she said.

I waved and thought, *I guess I have a date.*

I rushed home after work and downed my grilled cheese sandwich. I put on my church pants and grabbed my favorite shirt. When I told Mom I was going to the movie with Shannon, she added, "She's such a nice girl."

Shannon was wearing a tight gray skirt and white blouse. It was hard to believe this was the same girl I had played baseball with. I was glad she was wearing flat shoes, this made both of us five-foot nine.

She drove fast, getting us to the movie early. The place was packed; it must've been a popular movie. We walked down the right aisle and took a seat on the fifth row. As soon as we were seated, she wanted popcorn so I got back up and headed to the concession stand. After getting popcorn and drinks, I was making my way back to my seat when I saw Diane, Mary, and Lucy sitting together on the right side of the aisle.

When my eyes met Diane's, I felt her stare go right through me. I managed a small smile; she looked disappointed.

The movie opened up with a newsreel about United States military activities in the war. The movie was better than expected.

I made Shannon laugh every time I said, "Play it again Sam."

Afterwards, Shannon and I walked up next to Diane and her friends. Shannon immediately started talking with them, but I looked straight ahead. They were talking about their summer. When I glanced back at Diane, she let Shannon know she had gone to the river a few times.

Back at Shannon's, we saw her mother and father sitting on the front porch. They asked about the movie and we talked for a few minutes. I told them I had to open the store the next day and needed to get home.

"I had a good time," Shannon said.

"Me too."

I realized things could be complicated with girls; this was definitely new territory for me. The good did seem to outweigh the bad, however.

On Monday, Mary showed up at the grocery store around noon as I was getting ready to break for lunch. There was a picnic table next to the store where I always ate. Mary came up and sat across from me.

"Diane's coming over Thursday," she said.

"And you are telling me this why?"

"You know why," she replied.

I shrugged my shoulders. "I didn't think she wanted to see me," I said.

"She's just confused," Mary continued. "There's a lot going on, but she does want to see you though. Will you come by?"

"Maybe," I said.

Mary tapped me on the arm, "You know you want to see her," she teased.

Then Mary, the negotiator, stood up and proclaimed, "She also said to bring a blanket."

The rest of the afternoon, all I could think about was the blanket. Just the thought of lying on a blanket with Diane got me excited.

On Thursday, for some reason, my father quizzed me about the use of the car. This was new, he hadn't had enough to drink. When he drinks a lot, he can be mean, but he also reaches a point where nothing matters. I made up a lame story about running errands and going by the store.

I was going to take the quilt that was on the foot of my bed, but I needed to get out the door with it without drawing suspicion and questions from my father.

Even though it was a warm summer night, I rolled the quilt up and placed it in my leather jacket, which I carried under my arm. I walked down the hall and glanced in the family room. My mother was knitting and my father was listening to the radio. I walked quickly down the hallway and out the front door. I threw the blanket in the back of the Ford and drove to Mary's house.

This time Diane was on the porch swing by herself. When she saw me, she skipped down the steps and opened the passenger door. She was wearing short shorts and a blouse that was thin enough for me to see her bra. She wore her hair so that her bangs dropped over one eye. This was the Casablanca look complete with heavy eye shadow.

She smiled and we began to talk about the movie. After a few blocks, she moved over close to me. It was as if things had returned to normal. I drove the car to the most remote spot. Despite the bumpy ride, she never said anything. I turned the engine off, expecting us to kiss. Instead she said, "Let's go swimming."

I grabbed the blanket that was in the backseat and walked to the bank, dropping the blanket on the sand. Diane started to strip and I just watched her. Her body was perfectly proportioned. Quickly, I removed my clothes and waded into the water. Instead of splashing and swimming, we moved toward each other. Our heads were the only body parts above water. We embraced and began kissing. I could feel her body pressed against mine. I knew she could feel my stiff pole pressed against her stomach, she reached down and touched me while I touched her breast.

After some more petting, Diane asked, "Do you want to do it?"

I was so nervous I had difficulty getting my words out. Finally, I said, "Yes, but I don't want you to regret it."

"I won't regret it," she said. "Have you ever done it?"

I shook my head and said, "No."

In a low voice she replied shyly, "I don't want to get pregnant."

"You won't. I'll pull out."

"Will it hurt?" she asked.

I touched her left arm and said, "I'll take it slow." We came out of the water and laid down on the blanket. I wasn't sure what to do next but we started kissing and animal instinct seemed to follow.

Afterwards, we both were on our backs with the blanket rolled up over us; neither of us spoke. I wasn't sure if our experience had held up to the hyped expectations. I knew my body was totally relaxed and the touch of her body next to me gave me a feeling of peace. I heard her sniffle, and wasn't sure what to say.

The next week, I found myself thinking about Diane every waking minute. The anticipation of Thursday gave me unbelievable energy. My mother asked me throughout the week if there was something wrong with me.

The following Thursday, we followed the same routine but with an added level of excitement. Again, we stayed wrapped up in the blanket and gazed at the stars. We could hear the sound of the river flowing and feel the limpness of our bodies.

I broke the silence when I said, "Diane, why doesn't your father like me?"

"He thinks your family is white trash."

Sarcastically, I replied, "Thanks a lot."

"No, I didn't mean you," she said.

"Yeah, but you're talking about my family."

"It's mainly about your brother being put in jail."

I raised up on my elbow and explained, "That was a bar fight."

"Exactly, he was in a bar and got arrested for fighting. He also thinks your father is a drunk."

I returned to lying on my back and added, "Well, he's right, but is that a sin?"

"To my father it is."

"Do you think I'm like my father and brother?" I asked.

Diane patted my leg and replied, "We wouldn't be doing this if I thought that."

After a minute of silence I said, "I have a question. What do you want to do with your life?"

"What do you mean?"

"Exactly what I said. What do you want out of life?"

Diane crossed her arms over her breasts and replied, "I guess to get married and have kids. What about you?"

"I'd like to go to college. I've thought about teaching. I really don't want to end up in the steel mill. I may not have a real choice since I don't think the war is going to end quickly, and I graduate next year."

"I think you would be a good teacher. You're a lot better with school work than I am."

"What does your father want you to do?"

"I don't want to talk about him," she replied angrily.

We never discussed her father, or our future plans for the remainder of the summer. We didn't make it to the river every Thursday but we made it most weeks. Sometimes we met at Mary's and we also arranged it so we hooked up at the movies. When we met there, she would wear more conservative clothes and skip the makeup. Regardless of where we met, we would head to the river. We made every minute count.

One night it rained, so we stripped in the back seat of the car. It was tight and we had difficulty maneuvering. We were determined nothing would stop our summer passion. Even when I was at work, I could smell the scent of Diane. When I went to bed at night, I would roll my blanket around me and think of the river.

As school approached, I realized this was the best summer of my life. I couldn't imagine any summer being better. This had been the summer of my dreams.

The week before school started, Diane called me on the phone late at night. She was crying and I couldn't understand what she was trying to say; she started sobbing. I waited silently as I held the phone up to my ear. My heart was racing and I felt paralyzed. Finally Diane got her composure and between sobs, I heard her say, "I missed my period. I never miss."

CHAPTER NINE

Amiens, France, March 18-31, 1944

My communication with Camille was improving. I could not understand every word in a sentence, but I understood enough to comprehend what she meant. After my talk with William, I sat down with Camille and did my best to convince her that she and Joshua were in danger. Speaking and using gestures, I warned her that the new German Commander was obsessed with rounding up all Jews before any type of invasion by the Americans. I knew that she understood what I was saying. She looked directly in my eyes and listened to every word. When I had finished speaking, she focused her gaze on me.

Eventually she said, "This is my house."

Each day I brought the topic up again. I knew she understood the problem; she just couldn't think of a viable solution.

We established a set routine of working and eating. Early each day I milked cows and churned butter; Camille worked in the garden while Joshua played next to her. I would take the cows to pasture and then we met at the house for lunch. I enjoyed the work, and there were times when I didn't think about being an American in a Nazi-held territory. I would lose the fear that always seemed present.

One afternoon, I decided to help by getting eggs from the chickens in the hen house. I wasn't sure what to do but it didn't look that hard. As I reached underneath one of the chickens, the hen pecked my hand. I immediately pulled my hand back. I found a piece of wood, hoping I could get the chicken off the nest by poking it with the wood. Behind me, I heard a laugh; it was Camille. She walked over to the hen, pushed it off the nest, and took the eggs. It was the first time I had heard her laugh. As we walked out of the hen house, she started laughing again. I told her it wasn't funny, which caused her to laugh even more.

Camille had a wonderful smile, I tried to get her to smile as often as I could. In the evenings Joshua wanted me to play with him and read to him. After reading a book for the umpteenth time, I walked around the room, pointing to objects, naming them in French; then Joshua would repeat each word. This game helped me practice speaking in French. When I mispronounced something, Camille would laugh and correct me. Slowly, I began to speak in complete sentences. When I was correct, Camille would give me a thumbs up.

One evening, when Joshua came to me with a book, he called me Papa. I was taken aback. Camille had heard, but she did not correct him and I ignored his reference to Papa.

In the afternoon when Joshua took his nap, I would join Camille on the back porch steps. Occasionally she would ask questions about America. I admired this woman, she had gone through a lot of hard times in her life. Although she was small in stature, she was spunky and could outwork most men I knew. She had lost her husband and was working hard at keeping a stiff upper lip. She was trying to move on with her life. Apparently, she enjoyed my company. She always said 'merci' after I answered her questions.

One afternoon after Joshua had gone to bed, she told me that I needed a bath. I knew that I must smell but wasn't sure how to ask about taking a bath. There was an old tub located in her bedroom. The hot water needed to be heated on the stove. I hadn't wanted to create extra work for her. She prepared the water for her bath first. When she was finished, she put on a robe and walked to the kitchen area to let me know it was my turn. She also asked me to bring her my dirty clothes when I had finished bathing. After my bath, I put on clean clothes that had belonged to her husband and joined her on the back steps.

I could smell the soap that we had both used. Her hair was still wet and hung straight against her face. Again, I couldn't get over how young she looked. I looked at her and asked her age.

Shyly she responded, "I'm nineteen."

Camille was a year older than me but looked five years younger.

I told her that I would be going to town with William tomorrow to trade goods and that I would try to get shoes for Joshua. I then brought the topic of safety up again. She told me she was still thinking about it so I didn't push the point. I would ask William if he had any new information.

There was a greater German presence in town. Trucks and military personnel were everywhere. People were continuously being stopped and questioned. The Major in charge had taken over the old courthouse-looking building, which now displayed a huge Nazi flag. William figured the additional troops were probably a result of the anticipated invasion. Things around town were more tense, causing me to feel uneasy. Again, soldiers came by our truck and took produce. We kept our heads low and said nothing. I was able to get the shoes for Joshua, something he really needed. On our way back to the farm, William expressed concern that things were going to get worse.

He stressed that we were in real danger; I noticed this time he included me in the equation.

As he turned down the road that led to the farm, we came upon an old woman walking on the side of the road. She was wearing a dark dress that came down to her ankles. She had a stooped posture. William said, "That's old Mrs. Claire. She's your neighbor." I was aware he said 'Your neighbor.'

When William stopped the truck, Mrs. Claire told him she was on her way to see Camille.

William said, "You walked two miles?"

In a labored voice she answered, "Yes. It is important." Mrs. Claire then turned to me and asked, "Who are you?"

I told her that I was Joseph's cousin. She asked about Joseph and I told her that he had gone out of town. William insisted that Claire ride with us. After a little coaxing, she climbed into the truck.

I helped William unload the truck and then joined Mrs. Claire and Camille in the kitchen. Camille had given her a glass of water and a towel to wipe the sweat from her face.

After Camille had poured her a second glass of water, Mrs. Claire said, "I had a visitor come to my house yesterday. Before I went to bed, I heard a knock on my door, and my dog started to bark. When I went to the door, there was a German soldier standing there. He was some type of officer. He had other soldiers sitting in a car parked out front. He invited himself in and said he had questions for me. He acted very nice at first and then began to make threats. He kept asking questions about Jews. He wanted names. When I told him I didn't know any Jews, he got angry and told me I better not be lying. I'm old and I don't care if he threatens me. He did ask about Joseph, I'm afraid other people will be asked. Before he left, he told me he would be back. That's why I walked to your house."

Camille thanked her and asked if I would drive her home. Before we got up from the table, I asked her, "Was this man a Major?"

"I'm not sure of his rank, but I know he was an officer. He had a driver and acted like he was an important man."

I took Mrs. Claire home. When I returned, I sat down with Camille and talked with her about leaving. She told me that it would take a couple of days to get rid of the animals and get things together. The plan was to go south toward Paris. I was hoping the invasion would result in a quick liberation of Paris. If we could get close to Paris and hide, we had a chance to be liberated.

CHAPTER TEN

Allentown, Pennsylvania, Fall 1943

After Diane told me about missing her period, I retreated to my room and locked the door. I sat on the bed while a thousand thoughts rushed through my head. None of the alternatives were good. I still had hopes of getting a call tomorrow, telling me it was a false alarm. I felt paralyzed and helpless. I didn't go back downstairs; I stayed in my room staring at the ceiling.

The next morning I went downstairs and poured a cup of coffee. My father was at the kitchen table reading the paper and my mother was frying eggs. I wanted to talk with my mother, but decided against it. I did not want to cause a panic. I sat across from my father and found myself glancing at the back of the paper. The headlines reminded me we were in the middle of a war where people were dying.

My mother placed two eggs on a plate and set it before me. She then took a loaf of bread and walked over to the toaster.

While she was waiting for the toast to pop up, she gazed out the window and said, "What is Reverend Clark doing here?"

My chest felt tight. I had difficulty getting my breath. We heard a loud knock.

My father went to the door and standing outside was Reverend Clark. "I'm here to speak with you and your son," he said in a harsh tone.

Diane was standing next to her father; she looked terrible. Instead of her long flowing hair, she had really short hair. It looked like someone had placed a bowl on her head and given her a haircut. She was wearing a dress that was way too big for her and could have been her mother's. Her eyes were red and swollen and she wouldn't make eye contact. We all gathered in the family room. My mother grabbed the beer bottles that had been left from the night before. When she returned, she took a seat next to my father.

Reverend Clark pointed his finger toward my father and shouted, "Your son has defiled my daughter. He has taken my innocent child and defiled her."

My father was still not sure what the Reverend was saying.

The Reverend added, "That's the trouble with you people; you have no respect for values and decency."

This got my father's attention, he stood up and pointed a finger at the Reverend. They both began to yell but nobody was listening. I looked over at Diane but she kept her head down as her tears dropped on the floor. I knew she had been shamed to the point of complete submission, I walked over to her and put my arm on her back; she didn't move. Her father jerked my arm off of her.

My father finally comprehended that Diane was pregnant and that I was the father. He said nothing to me but instead continued to exchange words with the Reverend. I think he was more upset about being referred to as "you people" than with me being a father.

The conversation turned to standing up and doing the right thing and being a man. I began to feel like Diane. It was as if we were the children who had no say in such matters. Like Diane, I lowered my head and listened to what needed to be done with their bad children.

My father got louder. Pointing his finger at the Reverend he said, "My son will do the right thing. He will marry your daughter."

I looked over at Diane who remained in a trance, she continued to stare at the floor. Although it was a shock to hear my father mention marriage, I thought to myself, *Maybe he's right.* Reverend Clark was silent when my father mentioned marriage. The thought of having me as a son-in-law disgusted him.

Finally, he said, "I will not marry them. It will only bring more embarrassment to the church."

My father started pacing in a circle like a caged lion. Finally, he said, "Then they'll go to the Justice of the Peace."

"When?" Reverend Clark demanded.

"Today is Saturday. We will go Monday."

My mother contributed to the conversation by asking, "Where will they live?"

My father replied, "They can live here."

Reverend Clark mumbled, "They can live at my house but there will be certain rules."

After sitting and listening to my future being planned, I said, "How will I support a wife? I'm in high school."

My father responded, "You will get a job. That schooling is a waste of time anyhow." Before Diane and her father left, a time was set to meet at the courthouse on Monday. Diane and I never had a chance to say a word to each other.

When the door closed my father yelled, "What in the hell are you doing knocking up the preacher's daughter? Your brother knew a lot of girls, but never knocked one up."

He went to the phone that was located on the wall near the kitchen. I walked up to my room and threw myself on the bed, this was an absolute nightmare.

Within an hour my father opened my bedroom door with a bang and yelled, "You've got a job; you start on Tuesday. You are going to work for Smitty as a laborer to block masons. It's a good starting job and you will have a chance to become an apprentice." I said nothing. He closed the door.

I walked down the stairs, meeting my mother in the hallway. "Mom, I need to use the car."

"I'm not sure, honey. I need to ask your father."

With a disgusted look I said, "I'll be right back."

"OK, but don't be gone long."

I wasn't sure why but I decided to drive to the river, I parked in an isolated spot. After staring at the water, I began to cry. The crying turned into deep sobs, I held so much inside that it felt good to cry. Everything was about to change. I guess I needed to go to the river one more time. For me the river represented a happy time that I knew I would always remember.

As I stood in front of the courthouse with my mother and father, I wondered if Diane had gone to church on Sunday. If she had, the additional shame would have been unbearable for her. It was past the time when we were supposed to meet. I was beginning to think that maybe the Reverend had changed his mind about Diane being married. I was pacing back and forth. Then the Reverend's car turned the corner near the courthouse. Diane was driving the car and she was alone.

She parked by the curb and got out. She was wearing a nice church dress. She had tried to salvage her hair, but it was still a mess.

She walked toward us and said, "It's just me. My parents aren't coming."

Soon we were standing before the Justice of the Peace. There were no flowers, no white dress, no music, no bridesmaids, and no smiles. My mother gave me a ring that belonged to her mother. As I put it on Diane's hand, she kept looking straight ahead. When it came time to kiss the bride, I kissed Diane on the cheek. When I did, I felt the salt on my lips from the tears that were trickling down her cheeks. I had packed a suitcase with my clothes to bring to the courthouse. I placed the suitcase in the back seat of Diane's car, and got in the passenger's seat and Diane drove off. We were now married.

CHAPTER ELEVEN

Allentown, Pennsylvania, Fall 1943

On the drive to Diane's house, the silence was oppressive. We were now legally married; yet there was no excitement, laughter, or even a word spoken. I looked over at Diane. She looked tired, sad, and ten years older.

Finally, I said, "Pull over." She continued to drive and look straight ahead. "Dammit, I said pull the car over."

She slowed down and came to a stop next to the curb. She continued to look straight ahead.

"Diane, look at me." She slowly turned her head, "I don't know what to say to you. I've tried to think of words to say. I am so sorry things are the way they are; I didn't want this to happen. I know I can make a go of things. I'll try hard to make things work. If I have to get two jobs, I will. I don't want to live at your parent's house. As soon as I can make enough money, I want us to have a place."

I stopped and waited for her to say something. When she didn't, I said, "Talk to me. Say something."

Tears started to roll down Diane's cheeks. In a low voice she replied, "What do you want me to say?"

"Tell me how you feel."

"I don't think it is a good idea to move out of my house. I have shamed my family and I need to get their trust back. Besides, my mother can help with the baby. You don't even have a car."

"I can get a car."

"My father will never allow it," she said.

"What do you mean your father won't allow it? I'm your husband."

Diane didn't say anything, which really hurt. She never responded to my comment about "making it." I wasn't sure what we were doing.

She did say, "We need to get going."

"Wait. Before we go, I have another question. What happened to your hair?"

"My father cut it. That night when he found out, he went crazy. He called me a whore and then cut my hair. He also threw out all my makeup."

Tears began to form in my eyes. I lowered my head and whispered, "I'm so sorry."

"It's not your fault," she said.

As we drove to her house I couldn't help but think of the girl wearing short shorts, make up, and being full of life. I wasn't sure if I would ever know that girl again.

I dreaded the thought of living at Diane's house. When I got there, I carried my suitcase to her room, realizing it was going to be worse than I had expected. Nobody said anything to me. I felt like a person with leprosy who lived in biblical times. Her brother gave me a look like he wanted to pounce on me. At dinner, conversation was avoided unless the Reverend asked a question. Diane looked at her food instead of making eye contact with anyone. When dinner was over, I started to help with dishes but was stopped by Diane, this was her job. When I went to the family room, I purposely sat next to Reverend Clark.

He set down the newspaper he was reading and said, "I want you to know my rules. I expect you to pay me rent and to pay medical expenses for Diane."

"I can do that," I said.

In a harsh tone he added, "I'm not finished. I don't want any drinking, smoking, or playing music in this house. I don't want any of your friends in my house. Your parents can visit if I know about it."

"Reverend Clark, I want to take care of Diane. I would like for us to have a place of our own."

"I think you have already taken care of her. She needs her family now."

There was part of me that was ready to walk out the door, but maybe things would get better. That night when I crawled into bed, I placed my arm on Diane's shoulder. After a few moments, she took my arm and moved it away.

The next morning, Smitty picked me up for work. Smitty was a man my father had known most of his life, he was a big man who had red hair and a sporty red moustache that was turned up on the ends. I heard his old truck rattle up to the house. I grabbed the lunch Diane had packed and jogged to the truck.

I wasn't sure what a block mason laborer did, but it didn't take long for me to learn the job was damn hard. I learned to make mortar by mixing powdered mortar, sand, and water together in a large flat looking tub. I then used a hoe to mix everything together because the mortar had to have the right consistency. Then shoveled mortar into a wheelbarrow and hauled it to where the masons were working. I took my shovel and dumped mortar on a flat board. There were other boards a few feet away where I would place mortar. That way the mason could lay block without having to move one of the boards. It was also my job to stack block near a mason so he wouldn't have to move.

Sometimes when I was mixing, I would hear Smitty yell, "mud!" I would then grab the wheelbarrow and get more mortar placed on the board. I was in constant motion, I learned to get ahead by having blocks stacked near the different boards. Occasionally, the mortar would dry out and it was my job to bring a bucket of water and splash it onto the drying mortar. The two masons worked my ass off but they were likable guys. They were always teasing each other and me. I even began to dish a little sarcasm back at them. When we broke for lunch, they expressed an interest in me. They questioned why I had dropped out of school. At day's end, I was exhausted. Since we were working on an office building that was enclosed by a temporary fence, I didn't have to load equipment back in the truck. Smitty invited me to go for a beer. I declined but was glad he asked. It was nice to be treated like an adult.

When I returned home, I showered and met everyone at the dinner table. Again, we ate in silence. Diane did ask about my first day, which was a nice surprise. I gave all the details and also told her about Smitty and his partner Charles.

That night I got in bed and again placed my arm on Diane's shoulder. When she didn't remove it, I moved closer and began kissing her on the neck.

In a whisper she said, "We can't, my brother is next door." I was angry but held my tongue. I rolled on my back, staring at the ceiling.

The next two weeks followed the same routine. But one morning when Diane handed me my lunch for work, she actually kissed my cheek. *Maybe this could work after all,* I thought to myself.

At the end of the second week, I got paid and paid Reverend Clark for rent. He seemed thankful but was quick to remind me that he wasn't charging anything for food. On that same evening, I was sitting at the table for dinner when my right hamstring cramped so badly I fell out of my chair. I immediately grabbed the back of my leg and tried to straighten it. When I did, my other leg cramped and I began to roll on the floor. When I looked up, Diane's brother was laughing.

"It's not funny," I said.

"Maybe you're not cut out for man's work," he replied.

"Kiss my ass!" I shouted.

Reverend Clark stood up and yelled, "I'm not going to have that profane language in my house."

Without the help of anyone, I made it to my feet and tried to walk off the cramps. I walked on the front porch, pacing back and forth.

In a whisper, I kept repeating, "I can't take this shit."

Although the next day was Saturday, it was still a work day. We were fighting a deadline and Smitty wanted to have the west wall up before Monday. This time when Smitty invited me to stop for a beer, I said yes. We went to a small tavern frequented by construction workers. Since I was with Smitty and Charles, nobody asked me my age. The first beer was quickly downed as a second round was placed on the table.

Halfway through the second beer, Smitty asked me what Diane was like. For some reason, I told him everything about my situation, including Diane's family and the lack of affection between Diane and myself. Smitty ordered another round of beer and encouraged me to keep talking. I went into every detail; it felt great to get this off my chest. Smitty and Charles were in their forties and excellent listeners. They didn't interrupt me or make wise cracks about my predicament.

Smitty lit a cigarette and took a long drag.

He leaned forward and said, "I could be wrong on this, but when the baby comes, you are probably going to get a visit from an attorney."

"What do you mean?"

"Like I said, I could be wrong. I'm thinking it is important not to have some bastard's child. Once the child is born and has a proper name, it would be okay to cut ties."

"You mean like divorce?"

"I'm just saying, it seems like you are merely being tolerated for now."

For some reason, this actually made sense. Diane had been shamed into going along with her father. Maybe she did have feelings for me but didn't want to encourage anything. Maybe Smitty was wrong and this was just beer talk. This time I bought the round.

When Smitty dropped me off, it was already dark. I felt like a child trying to sneak into the house. I tiptoed across the porch. I had my right hand on the doorknob when it opened. Standing in the doorway was Reverend Clark.

"You're late!" he yelled.

"It was a long day," I said.

He slammed the screen door and got directly in my face.

Before I could say anything he asked, "Have you been drinking?"

"I had a couple of beers," I admitted, lowering my head.

"Then you can't come in this house."

"Where am I supposed to go?" I asked.

"I don't care. I told you no alcohol."

Without saying another word, I turned and walked away. I walked down the sidewalk trying to decide what to do next. I walked for miles until I reached the house of my friend Jonas Williams. I was greeted like the prodigal son returning home. Mrs. Williams fixed me something to eat. I had no trouble getting to sleep. The next morning I shared that I'd had a disagreement with the Reverend Clark and left. I took my time getting to the Clark house. Nobody said a word when I walked in the door; it was like business as usual.

The next day was my birthday. The Clark family was not aware of this, but it wouldn't have made any difference. I didn't expect to hear anything from my parents unless I got a card in the mail. After work, I had Smitty drop me off near the post office. The army recruiting office was located next door, it was still open and not too crowded. The sergeant took a lot of time with me and explained every step of the process. He was pleased when I asked about airborne.

A few days later, I told Smitty I would be late to work because I had to take a physical for the Army. He was very understanding and even offered to pick me up and bring me to work. The following Monday, I was back in the recruiter's office. I had passed the physical with flying colors and there was no reason I wouldn't be able to go airborne. I took my oath in the recruiter's office and was then asked when I wanted to leave. I told the recruiter as soon as possible. He handed me paperwork and told me to be at the Greyhound station tomorrow night; at nine o'clock.

At dinner, I announced to the Clark family that I had something I wanted to share and that I also had one request. Everyone in the family looked directly at me.

I took a sip of water and said, "Today I enlisted in the Army. I'm sure you won't be disappointed to see me go. I'm so sorry all of this happened. I would never willingly do anything to hurt Diane. Living here will not work for me. I also think it is time for me to do something good and to serve my country. Reverend Clark, I will send everything I make in the Army to Diane. I want to do the right thing by her. I do have one request. Diane, I would like for you to take me to the bus station tomorrow night; I would like to say goodbye to my wife alone."

Nobody said a word. When I looked over at Diane, she had tears rolling down her cheeks. Before the meal was completed, Diane excused herself and went to her room.

The following night, I gathered my paperwork and met Diane at the car. She drove while I sat on the passenger side. Again, little was said. When we got to the Greyhound station, I gave the clerk a military voucher in return for a ticket. Some people had already boarded the bus. I stood next to the bus and took Diane's hand, asking her to look at me.

I said, "I want you to know that whatever happens, I will always remember the river."

I then took her in my arms and kissed her. She was also kissing me. She pulled closer and the kiss continued. When our arms dropped, tears formed in her eyes.

She said, "John, I'm so sorry."

Once I was on the bus, I had mixed feelings. I was glad to be away from the Clark family but I knew I would miss Diane. The realization that I was going to boot camp and would be going to war also began to sink in. The thing that bothered me the most was that the only thing Diane said to me as we parted was, "I'm so sorry."

CHAPTER TWELVE

Part II

France, April, 1944

With some persistence, I finally convinced Camille that we needed to get away from here. I didn't think it was a good idea to sell the cows. If we sold something to a neighbor, they would ask questions. Even though the neighbors had known Joseph and Camille for some time, I thought it was best to trust no one. William told me that it wasn't uncommon for the Major to hold a pistol to someone's head when questioning them.

I had no idea what to do with the livestock. Camille had a name for each cow. She would be reluctant to just leave them. I came up with the idea of leading them out to pasture and breaking the fence of our neighbor's farm. This way the cows would roam onto the old lady's farm. It would look like the cows broke the fence. I told William of the plan so that he could stop by and let her know about the cows. William would then be in the position to take the cows off her hands.

Camille closed up things and packed two suitcases. I took all our money that we had and drove the truck to town. It had been hard to purchase any gas, but as a farmer who supplied goods for the German army, I was sure I could get some. I also carried eggs and milk. I did not want to trade. I wanted money.

I had no trouble getting fuel. I was only allotted a certain amount. At the market area, I parked the truck and looked for the old Frenchman who walked with a cane. He would sometimes give William cash for milk and butter. I walked in the front door at the grocery store, but did not see anyone. When I walked back outside, there were two German soldiers next to my truck. In broken French they asked me if the truck was mine. I nodded yes. One of the soldiers motioned to a man in a military truck to move forward. The soldier in the truck parked next to my truck and began loading everything I had in the back onto his truck. I started to say something but decided I just needed to leave. Both soldiers laughed, pushing me against the truck. The tall, skinny soldier asked me for papers. I shook my head like I didn't understand. He then stuck his hand in my jacket to see if I had anything in my pockets. He located the cash and pulled it out. It wasn't a lot but it was all we had. He started counting the money when the other soldier told him to let me go. The tall, skinny soldier took the cash and threw it in the street. I didn't move immediately, but as soon as they turned and walked away, I scooped it up and put it in the pocket of my jacket.

When I got back to the farm, I explained to Camille what had happened. Things were getting worse by the minute. I grabbed the two suitcases and she took Joshua by the hand. We walked out the front door and closed it tightly. As we started to walk down the steps, we heard a car coming. We could also see the dust flying as the car turned the corner. Whoever it was, they were driving fast. We hurried back in the house and closed the door. I looked out the window and saw a car with two Nazi flags mounted on the front of it. It looked like a car that belonged to someone important. Camille said, "Oh, my God. Oh, my God."

I said, "Let me do the talking."

I wasn't sure why I said that. If the soldier spoke good French, I was screwed. The car came to a stop and an officer got out of the backseat. He stretched his arms and placed his hat on his head. The insignia on his uniform identified him as a major. This was the devil William had warned me about. The driver stayed in the car and lit up a cigarette. The Major pulled a nightstick from his belt and walked toward the house. He wasn't a big man but he walked as if he was somebody people should fear.

Camille held Joshua close to her and again said, "Oh, my God."

The Major did not bother to knock; he opened the door and walked inside. The three of us were standing side-by-side. I had my arm around Camille's shoulder. The Major said nothing. He slowly walked through the house, placing the nightstick in his right hand and hitting it against his left hand. He was hitting his left hand hard enough for it to hurt. He walked through the house and looked in every room; he looked in the closets and the cabinets. He continued to smack his left hand as he slowly walked in a circle. Then he noticed the suitcases behind us. He pushed us to one side and kicked one of the suitcases. He bent over and dumped the contents on the floor. I could feel Camille trembling. Joshua started to cry so she placed her hand over his mouth.

After what seemed like an eternity, the Major looked at me and in broken French said, "Mr. Bernhardt, are you going somewhere?"

"We are going to visit family," I replied, trying to remain calm.

"I see. And where is your family?"

"Paris."

He screamed, "You are a liar."

I didn't say anything. The Major again started pacing and hitting the nightstick in his left hand.

I said, "My parents are sick."

In a calmer voice he replied, "You are a liar. All Jews lie."

"I am not a Jew," I said.

"You are a liar."

This time his voice was full of hate and anger, "You are a Jew, liar."

As he came close to me, he swung his nightstick like a baseball bat, striking me on the side of the head. I fell to my knees. He struck a second time, striking me in the same place. I heard Camille scream as I felt another blow. After that, I didn't hear anything.

I could hear voices but I wasn't sure where they were coming from. I tried to open my eyes but everything was a blur. I could feel blood running over my eyes. I raised my hand to my face to wipe the blood away. My ears were still ringing but I could hear voices and screams. I rolled to my side and attempted to get up, but my legs were too wobbly. I lost my balance, falling to the floor. The screams were louder and I could now hear one voice. The voice was saying something about a Jew. The scream sounded like a child's. I remembered why I had been hit and slowly came to my feet. My vision started to clear. I could see Joshua screaming in the corner of the house. I turned my head slightly and saw the German Major with his pants around his ankles; he had his back to me. It became obvious he was raping Camille. She was lying on her back on the kitchen table. Her dress was up and her panties were on the floor. The Major was also choking her. He had both hands around her neck. Although he was yelling in German, I understood the two words, "Jew pig."

I took two steps, then I picked up one of the kitchen chairs that had been pushed to the side. The Major was still a blur but I took a swing at his head. I hit him hard and he fell to the floor. He wasn't knocked unconscious, but he was dazed and disoriented. He began to reach for his pistol holster. I fell to my knees and began to wrestle him for the pistol. I took a swing at his face, hitting him in the jaw. As his hand came off the pistol, I was able to pull the pistol from the holster. I was still weak from the blows I had received, blood continued to flow over my eyes, making it difficult to see him clearly. I took the pistol and held it close to what I thought was his face. I pulled the trigger then his body went limp.

I stood up and turned toward the kitchen table. Camille was standing, her body was trembling. I could see semen rolling down her legs. I took her panties and helped her put them on. She seemed better focused and her attention immediately went to the welfare of Joshua. She walked over to him, falling to her knees, to give him a hug; his crying immediately stopped.

Everything seemed to happen so quickly. I was still not thinking clearly. I felt like I was moving in slow motion.

Camille turned to me and in a whisper said, "The soldier."

I walked toward the window and stood to one side. I peeked through the curtain and saw the German soldier standing at the front of the car smoking a cigarette. He had his back to the house and apparently was not bothered by a gun being fired. Maybe the Major had planned to kill all of us. I still had the Major's gun in my right hand.

I walked back toward the kitchen and said, "I've got to kill him."

Camille's eyes grew big; she picked up Joshua, and went to the bedroom. I went out the back door and tiptoed down the stairs. I went to the right side of the house, slowly walking until I came to the corner of the house. I wiped the blood from my eyes and peeked around the corner. The German soldier was still smoking a cigarette with his back to me. I walked slowly toward him, doing my best not to make any noise. I was about fifteen yards from his back when he turned and looked at me.

He saw me holding the pistol. When he grabbed for his pistol, I fired, hitting him in the shoulder. He stumbled backwards as I fired three more shots. He fell to the ground and did not move. I walked toward him and fired another round in the back of his head.

I staggered towards the house and saw Camille and Joshua on the porch. As I walked up the steps, I stumbled and fell to my knees. Camille rushed over and helped me stand.

Once inside, I said, "We leave now!" She rushed to the bedroom and came back with a wet cloth. She wiped the side of my head with the wet cloth and then tied a rag around my head. Although it didn't stop the bleeding, I could see better than before.

She grabbed the two suitcases and the three of us made our way to the truck. She placed the suitcases in the back and I walked to the driver's side. She grabbed my arm and shook her head.

When I didn't move she said, "I'll drive."

I didn't argue, everything was still blurry and my head was throbbing. I was beginning to feel the pain and was starting to have difficulty concentrating.

Camille could barely reach the pedals. She pulled up her dress to her waist so she could better operate the clutch. Once she had the truck in first gear, the tires spun and gravel turned beneath the tires. We were bouncing down the road that led to the farm. Once she reached the fork, she turned left. We were going in the opposite direction of Amiens. The road was still bumpy and it was exaggerated by the high speed we were going.

We had traveled at least ten miles before I asked Camille, "Where are we going?" She didn't answer. Maybe I had used the wrong French words.

Again I said, "Where are we going?" She shrugged her shoulders.

Holding my head in my hands I calmly said, "Stop. We need a plan."

She pulled over and stopped the car.

I looked at her and said, "If you don't understand, raise your hand." She nodded as I continued. "Once they find the bodies, they will hunt for us. All roads will be blocked and the train station will have German soldiers looking for us. They will have a perimeter established. I'm not sure how much farther we can go in the truck before we run into a roadblock. Do you understand?" She shook her head affirmatively.

"Do you know a place we can hide?" She didn't say anything. She was thinking.

Although she didn't seem convinced, she said, "Andre Bellamy."

"Who's he?" I asked.

"He is the farmer who helped Joseph get started."

"Why would he help?"

Camille took my hands from my face and looked directly at me. "He's a good man. He liked Joseph."

"Does he know Joseph is a Jew?" I started to say 'was a Jew' but caught myself.

"Yes."

"Where is his farm?"

She pointed to the right and said, "Not far. He has a big farm."

We started traveling again and after three miles, she turned down a smaller road that was mainly mud. A short distance later she pointed to the right and said, "Bellamy farm."

CHAPTER THIRTEEN

Camille told me all about the Bellamy family. The family had been there for many years and had one of the largest farms in the area. Mr. Bellamy and his wife lived with their oldest son and his family in the large farmhouse. They also had another son who lived with his family nearby.

When Camille stopped the truck in front of the house, a short stocky man wearing a straw hat walked out the front door. He reminded me of the Amish farmers in Pennsylvania. He recognized Camille and gave a smile. Next, a heavyset woman walked out the front door and slowly walked toward the truck.

Mr. Bellamy came to the driver's side and said, "It is good to see you."

"Andre, this is Joseph's cousin, Jean. We need your help," Camille responded.

Looking confused, Mr. Bellamy asked, "Where is Joseph?"

"Joseph is dead," Camille said.

"Dead. What happened?" Mr. Bellamy asked, as he opened the car door for Camille.

"He was killed by the Germans," she cried out, trying to keep her composure.

A look of panic came over his face, "Are you in trouble?" he asked.

"Yes. We had to leave. They are looking for Jews."

"Are they looking for you?"

"Yes. That's how Jean got injured. We need to hide."

Mr. Bellamy looked toward his wife as he rubbed his chin. He looked at me and then looked toward the woods. He opened the car door and said, "I will help you. My son and I will take your truck and hide it at the old mill about three miles from here. The mill has been abandoned for years. There's an old barn on the property. My wife will look at Jean's head. She has patched up our boys for years. I will hide you in the small barn next to the woods. I only use it to store things."

We got out of the truck and took our suitcases. Mrs. Bellamy told us to follow her. Mr. Bellamy went to the farmhouse and returned with his son. His son was taller, but looked a lot like his father. Within a matter of minutes, they were driving the two trucks away from the farm.

When we reached the old barn, Mrs. Bellamy showed us where to put the suitcases and pointed to the small hayloft where we would sleep. She told me to sit down on a bale of hay. She removed my bandage, squinting her eyes as she checked my head.

She looked at me and said, "This is a bad cut. I can sew it up, but it will hurt."

Camille looked at her and said, "His French is not good. He speaks English." She looked puzzled.

I responded that I understood. "It is okay to sew."

She smiled and walked toward the house. A few minutes later she returned with a bucket of water, soap, and a sewing kit. She cleaned the area on the side of my head and she explained to Camille that she no longer had anything to numb the area. She looked at me and smiled. She had me lay on my side as she began to sew my scalp together. My head hurt from the blows I had received from the Major. I was already in pain so the sewing wasn't as bad as I had anticipated. She put a new dressing on the wound and told me to lie down. She told Camille that she would return with food and blankets.

I closed my eyes, trying to focus on something other than the pain I felt in my head. When I heard the truck coming, I tried to sit up. Camille pushed me back down and told me it was just Mr. Bellamy. I closed my eyes. I could hear Camille talking to Joshua. I relaxed and thought I could sleep when all of a sudden I felt nauseous. I made it outside the barn just in time. When I was finished throwing up, I went back inside and sat on the ground with my back against the wall.

At dusk, the entire Bellamy family came to the barn. Mrs. Bellamy brought buckets that contained food and water while Mr. Bellamy brought blankets. His son and daughter-in-law followed them in the barn and took a seat on a bale of hay. They insisted that we eat before we talked. Camille prepared a plate for Joshua and then fixed a plate for me. The three of us wolfed down the food.

Mr. Bellamy took a seat on another bale of hay and motioned for his daughter-in-law to join him. His daughter-in-law said in English, "I speak some English. Mr. Bellamy has asked me to interpret what he says." I nodded that I understood. Mr. Bellamy began to speak. When he was finished, his daughter-in-law said, "The truck is located at the old mill barn. On the way back, we saw many German trucks. You are safe here for now. The Germans come here every week to get food from the farm. It has gotten very bad. Now they take most everything and leave my family with little. You should stay in the barn at all times. If you see Germans, you can sneak out the back between the broken boards. The barn is next to the woods. Once you are in the woods, you can go down the hill and hide behind the large rock. My wife will bring food and water every day in the buckets. There is a hole in the ground that is covered with boards. You should keep the suitcases there. If you have to leave the barn, take your blankets with you. The Germans have never searched our farm but things are different now."

I looked at the interpreter and said, "Please thank Mr. Bellamy. Tell him we need to rest and then decide what to do next. We do not want to put his family in danger."

When I was through speaking, Mr. Bellamy responded and the interpreter said, "Why are the Germans after you?"

"We are Jews and I killed the German who was going to kill Camille."

He looked startled and rubbed his face with both hands.

He then stood and said, "We must be careful and smart."

Camille prepared a place for Joshua to sleep in the loft. The loft contained hay, which could be spread on the wood planks. She then placed blankets on top of the hay. All the places, including mine, were together. Within minutes, Joshua fell asleep which didn't surprise me. All of us were drained from our experiences.

I climbed the ladder and sat next to Joshua. I took off my boots and stretched out on my back. My head was still throbbing, but I was doing a good job of ignoring the pain. I was so tired, I felt like I had been drugged. Instead of turning off the lantern and going to sleep, Camille took the lantern and went down the ladder. I heard her raise the floorboard to lift out the suitcase. I rolled to one side to see if I could see what she was doing. When she returned the suitcase under the floorboard, I noticed she had a pair of panties in her hand. She then reached under her dress and pulled down the panties she was wearing so she could put on the clean pair. Her next move surprised me. She took the worn pair, dug a small hole in the dirt floor, and buried them. She wiped her hands on a bale of hay, and climbed the ladder to the loft. I had forgotten that her panties were stained. It was her way to feel clean again and to bury a part of her painful past.

She settled down on the other side of Joshua and turned off the lamp.

I closed my eyes, immediately feeling my body drifting off to sleep. I was almost asleep, when I heard Camille say, "Merci."

I responded by saying, "De rien."

After all that had happened to her, she thanked me. I rolled to my right side and looked at her. Even though it was dark, I could see her small features and dark hair that was covering part of her face. For the first time, I realized how dark and thick her eyebrows were. I thought to myself, w*hat a remarkable woman.*

Before I drifted off to sleep, I thought of everything that had happened to me since that evening when I had jumped out of the plane. Joseph had saved my life and I, in turn, had saved his wife's life. Now I was fleeing for my life with his family. I wasn't sure why I decided to stay, but I did know that I had no regrets. My thoughts turned to Allentown. My family would have been notified of my death by now. I knew my mother would grieve and Reverend Clark would be relieved. I wasn't certain about Diane.

CHAPTER FOURTEEN

I woke up to roosters crowing and the smell of coffee. Mrs. Bellamy had brought food and coffee to the barn. Camille was attending to Joshua. They had let me sleep. When I sat up to put on my boots, I felt pain on the left side of my head when I came down the ladder, Mrs. Bellamy was waiting for me with a cup of coffee.

After Camille made sure Joshua had eaten, she took the food that Mrs. Bellamy had prepared and brought me a plate. I noticed the bruising around her neck; Camille had been choked so hard that a ring of black and blue covered her throat. When she caught me staring, she pulled her dress up to partially cover the bruises. Mrs. Bellamy had noticed the bruises too, but she said nothing. After eating, Mrs. Bellamy checked my dressing, and she seemed pleased. She commented on my bruises. I didn't have access to a mirror but realized I must look pretty bad.

Mrs. Bellamy reminded us of the outhouse, and informed us she would return with soap and water. Camille made sure Joshua was clean. I never asked Camille the age of Joshua; he may have taken after his mother and was small for his age.

We remained in the small barn throughout the day. After eating a bowl of soup for lunch, I asked Camille if she wanted to take Joshua for a walk in the woods. We crawled through the broken planks in the barn and within ten feet entered the thick wooded area. We walked down the steep hill and came to a narrow path next to the rock Mr. Bellamy had mentioned. Camille and I started walking down the path while Joshua ran and hopped. He was definitely glad to be outside.

As we were walking, I said, "I want to speak French."

She smiled and replied, "You are speaking French."

"It needs to be better. You teach me."

Camille took my hand, "I will help you," she said.

"Good. Talking more with you will help me," I said confidently.

She smiled and looked embarrassed. As I talked about trying to make our way to Paris, she kept interrupting me by giving me the correct pronunciation of various words. It was making our conversation somewhat difficult, but I realized she was serious about helping me learn French. I was able to make her understand we needed rest and that I needed to get the stitches out of my head. We could then meet with Mr. Bellamy to formulate a plan to make our way to Paris. The Germans would not forget about us.

The next two days were the same routine. I was getting back to normal and was able to concentrate for longer periods of time. My French lessons were going well. As we walked, Camille would point things out and then use the words in a complete sentence. I would repeat her words and could tell how well I had done by the expression on her face. Occasionally, I would say something terribly wrong and she would slap me on the arm. Although she realized I was doing it on purpose, she continued to play along.

On the fourth day, before Mrs. Bellamy brought our breakfast, we heard the sound of trucks approaching. I took the blankets and tossed them in with the suitcases below the floorboards. Camille grabbed Joshua and we crawled through the opening and sprinted to the woods. I motioned for Camille to take Joshua down the hill. I crouched behind a tree. Camille waved her hand for me to come. I shook my head no and motioned for her to go.

Mr. Bellamy and his son came out the front door and walked toward the lead truck. A German soldier got out of the truck and stood in front. Two other soldiers got out of the back of the truck. I noticed the large military truck was pulling an open trailer with very large sideboards. The soldier who was driving walked toward Mr. Bellamy and the two of them started talking. I saw Mr. Bellamy lift his arms and drop them like he was disappointed with what he was hearing. The three men stood for some time before Mr. Bellamy and his son motioned for the truck towing the trailer to follow them. They went around the farmhouse so I could no longer see what was happening. Thirty minutes later the truck and trailer returned. The truck was full of corn and other boxes. The trailer now contained a large beef cow. When the truck pulled away, I walked down the hill and had Camille and Joshua return with me to the barn.

An hour later Mr. and Mrs. Bellamy returned with the buckets full of bread and coffee. While we were eating bread, Mr. Bellamy started to speak and then stopped. I knew he was concerned that I would not understand.

I said, "My French is better. If I do not understand, I will shake my head."

He told me that he knew some English.

He then proceeded in French, "The Germans are coming more often. They take my crops and now my cows; this is hard. We make do with what we have. We can continue to provide food but it may be less."

Camille and I responded at the same time, "Merci."

Mr. Bellamy added, "They are looking for you." He looked at me and said, "They do not know Joseph is dead. They think they are looking for Joseph and his wife. The soldier wanted to know if we knew you. I told him I sold cattle to you."

I realized he was talking to me as if I was Joseph. I chose not to correct him with the hope he would continue talking.

"The soldier wanted to know if I had seen you and if I knew you were Jews. I answered no. He then told me I am to report to him if I see you or know of your whereabouts. He reminded me that failure to do so would not be good for me or my family."

"Do you need for us to leave, Mr. Bellamy?"

"I don't think they have found the truck. As far as they are concerned, you could be kilometers away. Fuck the Germans."

Although his talk was defiant, I could tell he was worried. I glanced at Camille and then said, "It might be good for us to get to Paris. Maybe you could draw a map."

Mr. Bellamy surprised me when he motioned for me to follow him. We walked out of the barn and into the woods.

He stopped and said, "Who are you?"

His question startled me. "What do you mean," I asked.

"You are not Joseph's cousin."

"No, I'm not. I'm an American soldier."

Mr. Bellamy turned to look at me, "Why are you with Camille?" he asked.

"Joseph saved my life," I replied.

He didn't say anything. He looked like he was thinking about what he wanted to say next. "When are the Americans coming?" he asked.

"Soon," I said.

As he continued walking, I followed next to him. After a short distance he asked, "So you might be safe if you go to Paris?"

"I'm not sure, but it makes sense to me."

"I will find a map and we can study it," he said. "You will need to stay off the main roads. Your truck is no good."

"Why?" I asked.

"Too dangerous. Besides, they will be looking for it."

We returned to the barn and I finished my cold coffee. Mrs. Bellamy said it was time for the stitches to come out. I laid on two bales of hay while she removed the stitches. She had done this before, within a few minutes the stitches were removed; she admired her work. She congratulated me on my fine new scar.

CHAPTER FIFTEEN

We had been at the Bellamy farm for a week; we had established a routine and for periods of time, I actually felt safe. Mrs. Bellamy offered to wash the clothes we were wearing which was appreciated. We continued bathing with the bucket of water and soap she would bring to the barn.

One evening, Mr. Bellamy accompanied his wife when she brought food. After eating, the two of us sat on bales of hay. Mr. Bellamy pulled out a map, which contained roads and city names. He had taken the time to draw a detailed route we could follow to Paris. He lit a kerosene lamp and set it next to the map.

He went on to explain, "I have marked a path that will keep you off the main roads. I'm not sure of some of the landscape. You may encounter streams and you will certainly have fences to go through. At night, you could probably walk along the roads. When you see lights, you can duck in the woods or lie low to the ground. You cannot carry enough food or water; you will need to rely on the help of villagers and farmers. Most people support the French resistance. Be careful what you say at first. If they identify you as resistance, they will probably help you. I would not say anything about being a Jew. I would stay away from the train stations. I'm sure there are soldiers looking for a man and woman with a child. When you get to Paris, stay off the main streets. You should look for people who support the resistance."

"Thank you for all you have done. We will get our things together."

"It looks like the weather is turning bad. I would wait until you have better weather. I have a question. How long before the Americans come?"

"I think it will be soon," I said, trying to reassure him.

"Months or weeks?" he asked.

"Weeks."

He smiled and patted me on the arm. I was never sure when an invasion would take place. Along with the British, we had been getting ready for a long time. In a few days it would be June. I was praying it would be soon. I was also hoping a major objective would be to retake Paris.

I explained everything to Camille about the route, and the advice Mr. Bellamy had given me. She listened carefully but gave me no indication what she thought about the plan. She reminded me that Joshua was small and could not walk long distances. I told her we would move slowly and rest when necessary; she seemed to understand. I also explained that I could carry Joshua.

That night after Joshua went to sleep, we both laid on our blankets looking at the barn roof. The rain was pounding the old roof. It became necessary for us to slide over so we wouldn't get wet from water coming from a hole in the roof. The sound of rain was soothing as I tried to sleep. I was going over in my mind the route Mr. Bellamy had shared. I heard Camille moan and then realized she was crying. She certainly had many reasons to cry; she then began to sob. I got up and walked around Joshua to sit beside her. To my surprise, she rose up and put her arms around me. She continued to sob and place her face tight against my neck. I could feel her heart pounding and her tears running down my neck. I didn't say anything; I just held her tight and stroked the back of her head.

When the deep sobs ended, she said, "I missed my period." Like before, this sentence caused me to freeze and feel numb. This time, however, I didn't feel panicked. I remained silent for almost a minute and then said, "Are you sure?"

She pulled away from the embrace, looking into my eyes, "Yes, I'm sure."

"Joseph?" I asked.

"No."

Again I waited for a while and then added, "The German soldier?"

Sadness filled her voice. "Yes," she replied

I continued to hold her and listen to the pounding rain on the roof.

She said, "I don't want this baby." I didn't know what to say so I chose to remain silent. Finally, she added, "We must go to the Lille. I know a doctor there."

"I don't understand."

"I don't want this baby. Dr. Benoit will remove it. He was a friend of my father."

"Where is Lille?" I asked.

"It is north near Belgium."

"What about Paris?" I whispered.

"We must first go to Lille."

"Okay, I will talk to Mr. Bellamy and get directions."

"Merci."

I continued to hold Camille until she eventually fell asleep. I placed her on the blanket and returned to mine. The rain continued to pound on the roof as thoughts raced through my head.

The next day I told Mrs. Bellamy I needed to talk with her husband. After noon, Mr. Bellamy came to the barn. He had been working in the fields; he was sweaty and had large clumps of mud on his pants.

Although the rain was a welcomed sight for him, he now had to work in mud. Again, we went to the woods to talk.

"Mr. Bellamy, I need to change my route. I need to go to Lille."

He stopped, "Why would you go there?"

"Camille needs to see a doctor."

"Is she sick?" I asked.

"No. She is going to have a baby."

"I don't understand," he said.

"She was raped by a German soldier. She wants to end the pregnancy. She knows a doctor in Lille who would do this."

Mr. Bellamy seemed disappointed and even frustrated with my comment.

He added, "Getting to Lille will be difficult and dangerous. I will bring you another map. You will see this is not a good idea."

Later that evening, I again met with Mr. Bellamy to map out a new route. It was easy to understand why it would be more dangerous. There were fewer side roads and there was an increased likelihood of seeing Germans. There were many potential German checkpoints and the terrain would be more difficult. The only advantage of going to Lille was that the Germans looking for us would more than likely rule it out as a destination.

I went over everything with Camille. Instead of being frightened about the potential danger, she seemed relieved and even anxious to go. Mr. Bellamy said the weather would be improving soon, so I told Camille we needed to pack our things and be ready to go.

Mr. Bellamy handed me a WWI canteen and an old compass. He didn't know if the compass was accurate. I told him he had saved our lives and that we would always be grateful.

That night I could hear Camille tossing and turning; neither of us really slept. The trip to Lille would be risky. My one positive thought focused on the invasion. If it didn't happen in the very near future, our chance of survival was slim.

I had barely fallen asleep when it was time to get up and go. Camille was returning from a visit to the outhouse with Joshua when I came down the ladder. We had the suitcases next to the opening in the wall. We sat on the bales of hay waiting for Mrs. Bellamy to arrive. For some reason, she seemed to be running late.

I peeked between the boards of the huge barn doors and saw her coming. She had the familiar buckets that contained bread and coffee. I opened the door and let her inside. She sat down the buckets and told Camille she would return with food that we could take on our trip.

I started to pour coffee in the tin cup when all of us heard what sounded like a truck coming. I peeked through the crack, and could see dust rising in the distance. Whatever was coming it was moving at a fast speed. Camille grabbed Joshua and went to the opening next to the suitcases. I kept looking through the crack, waiting to see what was coming around the corner heading toward the front of the farmhouse. I saw an old truck that seemed familiar. I turned to Mrs. Bellamy and Camille and said, "It's William."

William jumped out of the truck and ran toward the front of the house. Before he got there, he was stopped by Mrs. Bellamy. I could not hear what they were saying but they both looked excited. All of a sudden, Mr. Bellamy came sprinting toward us. Before he got to the barn, I opened the door. He was excited and had trouble getting his breath. He paused for a brief second and then said, "The Germans are coming.

They found your truck and they are searching all the nearby farms. You must go now."

He grabbed a bale of hay and gave it to his wife and said, "Take it to William. He is going to say he came for hay. I'll bring two more."

Mr. Bellamy then went to the back of the barn and opened the lid of an old chest. He pulled out a large brown sack that contained pot ashe, phosphate and lime. I remembered asking Camille about the contents of similar sacks when we planted beans. He spread the contents on the ground and kicked straw over it. As he went out of the barn door he said, "Take everything with you. God be with you."

I grabbed the two buckets and blankets. I then ran toward the opening and grabbed a suitcase. Camille grabbed the other suitcase and we crawled through the opening. Once in the woods, I motioned for Camille to take Joshua down the hill. She looked worried so, I calmly said, "I will come in a minute."

Camille slipped as she went down the hill. She was holding Joshua's hand so they both fell. She got back up and they both continued downhill.

I put the buckets and suitcase on the ground and crouched down next to thick brush. Within a minute, two German trucks arrived. There were soldiers in the back of the trucks. When the trucks stopped, the soldiers exited. There were at least ten soldiers and two dogs. William loaded the last bale of hay in his truck and started to get in the cab. He was stopped and remained standing next to his truck instead.

The soldier in charge was yelling at Mr. Bellamy. After he was through yelling, all the members of the Bellamy family filed outside and stood next to Mr. Bellamy. The German soldier then pulled out his pistol and started waving it around, occasionally pointing it at a family member. I wasn't sure what was being said, but I did know the conversation was about

Camille and me. I wasn't sure what to do; I felt so responsible but helpless. I picked up the buckets and suitcase and went down the hill.

Camille and Joshua were crouched behind the rock. I left the buckets behind the large rock and motioned for Camille and Joshua to follow me. I picked Joshua up and placed him on my right shoulder. I could see Camille carrying the other suitcase in one hand and a loaf of bread in the other. The canteen with the long strap was hanging around her neck. The loaf of bread was our only food. We at least had a canteen. Hopefully, Camille had the compass. We kept moving at a fast pace. I did not hear gunshots or the sound of barking dogs. I could only hope the soldiers would search, find nothing, leave, and go to the next farm. I realized the sack of pot ashe, phosphate and lime was for a dog that might enter the barn. The smell would be too much for even the best tracking dog.

CHAPTER SIXTEEN

We made our way through several pastures, though some of the land had fences we had to climb. Joshua would walk for a while and then become tired; when I carried him, Camille would carry the two suitcases.

When we came to a wooded area, we rested and ate the bread. Camille did have the compass, which was a great relief. She also brought the tin cup that we used for coffee. We never stopped to fill up the canteen; I would eventually need to locate a stream or possibly a well pump. If possible, I wanted to avoid going near a farmhouse. I was not sure who we could trust.

We continued walking through farmland and eventually came to a road. Fortunately, there was a wooded area near the road. I told Camille we needed to wait here, the decision to wait proved providential. Within a matter of minutes, a large caravan of German military trucks and equipment passed. The trucks were full of soldiers; they were moving at a fast speed. Perhaps this had something to do with an American landing.

When the last truck passed, I motioned for Camille and Joshua to follow me across the road. Once on the other side, I studied the map Mr. Bellamy had given me. We had traveled less than seven miles. We had a long way to go to Lille and no food or water.

When we crossed a stream, I filled up the canteen. Joshua told his mother he was hungry. She said nothing to him. We just kept walking. The compass did work, but I wasn't sure if I was using it correctly.

I wished I had paid more attention to the drill instructor when I went through boot camp.

By evening, we were exhausted and hungry. We needed to stop in the woods for cover. I knew it was too risky to build a fire. We slept on the ground huddled together. I knew we had to find food the next day or we would be in serious trouble.

The next morning, I spotted a farmhouse in the distance. I told Camille to stay while I went in search of food.

"Do you know what you are looking for?" she asked.

"No," I replied.

"Look in the garden; if you see asparagus, pull it up. Any kind of vegetable is good; if you see corn, pick a few ears. They may have a chicken coop. You can get eggs if you remember how to get the hen off the nest." This brought a grin to my face.

As I approached the farmhouse, I didn't see any activity. I slowly made my way closer to the house. I heard a dog bark and thought, *Oh shit, this is not what I need.* I located a small garden that was enclosed by a fence. I entered through the gate and immediately started pulling asparagus. I stuffed the stalks in my shirt and looked for other things to pull up. I saw some radishes and pulled up several clumps and stuffed them in my shirt.

When I eyed the hen house, I crouched down to see if anybody was around it. Seeing no one, I stood up and slowly walked toward it. Once inside, I retrieved four eggs and carefully placed them in my shirt.

As I left the chicken coop, I walked to the edge of the barn and peeked inside. Again, I didn't see anyone. Everyone must be working in the fields. Two milk cows were eating hay and there were four milk pails nearby. I took one of the pails and put my milking skills to work.

When I returned to Camille, I looked like an overweight farmer carrying a bucket. We went back to the woods, and Camille washed off the vegetables and told Joshua to eat. When he refused, she sternly told him again. She poured milk in the cup and cracked an egg in it. I was surprised how quickly Joshua downed the milk and egg. At least we had something to eat, but I wasn't sure how we could continue to find food. We needed to go on faith.

Camille took the vegetables we didn't eat and placed them in a suitcase. Shortly after we resumed our journey; I was carrying Joshua. Because the terrain had become more difficult, we were constantly stopping to rest. We crossed over two roads that were shown on the map; I was confident we were at least going in the right direction.

While walking up a steep hill, Camille fell and dropped a suitcase. When the suitcase fell to the ground, it opened and all of the contents flew out. When I started to stuff clothes back into the suitcase, I noticed the latch was broken.

I looked up at Camille and said, "We need to get rid of the suitcases."

She didn't say anything. She grabbed the jacket on the ground that belonged to Joshua, dropping the other suitcase on the ground. She then took Joshua's hand and started walking. I continued to find reasons to admire this woman.

We walked in this fashion for two more days, living off the vegetables I had taken and pears that we had picked from a tree. We were tired, hungry, and low on water. I thought it might be time to make our way to a village to see if someone would help us even though the Germans were everywhere. It wasn't a good idea to go where we would likely encounter them, but we were getting desperate.

As darkness drew near, I saw what looked like a campfire in the distance. We were able to get close without being seen. There were two horse-drawn wagons next to the campfire. There were at least twenty people in the area, including some children.

Camille leaned toward me and whispered in my ear, "Gypsies."

The three of us walked slowly toward the campfire; we looked like refugees. As we came into sight, a large man with a full beard stood and looked at us. I could tell he was sizing me up. We obviously offered no threat.

He said, "Welcome to our campsite. Are you hungry?"

Camille responded, "We are very tired and hungry. If you have anything to spare, it would be appreciated."

"You are welcome to eat what we have. We have rabbit stew, and my wife has also thrown in a few squirrels. These are hard times. My name is Anton."

"This is my husband, Joseph, and our son, Joshua. My name is Camille."

When Camille referred to me as her husband, I glanced at her, she gave me a stare letting me know it was better to be traveling as a family. We sat down on an old log. Two of the women scooped up the stew and placed it in a bowl. All of us were so hungry we didn't say anything. We ate ravenously until the bowls were empty. I could have eaten two more bowls but didn't want to take advantage of our generous host.

The campsite was in a perfect location, in the woods close to a river. There were signs they had camped here for a long time. Once our bowls were collected, Anton took a seat on another log and lit a pipe. His clothes were worn and he had a huge hole in the sole of his right boot. He took a few puffs on his pipe and stroked his beard. A few of the women joined us around the campfire. Joshua was so tired he laid his head on Camille's lap.

Anton looked directly at me and asked, "Where are you going?"

"Lille," I replied.

"That is a very dangerous place. Especially for a Jew."

"How do you know we are Jews?" I asked.

"Because like us, you are running from something. Why go to Lille? You should stay with us here."

"We need to find a doctor."

"I see. Your boy has a bad cough."

I knew Joshua had a cough. I guess I was so focused on moving and getting to Lille that I failed to realize his cough had gotten worse. By the look on Camille's face, I could tell she had blocked his cough from her mind.

"Yes. We need to get to a doctor."

Anton stood and walked closer to the fire. "Your accent is different. Where are you from?"

Although my French had improved, I knew I stood out. I'm not sure why, but I answered, "At one time, I lived in Canada."

I then switched the topic and asked, "How long have you been here?"

"We have been here two weeks. We escaped from the camp and are hiding here."

I asked, "What camp?"

"We were in a camp for Gypsies. The Germans gathered us up and put us in the camp. It is the French who kept us there. My own countrymen were my guards. The Germans called us spies. We did not have enough to eat at the camp; my family was starving so I found a way to escape."

I inquired, "Are the Germans looking for you?"

"I don't think so. They seem more concerned with moving troops."

I replied, "They are getting ready."

"Ready for what?" he asked.

"The invasion by the Americans and the British."

Anton looked excited and his eyes opened wide. He looked quickly at the people around the campfire and said, "Do you think this will happen?"

"Yes, I do."

"Will it happen soon?" he asked.

"I think it will happen very soon."

"Then you must stay with us and hide until the Americans come."

"I first must go to Lille."

"Then you should stay with us and rest before you leave."

"Are we near Lille?" I asked.

"You are close to Cambrai. You still have a long way to go."

I remembered seeing Cambrai on the map. We had not traveled in a straight line, so we were at least thirty miles farther right on the map. Anton was correct. We still had a long way to go.

Joshua was asleep in Camille's arms. He was breathing so deeply he started to snore. Anton stood and turned to his wife and said, "Fix them a place to sleep. We will talk more in the morning."

Anton insisted that we place our blankets close to the campfire. Camille rolled Joshua up in his blanket and placed him between us. It was the best night's sleep we had had in a long time. I liked the secure feeling of being with other people.

In the morning, we were handed a bowl of porridge. It was mushy and had little taste. We were, however, thankful to have something to eat.

After eating, Camille suggested we go to the river and wash up. The water was refreshing and all of us smelled better. Camille looked at me when Joshua began to cough; the cough was getting worse. Now we needed to get to Lille for two reasons.

When we returned to the campsite, some of the men were missing. I assumed they were out searching for food. For the gypsy camp, it was a matter of survival.

We rested most of the day, which seemed to help Joshua. He looked better, but his cough had not improved. In the evening, everyone gathered around the campfire. We had another bowl of stew, and this time Anton gave me a cup of coffee to drink. I wasn't sure how he had obtained coffee, but I was not about to ask.

As we sat around the campfire, Anton said, "I may know somebody who can help you get to Lille."

Camille and I both turned our heads toward him. I said, "Who would help us?"

He replied, "A priest."

"Why would a priest help us?"

"Because you are Jews."

I shook my head and said, "I don't understand."

"There is a priest in Cambrai who has helped Jews hide and escape. Father Glaize is a brave man; he has helped many people. He is also careful and he knows many people."

"Do you know this priest?" I asked.

"I know him but not well."

"Do you think he might help us?"

"I'm not sure. Your son is sick, so maybe he will."

I stood and walked toward Anton. As I got close to where he was sitting I asked, "Can you take us to him?"

"Yes, but we will need to leave at night. It is too risky during the day. We can leave tomorrow night. You should get your rest."

"Anton, I have a question for you; you said the Germans are not as interested in finding you as they have been. Are they still interested in finding Jews?"

"They are always interested in finding Jews," he replied.

CHAPTER SEVENTEEN

I had a sleepless night, so did Camille. It was a combination of worry and being awakened by Joshua's cough which brought about more worry. The cough was getting worse, he was so congested he had trouble breathing at night.

One of the ladies in the camp brought us some sassafras tea to drink. Although Joshua was reluctant to drink the tea, it helped ease his cough. We rested in the morning as much as possible and ate a type of mush for breakfast. It wasn't tasty but it was filling. Anton again served coffee, which was a treat.

Since the plan was to arrive in Cambrai at night, Anton surprised us when he said it was time to get our things together. It was still daylight and Anton would not want to be seen. We were going to leave earlier than expected because I had miscalculated the distance to Cambrai. Anton said we had a seven-mile hike over some difficult terrain.

I carried Joshua; after a mile I had to rest. Anton put Joshua on his shoulders, and Joshua placed his head on the large pile of curly hair on Anton's head. Instead of resting, we continued walking down the narrow path. Just before darkness we came to an open field. We heard the sound of airplane engines. Anton motioned us to fall on the ground. Several planes flew overhead in a tight formation, they were German and heading east.

When we resumed, we moved at a quick pace until we reached the tree line. There was not a path to follow so we went through brush with no clear direction. Anton did not seem to be concerned, and I took this as a good sign. Joshua was limp and almost lifeless. We paused, and Anton put Joshua down. Camille ripped off a piece of her dress that was part of the hem and poured water over it. She wiped Joshua's face and then tied the cloth around his forehead. I offered to carry Joshua, but Anton scooped him up and continued to forge through the dense brush.

In the dark, I had no idea how Anton knew where to walk. We came down a steep hill and reached a road that looked like it would lead us to town. Anton motioned for us to stay by the road. He walked a few hundred yards, peering in both directions and then waved his arm signaling us to join him. We walked on the side of the road for about a mile and saw headlights coming toward us. We dove in the brush near the road. Camille took Joshua and held him close to her. I peeked through the brush and watched trucks carrying troops pass by us. I started counting and then lost track of the number. The trucks were moving at high speed. They were followed by seven cars. One car had Nazi flags mounted in the front.

Once the trucks passed, Anton stood up; we resumed our journey. Anton was searching for something. After about thirty yards, he waved for us to catch up. He left the road and went down a path into the woods. It was dark and visibility was poor. Anton showed no concern and obviously had been this way many times. Before long, I saw lights. As we drew nearer, I could see the outline of buildings. Finally, just before we emerged from the woods, Anton stopped and pointed to the Cambrai Cathedral.

It was a magnificent looking structure with tall spires reaching toward the sky. We walked slowly past the cathedral, until we reached a house in the rear. We squatted down and Anton went to a side door and knocked. After a small delay, a man in a robe opened the door. He was shorter than Anton and wore wire-rimmed glasses. I couldn't hear anything that was being said. Anton was doing his best to convince the man he needed to help us.

Anton gave the OK signal. I picked up Joshua and the three of us joined Anton who said, "This is Father Glaize. He will help."

I held out my hand and said, "I'm Joseph Bernhardt, this is my wife Camille, and this is our son, Joshua." Father Glaize shook my hand and said, "I will put you in my guest room tonight. We will talk more in the morning."

Anton grabbed and hugged me. I felt like a child when his huge arms wrapped around me. I told him, "I will never forget your kindness."

He answered, "Maybe one day we will meet again."

Father Glaize took us down a small hallway until we reached a room that contained a bed, a dresser, and a wash bowl. I laid Joshua on the bed. Camille removed the cloth from his head. She said, "He is so hot."

I took the cloth and poured cool water over it and returned it to Camille. Shortly, Father Glaize returned with bread and cheese. He told us we would be safe tonight but other arrangements would be needed in the morning. When I started to ask him a question, he told me we would talk in the morning.

Camille slept next to Joshua in bed. I took the blanket and slept on the floor. As I closed my eyes, I thought about the day's journey. Once again, I had told someone I was Camille's husband. I rationalized in my mind, *it just simplifies things.*

The next morning, a knock on the door woke us up. I opened the door and Father Glaize was standing there. He was wearing slacks and a shirt with a white collar. "May I come in? It is best to speak here."

"Yes, please come in."

Camille sat up in bed and I sat next to her, Joshua was still asleep. Father Glaize pulled over a chair and sat down. In a low voice he said, "Anton told me you are Jews on the run and you need to get to Lille. Why Lille?"

"Our son is very sick and we know a doctor there."

"I can probably get a doctor to come here to look at your son."

"Camille trusts this doctor."

Father Glaize was risking his life, but I could not bring myself to tell him about the rape. He was already helping others and staying at the church would complicate things for him. He stared at us and said nothing. Camille started to cry. He placed his hand on her head and said, "I will take you to Lille, but not today. It is too dangerous. There are Germans everywhere. It seems the troops are being mobilized. Word is they are going to Normandy. This is where the Americans and British came ashore."

Camille looked at me. In an excited voice, I asked, "The Americans and British have started the invasion?"

"Yes, it started yesterday; at least that's what I've been told."

Camille and I embraced as our eyes filled with tears. Father Glaize continued, "That's why it might be helpful to stay here."

Camille said, "My son is very sick, he comes first. I do know a doctor in Lille, he is a family friend so being a Jew is not a problem."

"When I think it's safe, I will drive you to Lille. Camille, you will need to stay with the two nuns, they will give you clothing. You will be Sister Camille. Your son is an orphan staying with the three of you;

that way you can take care of him. Joseph, you are a caretaker for the cathedral. I will give you appropriate clothes to wear. The SS is here all the time. The Americans bombed the prison at Amiens. The bombing helped many French resistance fighters to escape. They are looking for them. I am always a person of suspicion."

I asked, "The prison was bombed?"

"Yes, it was bombed in an air attack. Joseph, you have an accent, and your French is not always correct."

"I used to live in America."

Once Father Glaize left, a nun brought us something to eat and clothes for Joshua. After we finished our rolls and coffee, the nun returned and asked Camille and Joshua to follow her. Father Glaize returned and led me to a storage room that was located in the back of the Cathedral. The room had a small bed next to the shelves that contained cleaning supplies and tools. The clothes I was given fit remarkably well. Luckily, Father Glaize and I were the same size and I could wear his clothes. I still wore Joseph's boots. I hadn't been so lucky with them. They were tight on my feet, but I had developed callouses which helped with the discomfort. After changing clothes, I waited. After an hour, a worker entered the storage room and told me I could help him clean the church. He handed me a mop, bucket, and cloths. Once in the church, I mopped the narthex. I had logged a lot of experience mopping and cleaning. When I worked in the grocery store, I finished each day mopping the floors.

At lunchtime, I stayed in the storage room and ate a sandwich. I looked out the small windows and saw three nuns walking across the courtyard. It wasn't hard to recognize the short nun.

The next day I was polishing the pews in the Cathedral when an SS officer walked in the main entrance and said to me, "Get Father Glaize." I didn't say a word. I went to find Father Glaize. He was in his office and I told him about the SS officer. He looked alarmed, but grabbed his robe and put it on. He walked down the hallway and met the SS officer near the alter. I stayed in the hallway out of sight. Father Glaize and the SS officer spoke in German, so I wasn't sure what was being said. The officer's voice on two occasions became very loud. The SS officer then turned and walked out of the church. Within a minute, he returned with four soldiers. When the soldiers entered, they dispersed and began searching every part of the church. Next, they entered the courtyard and headed toward the house for nuns. While they were searching, the officer lit a cigarette and flicked the ashes on the floor.

I went back to the storage area and started polishing a set of candlesticks. When a soldier opened the door and looked at me, he said something in German. I responded in French that I was a caretaker. He seemed confused but said nothing.

I remained in the storage room. After what seemed an eternity, Father Glaize returned and sat next to me on the bed. He was still wearing his long robe. He had sweat pouring down his face and a worried look on his face. He wiped his face and said, "They're looking for French fighters. They also wanted to know if I had helped any Jews. They asked me about you, I told them you worked here part time."

"What about Camille?"

"To them, she was just another nun."

"I heard the officer yell at you."

Father Glaize stood and walked toward the door. As he turned the knob he whispered, "I'm always a suspect, he wants to intimidate me. He told me that a cat only has nine lives not ten. He's waiting for me to screw up."

"Aren't you afraid," I asked.

"Most of the time I'm terrified. I believe, however, that I'm doing God's work. This gives me strength and courage."

"You're very brave to help us."

"Not as brave as you think. Tomorrow will be an interesting day."

CHAPTER EIGHTEEN

Father Glaize wanted to get an early start, so I awoke before daybreak. I met Camille and Joshua in Father Glaize's kitchen. She was still wearing nun's clothing. I started to tell her she was a cute Jewish nun, but I didn't think she would appreciate the humor. Joshua seemed glad to see me and gave me a big hug. When I picked him up, his body still felt warm. His face appeared thinner. I was glad we would be seeing the doctor soon.

As we finished our bread and cheese, Father Glaize poured us a second cup of coffee. He explained that he would drive to Lille and return the same day. There could be checkpoints; when we were stopped, he alone would speak. He was praying the Germans would be so preoccupied with the invasion that they wouldn't be concerned with a priest transporting a sick child. He wanted the Germans to think he and a nun were transporting a father and his sick son to a doctor specializing in children's diseases.

He had trouble starting the old car. It had definitely seen better days. I rode in the front, while Camille and Joshua climbed in the back. There was a light rain hitting the windshield as we left Cambrai Cathedral. The traffic was light which was a good sign. Perhaps the military transport trucks had already gone through Cambrai. As we left town, I saw German cars parked by the side of the rode. They were stopping cars going in both directions. Father

Glaize said, "This is not a usual checkpoint, they are looking for someone."

Father Glaize pulled the car over and lowered his window. A German soldier walked over to the window and said something to Father Glaize in German. Father Glaize kept shaking his head and then asked the soldier a question. He then turned to me and in French said, "Get a pack of cigarettes from the glove box." I reached inside and took a pack of cigarettes from the box. Father Glaize then said, "Two packs." I reached inside and grabbed another pack. The compartment was full of French cigarettes. The soldier took the two packs and motioned for us to go. When we got further down the road I asked, "Who are they looking for?"

"French fighters."

"Why the cigarettes?"

"It's been my experience that with some people cigarettes help speed up the conversation. I just asked him if he was low on smokes."

I cracked the window of the car and asked, "How do you know German?"

"I served in a church in Munich for five years."

We continued our journey, occasionally passing a military car. We encountered no large convoys. Joshua had fallen asleep on Camille's lap. The rain continued to pound down, which kept the temperature cooler.

We went several miles in silence, Father Glaize seemed preoccupied. After a while I spoke, "Do you think the Germans will leave you alone?"

He glanced at me and said, "What do you mean?"

"Will they continue to come by the church and harass you?"

"Probably, but I will outlast all of them. I have managed to stay out of trouble while still helping people in need. Eventually the Germans will leave, I just need to keep a low profile."

Camille had packed cheese sandwiches. When we had eaten, Father Glaize pulled off the road for a bathroom break. Father Glaize stood by the car as the rest of us walked into the woods. When we returned, he was talking to a German soldier on a motorcycle. We got back in the car to continue our journey. Keeping his eyes on the road, Father Glaize said, "Do you know what the soldier asked? He wanted me to pray for him."

I didn't respond, but couldn't help but think of the strange circumstances that surround war. Father Glaize wanted to do God's work by helping people in need. In some cases, the enemy wasn't all that different from us.

We had traveled for hours when Lille came into sight. The city was larger than I expected. Trains were moving in every direction. Although the city streets were probably quieter than normal, there were still people and cars present. I saw no road blocks or checkpoints. I did see Nazi flags hanging from certain buildings. One building appeared to be a military headquarters for soldiers, including SS officers. Camille spoke up and gave us directions. "Go two more blocks, then turn left. In three blocks, you will take a right. Dr. Benoit's office is about halfway down the block on the left. You can pull over and park by the cobbler shop."

Father Glaize pulled over and we exited the car. As we crossed the street, an SS officer gave us the once over. A small sign hanging in front of a two story building had Dr. Benoit's name on it. After we entered the office, Father Glaize walked over to a lady who was seated behind a desk. The reception area was small. Two other people were seated in chairs near the window. When the woman at the desk looked up, he said, "We need to see Dr. Benoit. The boy is very sick." Camille added, "Tell him Camille Bernhardt is here."

We remained standing in the waiting area. I knew Father Glaize was anxious to be on his way but didn't want to leave us until he was sure we were safe. The door in the corner of the room opened, revealing a tall man with brown curly hair that was gray on the sides. He was wearing a white doctor's coat.

As the doctor entered the waiting area, he had a puzzled look on his face. Camille, still dressed in her nun's clothing, quickly walked over to him. In a low voice she whispered, "It's a long story, I can explain later. My son is very sick, can you help him?"

Dr. Benoit looked at Camille and then hugged her tight. He looked at me holding Joshua and said, "Is the boy your son?"

"Yes, he is very sick."

"Bring him into the examination room."

I carried Joshua in the room and placed him on the examination table. Father Glaize tapped me on the shoulder and said, "Joseph, I need to go." Dr. Benoit glanced at me and then turned to look at Joshua. He knew I was not the Joseph who was married to Camille. I walked with Father Glaize to the front entrance. He said, "You should stay in the building." I stuck my hand out, but he gave me a bear hug instead. When our arms dropped, I thanked him effusively for helping us.

"I will never forget you." I said.

"May God be with you all."

He stepped out the door, cautiously looking both ways before walking across the street to his car. I was relieved when I heard the car start. It was getting late and he had a long way to go. At least this time he wasn't transporting Jews.

I returned to the examination room and stood beside Camille as Dr. Benoit continued to examine

Joshua. The boy did not whimper or call for his mother, but he looked weak and listless.

Dr. Benoit placed his stethoscope on Joshua's chest and listened. He then sat him up and placed it on his back. He repeated this procedure three times. Next, he examined his throat and ears. Just when I thought he was finished with the exam, he placed the stethoscope back on Joshua's chest. Looking at Camille he said, "I think the boy has pneumonia. I'm going to give him a shot and some medication. I will monitor him for the next forty-eight hours to see if the medicine is working. If it is, he will not need to go to the hospital. I think we got it early enough, but I will know more tomorrow. For now he needs rest. You can stay with Mary and me."

Camille hugged him and said, "Thank you. I was so worried about him." She then turned and looked at me and said, "This is my friend, John."

Dr. Benoit shook my hand and commented, "I'm very confused about a lot of things. For now, why don't all three of you go upstairs so Mary can get you settled. I will join you when I'm finished with my patients."

After Joshua got his shot, I picked him up and carried him upstairs to the Benoit home. Mary Benoit was startled to see Camille dressed as a nun, but quickly showed us a place for Joshua to sleep. She hugged Camille. Their eyes filled with tears. Mary was a tall, thin, attractive woman who didn't have a hair out of place. She wore a pearl necklace and had rings on most of her fingers. After she gathered some food from the refrigerator, she looked at Camille. "Why are you dressed like a nun?" she inquired.

"I'll explain when Dr. Benoit comes upstairs. Do you have something I could wear?"

"I'm a lot bigger than you are, but I'll see what I have. Our daughter may have left some clothes here that might fit."

She returned with a nice dress and a pair of shoes. The shoes didn't fit but the dress was perfect. Again, it struck me how pretty Camille was.

Joshua went to sleep, but Camille stayed next to his bed wiping his forehead with a cool cloth. Mary was preparing something to eat, while I stretched out on the couch. Within a matter of minutes, I fell sound asleep.

CHAPTER NINETEEN

When I woke up, I could hear Dr. Benoit as he greeted Mary and Camille in the kitchen. He seemed so pleased to see Camille, I went to join them. Mary insisted that we sit down and eat before everything got cold. When I asked about Joshua, Camille told me he had eaten soup and was sleeping. The meal was more than we had eaten in a long time. We not only had fresh vegetables but we also had beef. This wasn't a typical wartime meal at the Benoit's house, but rather a special meal she had prepared for her guests. Halfway through the meal, Dr. Benoit left the table, and returned with a bottle of red wine. He told us he was saving it for liberation day but that this was a special occasion and we needed to celebrate.

When the meal was finished, Dr. Benoit poured more wine. He said, "I know it has been a long day, Camille, but I'm anxious to find out what has happened to you and Joseph."

Camille responded, "When we left Lille and went to Amiens, everything was going fine. Joseph was not a very good farmer, but he got a lot of help from friends. He was a hard worker."

Dr. Benoit understood that Camille was talking in past tense when she referred to Joseph. He did not, however, interrupt her.

"We were making a living, but it was hard. The Germans would take whatever they wanted from our farm. Joseph learned to trade goods and to sell food in town. When Joshua was born, it was harder because we needed more things. We were still making it, but there were times when we didn't have enough to eat.

"At first, we did not hide that we were Jews; this was a mistake. It became apparent that we didn't know who we could trust. Some Jewish families were rounded up and never seen again. After a while, things began to die down. Joseph was confident we would go undetected. He then met some men who were part of the French resistance. I told him he shouldn't become involved because he had a family to take care of, but he wouldn't listen. On his first mission as a freedom fighter, he was killed. He was killed saving John's life."

Dr. Benoit looked at me and seemed confused, so I explained, "I'm an American soldier. I was dropped from a plane in Amiens. After our parachutes opened, Germans started shooting at us. Joseph shot the man who was trying to kill me. He was killed saving my life."

Camille then added, "John found his way to our farm. He hid there, but he also helped me and Joshua. Things got worse when a new German commander came to Amiens. He was obsessed with finding Jews, and somebody gave us up. The Colonel showed up at my house. He raped me and was going to kill me, but John killed him. We had to run. We were hiding out at a nearby farm but had to leave because it became dangerous for us and the family that was hiding us. At first, we were going to Paris with the hope the city would be liberated. I talked John out of going because I wanted us to leave for Lille."

Camille began to cry. Mrs. Benoit stood up and patted her on the back. It took several minutes before she was able to continue. "I'm pregnant. I was raped and now I'm pregnant. I do not want this baby. That's the original reason for coming to Lille. When Joshua got sick, I knew we had to come. Father Glaize hid us and then drove us here. That's why I was dressed as a nun."

Dr. Benoit kept shaking his head as if he couldn't believe what he had just heard. Mrs. Benoit said, "We've got to help them."

Dr. Benoit folded his hands together and placed them on the table. "First of all, let's see how Joshua responds to the medication. I've only done an abortion once in my life, but if that's what you want, I will do it. It's been a long time. I don't know how long you would be safe staying here, things are not good. Since the invasion, it has gotten worse. I know of Jewish families that have recently disappeared. I have an idea about making sure you are safe. First, we will make sure Joshua is okay and you are fully recovered. Mary will get all of you new clothes. You should not leave this building under any circumstance."

That evening, after Camille and Joshua had gone to bed, I went to the kitchen. Dr. Benoit was sitting at the kitchen table. After getting a glass of water, I sat down. He was reviewing pages in a medical book. Once he realized I was sitting at the table, he said, "Would it be easier if I spoke to you in English?"

"Yes, even though I've learned a lot of French, I still haven't mastered the language yet. English would be much better."

"I have a question. I don't understand why you haven't tried to make your way back to an American unit."

"I'm not sure myself. I just wanted to help Camille."

"Are the Americans looking for you?"

I paused for a few seconds to take a sip of water before answering his question. "No, they think I'm dead."

"I see. Is this man John dead," he asked.

Confused, I asked, "What do you mean?"

"Have you left him behind?"

"I'm not sure what I've done or what I'm doing. Maybe I'll find my way back to a unit once this area is liberated. I just want to make sure Camille and Joshua are safe."

Looking over his reading glasses, Dr. Benoit added, "Camille is a very special young lady. She has gone through a lot in her short life."

"How do you know Camille," I asked.

Puzzled, he replied, "She has not shared this with you?"

"No, she just said you were a family friend."

"I knew Camille's parents very well. They owned the best bakery in Lille. I was one of their best customers. We would have them to dinner quite often. Camille became good friends with our daughter, Michelle. They would do everything together. Michelle is a gifted musician. We would often take Camille with us to recitals. When the Germans came, everything changed. Everyone was so guarded that many people would no longer go to the bakery. One morning, Camille's parents went to get fresh eggs from a nearby farmer and were killed in a wreck. A German military truck crushed their small truck. It was a foggy morning and visibility was terrible. When I couldn't find any family to notify, I asked Camille to live with us."

"How did Camille meet Joseph?"

"The Bernhardt family were close friends with Camille's family. The Jewish community is very tight. The Bernhardts were originally from Germany but moved to Lille when Joseph was an infant. They had a good jewelry business here, but decided to move to Paris. Joseph went with them and began his studies at the university. When Camille's parents died, he decided he would marry Camille."

As I crossed my arms and leaned back in the chair I said, "I don't understand. What do you mean by 'decided'?"

"When Joseph and Camille were young, their parents made arrangements for marriage. Although Joseph was seven years older, it was decided they would be married in the future. When Camille's parents died, Joseph stepped in and did what he thought was right. Camille was only sixteen."

Dr. Benoit asked if I would like a glass of wine. After he had filled our glasses, I asked, "What happened then?"

"Things became bad for Jews so Joseph got the idea of buying a farm in a rural area with the hope of hiding until the war ended. I helped secure a sale of the bakery. This gave them the money to buy a farm. Joseph's family helped, then Camille became pregnant almost immediately."

I thanked Dr. Benoit for sharing this information with me. It certainly shed light on several things. That night as I slept on the couch, I continued to think of all that Camille had gone through. I admired everything about her.

The next morning, Camille said that Joshua was doing much better and had more energy. It became more difficult to keep him quiet and from running through the house. Camille insisted that he rest. She accomplished this by resting with him.

Dr. Benoit went downstairs to see patients, and his wife had gone shopping. Feeling restless, I constantly walked to the window to peek out at the street below. As usual, there was constant military traffic, I saw more SS troops walking the streets. Maybe the Germans were planning some type of evacuation?

When Mary Benoit returned from shopping, she proudly showed us the clothing she had purchased for us. The new clothes were a welcomed sight. Once we had tried on our new clothes, she insisted on washing our old clothes. Mary gave Camille clothing that belonged to Michelle.

In the evening, when Dr. Benoit returned, he told Camille he would perform what he referred to as "the procedure" after dinner. After dinner, I insisted on washing the dishes and getting Joshua to bed. Dr. Benoit and his wife walked downstairs with Camille. He never spoke of what "the procedure" involved and nobody asked any questions.

They were downstairs for a long time; I laid on the couch while I waited for their return. Dr. Benoit returned after midnight, his white doctor's coat had blood on the front of it. He came and sat in a nearby chair. "Everything went well, Mary is staying with Camille in the examination room. I don't want her walking up the stairs right now."

"So everything is okay?'

"Yes, I don't see any problems. I want her to rest and I will check on her tomorrow."

I stood and extended my right hand, "Thanks, Dr. Benoit."

Dr. Benoit smiled and shook my hand. I wasn't sure why I thanked him, but he quickly replied, "You're welcome."

The next morning, Camille and Mary walked up the stairs. Camille was wearing a bathrobe and slippers. She looked remarkably well.

The only thing she said was that she was glad it was over. After breakfast, she bathed, washed her hair, and put on new clothes. For the first time since I had met her, she was wearing makeup.

That evening, Dr. Benoit examined her. He was quite pleased with her recovery but he insisted that she get more rest. After dinner, she changed into her night clothes and robe.

All of us were sitting in the living area listening to the radio when we heard a loud knock on the door. Dr. Benoit went to the door and motioned for us to retreat to the bedroom. In a loud voice he said, "Colonel Stackert, what brings you out so late?" Camille held Joshua and whispered to him to be very quiet.

The colonel walked into the living room with Dr. Benoit, and Mary greeted him. Before he took a seat, Colonel Stackert remarked, "I didn't know you had company." It was obvious he had noticed the water glasses sitting on the table and the two washcloths that were made to look like puppets.

Dr. Benoit said, "My daughter and son-in-law are visiting us. The puppets belong to their son."

"I'm so sorry to interfere with your family time," the Colonel said, with a bit of sarcasm in his voice.

"They were just going to bed, Michelle has not been feeling well," replied Dr. Benoit.

"I'm sorry to hear that," the Colonel continued. "How long are they staying?"

"Not very long. They will need to go back to Paris," Dr. Benoit replied.

As the Colonel placed his hat under his left arm, he commented, "I would like to meet them."

"Michelle has not been well. I told her she needed to rest," said Dr. Benoit. He was starting to become agitated with the Colonel's persistence.

"I may not get a second chance to meet this world class musician you talk about," replied the Colonel, with a smirk on his face.

There was a pause in the conversation. Dr. Benoit then said to Mary, "Why don't you ask Michelle and Sean to come out and say hello to Colonel Stackert. The little one is probably asleep by now."

When Mary returned, she took Joshua's hand. Since we had been listening to the conversation, we started walking toward the living room. Camille went directly to the colonel to introduce herself and then introduced me.

The colonel responded, "I'm so very pleased to meet you. Your father often brags about your music talent. What instrument do you play?"

Camille responded, "The violin."

"Oh, yes. The violin."

Looking around the room and then focusing his eyes on Camille, the Colonel added, "Your father didn't tell me how pretty you are. I really don't see any resemblance."

"Thank you, I take after my mother's family," replied Camille.

The colonel looked at me and said, "How long are you staying?"

"We will be returning soon," Camille said before I could respond.

"And how are things in Paris?" he asked as he looked at me.

"Confusing."

"Yes, just like every place else. Maybe one day when this war is over, we can return to the important things in life."

Dr. Benoit responded, "And what is that?"

"The arts, of course."

Nobody responded. Finally Dr. Benoit asked, "May I get you a drink?"

"No, I do need to go. I came by to invite you and your wife to the opera at the Opera de Lille. Although it will be in German, I thought you would still enjoy it. It is tomorrow night, but since you have company, we will make it for another time." Colonel Stackert took his hat and placed it on his head. He wished everyone a good evening, and walked toward the door.

Before he exited he turned to me and said, "If you have any difficulty with passage documentation, please let me know."

"Thank you."

Dr. Benoit waited until he was sure the colonel had left the building. He then fell back on the couch and removed his wire-rimmed glasses. He rubbed his face with his hands and said, "That asshole is nothing but trouble."

Camille said, "How does he know you?"

"I'm one of the few Frenchmen who continued to attend the opera after the occupation. Colonel Stackert is an art lover. He saw Mary and me at the opera and introduced himself. After that, he would just show up. He has come to my office and sought medical care for minor things. I'm not sure what kind of soldier he is. I get the feeling he has no friends, so he comes by to see me. I did tell him about Michelle playing the violin. That's why it surprised me when he asked what instrument you played. I always thought of him as a pain in the ass who will be gone one day, but I'm beginning to think he is more devious than I thought."

After the colonel left, I knew it would be impossible to sleep. Dr. Benoit must have felt the same way. We both made our way to the kitchen table. He poured us a glass of wine from the bottle he had opened the day before. Camille made sure Joshua was going to sleep, and Mary retired to her bedroom.

Dr. Benoit looked worried and was in deep thought. He took a sip from his wine glass and said, "I think I have a plan that will work."

"What kind of plan," I asked.

"A plan for survival; it isn't safe for you and Camille to stay here. At first, I thought it might be possible, but with Colonel Stackert poking around, I don't think it is safe. I have a hunting camp in Charleville-Mezieres that I haven't used in years. The camp belonged to my father. I haven't used it much, but it is in a great location. It is deep in the woods, miles from town. The road to get to the camp is in bad shape. The road has been washed out and there is a steep climb that last mile. I don't think it is possible to get there by car or truck. We can only go so far, and then we will have to walk. I could take you, Camille, and Joshua there. You could take food and other provisions with you. The cabin is located on a small pond. I fished there many times as a child. It was originally used as a hunting lodge, so I'm sure there is still wild game that can be shot. You can hide there and no one would know. Tomorrow is the first day of July, I don't think it will be too long before all of France is liberated. At least, that's what people tell me. Colonel Stackert even implied they were making plans to leave. What do you think?"

I smiled and said, "It could work, Camille knows about living in rough conditions. We would live like recluses."

"Will you talk with Camille about it?"

"Yes, I will. When would you want to leave?"

"Tomorrow, waiting any longer isn't wise. Camille and Joshua are doing well and I will give you medicine for Joshua."

"Dr. Benoit, you are both a brave and kind man. I can never repay you for all you've done."

"I'm glad to do it, but be cautious and trust no one. The Germans have created an atmosphere of fear, and people will do things unimaginable just to survive."

"I understand," I responded.

"I'm glad you are helping Camille. She's a wonderful person; she has been like a daughter to me."

The next morning, I talked with Camille. She asked no questions and immediately started packing things for our trip. Mary gave us a large bag full of provisions to carry. She also gave us a backpack that belonged to Dr. Benoit.

Dr. Benoit parked the car in front of his office. We hurried down the steps carrying our bags. Dr. Benoit stood outside making sure it was clear for us and then motioned for us to come.

Once in the car, Camille laid down in the backseat with Joshua. I sat up front with Dr. Benoit, pulling the hat he had given me down over my forehead. He then slipped two pieces of paper across the seat.

As he drove down the street, I looked at the papers. Although I couldn't read the French writing, I knew he had given me identification papers that belonged to his daughter and son-in-law; this was risky on his part. When he noticed I was looking at the papers, he said, "Hopefully you won't need them."

Dr. Benoit told us the trip would be about three hours unless traffic was being stopped at checkpoints. Although we saw military vehicles, we were not stopped. Apparently, since the invasion, traveling had become a little easier.

When we got to Charleville-Mezieres, we drove through town and continued on a small bumpy road. Dr. Benoit stopped the car in front of a building that resembled an old "General Store" I might see in Allentown. We needed to pick up provisions for the cabin. Inside, we were greeted by a short overweight man with thinning hair that was combed over to cover a large bald spot. Dr. Benoit told him we needed some supplies.

The man followed us through the store as he talked to Dr. Benoit, "You are not from here," he commented.

Dr. Benoit didn't turn to face the man. He continued to walk. "No, he replied. Just passing through Charleville-Mezieres."

"Have you checked in with the German authorities," asked the man.

"No, like I said, we are just passing through," said Dr. Benoit, annoyed by the man's inquiries.

"Where are you going," asked the man.

"Just passing through," said Dr. Benoit, repeating himself again.

Camille picked out canned goods, soap, and flour. I selected matches and two tin cups. Dr. Benoit paid for everything while I loaded the goods in a box.

I put the box in the truck, and we departed. As we continued down the bumpy road, I said, "Why all the questions from the guy in the store?"

"He's a rule follower, the Germans have scared him shitless. He thinks if he doesn't report something, he will get in trouble."

"Should we be worried, I asked. I'm very concerned about Camille and Joshua's safety."

"No, he has no idea where we are heading."

We continued down the road two more miles before Dr. Benoit turned on a side road that got worse as he drove; the road became treacherous. We were going almost straight uphill. The tires began to spin, occasionally causing the car to slide. Dr. Benoit did his best to maintain his speed, but was losing the battle. Finally, we reached an area in the road that had been washed out. He stopped the car and said, "This is as far as I can go."

I unloaded the car, and tried to figure out how I could carry everything. It would be impossible to carry Joshua. I put the backpack on and picked up the box from the general store. Before Camille picked up the other large bag, she hugged Dr. Benoit. He kissed her on both cheeks and then kissed Joshua on the top of his head. He gave me a pat on the back and said, "You have about a mile walk up the road. When you come to a fork, go right for a short distance and you will see the cabin. There should be a key in the old watering bucket on the back porch. Once I know everything is okay, I will come for you." He patted me on the shoulder and the three of us began our climb. It was cooler here, which helped us as we headed steadily up. Dr. Benoit turned his car around and started down the bumpy road.

We had to rest several times before reaching the fork in the road. Just as the good doctor had said, after a short distance, we saw the cabin. With some luck, it would be our refuge.

CHAPTER TWENTY

The cabin was nicer than Dr. Benoit had described it. The wood siding and tin roof were in good condition. We walked up the steps of the tiny front porch and peeked in the window. I remembered the directions for the key. I dropped everything I was carrying, went around the cabin, and located the old watering can. I reached inside and found the key, which was attached to a small key ring. When I returned, I opened the front door and we walked inside. Immediately to the right was a kitchen area consisting of a sink, a pump, and a wood burning stove. I walked to the pump and started pushing the handle up and down, but nothing happened. I checked the wood burning stove, it was in good working condition.

Around the corner of a support beam was a small sitting area with two chairs. On the wall next to the chairs, was a wooden cabinet that was locked.

Camille and Joshua climbed the ladder that went to the loft. The loft had a regular size bed and two twin beds, a dresser, and a small closet that contained blankets.

All of us walked out the back door. We stood on the porch that overlooked the pond below. I was expecting to see a small pond with a few trees, but it looked more like a lake than a pond. I spotted a small dock that could be used for fishing. In the back of the house, I located a tool shed and an outhouse. Camille seemed pleased with our new home. She immediately began cleaning the cabin. I found an old wooden toy train in the closet, which kept Joshua occupied as Camille swept and took out blankets to be aired on the porch.

I looked everywhere for a key to open the wooden cabinet. I eventually found it in a tin can located next to the stove. The cabinet contained rifles and ammunition. There was a shotgun and a hunting rifle, probably for shooting deer. The cabinet also had two fishing poles and a smaller cane pole, just the right size for Joshua.

I located a well on the slope that went down to the lake. The well had a pump that still worked. When I first started pumping, the water contained some mud. The more I pumped, the clearer the water became. I pulled back the boards that were over the well and peered down into the dark space. I heard a frog croaking inside. From what I could see, the water looked to be fine for drinking.

Camille soon had the wooden stove operating. There was plenty of wood stacked beside the cabin. I found an axe in the tool shed, which would be handy for chopping.

Camille was darting in and out of the cabin, she was excited about our new home. She had washed the plates with the water I had carried from the well and was baking bread. She stuck her head out the back door and shouted, "Do you think you two fishermen could catch some fish for dinner?"

"You're looking at the greatest fisherman in France," I yelled back. I took one of the larger poles and the small cane pole from the cabinet and told Joshua we were going to catch some fish. Before going to the lake, I was successful in digging near the tool shed and finding several good worms. I placed them in a small container I had found in the tool shed. As Joshua and I walked to the lake, he held my hand and asked to carry the worms.

The dock had a few loose boards, but overall was in good condition. I wasn't sure what kind of fish we might catch but we weren't going to return empty-handed. To my delight, within a matter of minutes, I pulled up a good size brim. Joshua really wanted to catch a fish, too. I put down my rod so I could help him. When the bobber went down, I told him to pull up. As the fish came out of the water, he started to scream with excitement. We had only been on the dock a short time and had already caught two fish. It took a little longer to pull in the third one. I placed the three fish in the bucket I had carried with me. We picked up our gear and headed back to the cabin.

Camille took the fish and cleaned them. When everything was ready, we sat down at the kitchen table to consume our first meal at the cabin.

The day had gone by quickly; we had been busy cleaning, preparing food, and fishing. I had totally forgotten about the war and the fear that had constantly haunted us. After dinner, we stood on the back porch and watched the sun set over the lake. As Joshua played with the toy train, I placed my arm on Camille's shoulder, she didn't resist. Instead, she placed her arm around my waist. This was one of the best days I had experienced in a long time.

Later that evening, we discovered the kerosene lamps did not have any kerosene in them. Fortunately, Camille found a few small candles which allowed us to see as we prepared for bed. Camille and Joshua slept in the larger bed while I slept in one of the smaller twin beds.

The next day became a repeat of the first day. I continued to be amazed at how Camille could prepare something to eat with only the provisions we had in the cabin. All of us worked together to get the cabin clean, including washing all the windows. My primary accomplishment was killing a large spider that had decided to make the outhouse his home.

Around noontime, I went to the large wooden cabinet to check out the rifles. Everything seemed to be in good working condition. I decided to take the shotgun to hunt for food in the woods. I told Camille I hoped to find a rabbit or a wild turkey.

As I walked through the thick woods on the other side of the lake, I saw a few squirrels. I made the decision not shoot them, hoping I would find bigger game farther in the woods. I walked a long way without spotting anything but a few more squirrels. When I was about to give up and walk back, I stopped dead in my tracks. Just twenty yards from where I was standing, a deer was looking straight at me. It was a rather large doe, I was surprised I hadn't spooked it. Unfortunately, I was carrying the wrong rifle to kill a deer. As I turned and walked back, I looked for a landmark that I would remember. I would definitely be returning to this area.

As I got closer to the lake, I saw two squirrels chasing each other. They were probably the same squirrels I had seen earlier. The squirrels were now sitting perfectly still on a tree branch not far away. I took the shotgun, slowly raising it to take aim. When it fired, both squirrels fell to the ground. I hadn't expected to kill both squirrels at the same time, but was pleased to have had such good luck.

I carried the two squirrels by their tails as I walked back to the cabin. As I started up the steps of the back porch, I heard Camille say something, but I wasn't sure what she had said. Although I was learning French quicker than I had expected, I still was not always certain of the pronunciation of certain words. As I put up the rifle, it dawned on me what she had said to me. She had called me "the great white hunter."

I went to the well to retrieve water while Camille
cleaned the squirrels. She told me she would use
them in a stew. As she cooked on the stove, I said to
her, "Tomorrow the great white hunter will kill a deer."
She laughed, and I told her about the deer I had
seen. She seemed pleased and asked if there was a
large knife in the tool shed. I told her I would check
to see. She informed me she would need help dressing
a deer. I told her I only considered myself a hunter.
She grinned, "Tomorrow you will learn to dress a
deer, also."

After dinner, the three of us sat on the back porch
as the sun was setting. Joshua went down the steps
to retrieve a can Camille had given him to play with.
I stood up and watched him kicking at the can. When
Camille stood up, I again placed my arm on her
shoulder. This time, however, I turned my head toward
her, our eyes focused on each other. I leaned forward
and kissed her. More importantly, she kissed me back.
We continued to kiss until both of us heard Joshua
walking up the steps.

Just like the previous night, Camille went up to
the loft to get Joshua to sleep. I stayed below, sitting
in one of the chairs with a lit candle, the only light in
the cabin. After a while, I heard Camille say, "He's
asleep." I climbed the steps of the ladder carrying my
candle. When I got to the top I held the candle up so I
could see my bed. This time Joshua was in my bed. I
moved the candle in the other direction and saw
Camille in bed looking at me. She lifted the cover,
inviting me to join her, and I realized she was not
wearing any clothes. I shed my clothes and joined
her in bed. Like a magnet our bodies were drawn to
each other. She felt warm, and the smoothness of
her skin felt like silk. I could feel and smell her hair
as it fell across my face. Camille lifted her head and
said, "Je t'aime."

No one except my mother had ever told me they loved me. Hearing it in French was even more romantic. I responded, "Je t'aime," and added, "Tell me again."

"Je t'aime."

I thought at one time we might wake up Joshua. When the love making was over, we both lay in bed with our bodies totally limp. I hadn't thought I could feel the way I did about Camille. I thought this was something other people could experience, but somehow I was not on the privileged list.

Joshua was still asleep when Camille rolled over and pulled herself close to me. I could feel the warmth of her breast against my chest. In a low, soft voice she said, "Do you have a girl in America?"

"I have no one, the people there think I am dead."

Placing her head on my chest she asked, "What are your parents like?"

I replied, "My father drinks too much and can be mean. My mother is sweet and kind, she would love you."

Camille added, "My parents would have liked you even though you are not Jewish."

I brushed back the hair from her face, "I forgot about the Jewish part," I said.

"It was important to my father, but my mother was different. I think she was always looking for love."

We didn't say anything for a while. I just enjoyed feeling Camille close to me. She then lifted her head and rolled on her back. She continued the conversation by saying, "What do you think you would like to do someday."

I placed my hands behind my head and replied, "After the war?"

"Yes."

"I would like to be a high school teacher. What about you?"

With excitement she responded, "I would like to have a bakery shop like my parents had; I loved working at their shop. I had thought that one day I would buy the shop they used to own."

"I know you can bake, everything you bake is incredible."

She pulled the cover under her chin and said, "But I love being here, I feel like I could just stay here and let the world pass by."

"I know what you mean. This place makes me forget about the war."

"Me too," she said.

We heard Joshua waking up. In a matter of seconds Camille was dressed. It took me a while longer as I had trouble finding my clothes. I had been in a hurry to get them off.

At breakfast, I was all smiles. When Camille poured my coffee, she kissed me on top of my head. For the first time in quite a while, I looked forward to the coming day.

I told Camille I would take my rifle to search for a deer. If I shot one, I would leave it and return to get her, then we would dress it out together. My plan was to have her be the supervisor while I did the actual work.

I walked miles in the woods and followed a few tracks, but I decided to give up. When I returned, Camille asked me to take Joshua and go fishing. I remembered seeing an old rowboat leaning next to the tool shed so I decided to haul it to the water to see if it would float. I cautiously pulled the boat away from the wall of the tool shed. I was afraid there might be a snake or some other animal using the boat for protection. Instead, I found the boat's oars underneath. I dragged the boat to the water with Joshua trying to help by pushing from behind.

The boat floated and seemed seaworthy. I placed our fishing poles and the bait in the boat. This time, I remembered to bring a small piece of rope that could act as a stringer in case we caught fish. I rowed a short distance from shore before putting our lines in the water. After about three minutes and no bites, I rowed farther out in the lake. Joshua caught the first fish; his smile said it all. I found myself staring at him. I realized by this time, I was a father. I wondered what my child looked like, and if he or she was accepted in the Clark family. I thought of Diane and hoped our child had brought some happiness to her life.

While we fished, I could see Camille in the distance as she walked toward the lake and carried a blanket and a small bag. She dropped the blanket and bag on the ground and walked toward the water. She took off her clothes and dove in. When she surfaced, I could see she had a bar of soap with her. I continued to stare at her. Once Camille had finished bathing, she put on her bra and panties, and returned to where she had placed the blanket. She was drying off in the sun.

Joshua out fished me three to one. I was using the latest rod and reel while he used the short cane pole. When the boat came to rest on the shore, he jumped out and ran toward his mother, dragging the fish behind him. When I walked up to Camille, she threw the soap at me and said, "It's bath time." Joshua wanted to come, so the two of us stripped and got in the water. After rinsing off the soap and splashing in the water, we both put on our underwear and returned to the blanket. Camille had baked bread that was stuffed with blueberry jam. She pulled a wine bottle from the sack and said, "Guess what I found?"

"Where?"

She grinned from ear to ear and replied, "There are two bottles behind the dresser in a sack, somebody hid them."

She had already removed the cork, and poured wine into our tin cups. The three of us were sitting on a blanket in our underwear, eating pastry. Camille and I were sipping wine.

After finishing our second cup, I leaned back and looked up at the sky. Camille and Joshua did the same. I said, "What a great day."

We continued to lie on the blanket staring at the passing clouds when Camille said, "Je t'aime."

I responded, "Je t'aime."

The next morning we were awakened by the sound of heavy rain hitting the tin roof. We continued to lie in bed holding each other, Joshua was still asleep. We stayed in this position until Joshua began to stir. He said, "I'm hungry."

As we sat at the table getting ready to eat our biscuits, I said, "If it stops raining, I'm going to try hunting again."

"Do you want us to go?"

"No, I'll come back for you if I shoot a deer," I said, hoping 'the great hunter' would be successful.

The rain stopped around noon, I grabbed the rifle and was walking toward the door when Camille stopped me to give me a kiss. She said, "Remember, we have a second bottle of wine."

This time I had only been out a short time when I came upon three deer getting a drink from a stream. My heart began to race, this was my chance. As I raised my rifle, I took a deep breath and set my sights on the large doe that was in the middle. I held my breath, slowly squeezing the trigger. The center deer dropped to the ground as the other two ran off. I walked slowly toward the deer. I was relieved that I had killed it with just one shot. I remembered hearing stories from my friends in high school who were hunters about how they had wounded a deer and then had to track it for miles with the hope of finishing it off. I dragged the deer under a tree and left it there. Camille instructed me on what to bring to dress out the deer. The knife was not real sharp but she felt it would be fine. I found rope and three burlap sacks in the tool shed that she said would be useful. All three of us made our way to the deer. I used the rope to string it up and then followed her carving instructions. Before attempting to bleed out the deer, she suggested I remove my shirt. I carved up several pieces of the deer and placed them in the sacks. I then buried the remains and the three of us made our way back to the cabin. As we were walking, I asked Camille what she thought of the great white hunter.

"Very impressive," she responded.

That evening, we had venison and rice. Joshua wanted seconds, which was a true compliment to the chef. We had plenty of salt to use as a preservative. Camille, however, told us we would be eating deer three times a day.

In the evening, we opened up the second bottle of wine. Camille and I sat on the back porch sipping wine from our tin cups as we watched Joshua try to catch a bug with a jar. Camille reached over and grabbed my hand. We sat there until the lake was no longer visible.

The next four days went quickly. Having the deer meat made things easier. Joshua and I did go fishing, but I didn't feel the pressure of having to catch our dinner.

On the tenth day, Joshua began coughing again; it soon became worse. Camille made him stay in the cabin and rest, but this was harder than she expected. Once he felt a little better, he wanted to go to the lake. There was no medication left in the envelope Dr. Benoit provided.

I walked down to the lake to make sure I had turned the row boat over so that it would not fill with water from the rain that appeared to be coming our way. When I walked back to the cabin, I heard Camille yell out a curse word which was highly unusual. She greeted me on the back porch and said, "Guess what?"

I closed the screen door and asked, "What?"

"I just burned up all of our matches," she replied, frustrated with herself.

I knew she was mad at herself so I put my hands on her shoulder and asked calmly, "How?"

"By doing something stupid," she blurted. "I left the box on the stove."

She already felt badly about what she had done, so I wasn't about to make another comment. This did create a problem for us, I knew there were not any other matches in the cabin or tool shed. I had looked on more than one occasion.

"Do you have wood burning on the stove?" I asked.

"Yes. But I can't keep it burning forever."

"We can keep it going for now," I assured her. "I'll look to see if there is any flint or something that might start a fire in the tool shed."

When we finished our meal and were still sitting at the table, I said, "I've got an idea."

"An idea about what," she asked.

"The matches and other supplies. Tomorrow morning I will leave very early and walk to the general store. It's about nine miles, so if I leave early I can make it back by sundown. Dr. Benoit left us plenty of money. I will get matches, kerosene for the lamps, and other food."

"You don't think it is too dangerous?" she asked. Her voice starting to quiver with emotion.

"I think it will be fine," I said calmly. "Maybe I'll be able to learn more about what's happening with the invasion."

Camille hesitated, "I don't know," she said. "Maybe we should wait longer."

"It will be all right, I'll be careful," I responded, trying to put her at ease.

"What about the creepy storekeeper?" she asked.

"I'll be in and out before he knows what happened," I said.

"We could use more flour and rice," Camille added. "If you see any type of tea, buy it. It helped Joshua when the Gypsies gave him some."

I patted her on the arm, smiled and said, "You can pack me something to eat and I will take the canteen."

"You have to promise me that you will turn back if you see anything suspicious."

"I promise."

CHAPTER TWENTY ONE

I left before daybreak. There was some fog, which was perfect for the long hike. I got several kisses and hugs before I left, which motivated me for the long day ahead. I made my way down the hill and turned on the old logging road. I walked at a good pace, only stopping to take an occasional drink from the canteen. By noon, I had reached the main road that would lead me to the store. I had miles to go, but I realized I was not in an area where I was likely to see people, so I kept to the side of the road with my eyes looking straight ahead. After an hour or so, I heard a car coming and ducked into the brush beside the road. The car that passed looked like it belonged to a local farmer. Just up ahead, something was lying in the ditch next to the road. When I got closer, I saw it was a dead body. The dead man had been shot. He could have been a French resistance fighter. By the look and smell, the body had been there a few days. I took the dead man's rifle and hid it under the tall grass. I then took a stick and stuck it in the ground next to the road. I planned to look for the stick on my return trip and take the dead fighter's rifle with me.

As I continued to walk, I saw a sign that showed Charleville-Mezieres was only two kilometers away. I was in a more populated area and I had passed a number of farms. The store sat in the distance at an intersection in the road. There were three German trucks and a jeep parked out front. I moved off the side of the road and hid behind a row of trees. There was a farm house behind me. I crouched down, staying out of sight. Suddenly I heard something behind me and when I turned, I saw three chickens pecking the ground near my feet. I breathed a nervous sigh of relief.

I kept surveillance on the store. The trucks were probably picking up supplies. After a half hour, six soldiers finally exited the store and left. I slowly walked back to the road, but then I heard the roar of more trucks coming. I quickly returned to my hiding place until the trucks passed. One of the trucks stopped at the general store. Again, I waited. Eventually, two soldiers exited the store and raced off in their truck.

I cautiously left my hiding spot and began to walk toward the store. After entering, I quickly walked to the shelves that were stocked with food. I grabbed flour, rice and some canned goods. As I placed the goods on the counter, the store keeper appeared on my left. With his combed-over hair, thick glasses, and bulging stomach, he definitely had the creepy look Camille had talked about. He examined me closely. Feeling a little uncomfortable, I said, "I'm just getting a few things."

The store keeper continued to follow me down the aisle of canned goods. When I stopped to examine a can of beans, he cleared his throat and commented, "I thought you were passing through."

"We decided to stay a few days," I replied, keeping my eyes focused on the canned goods.

"Have you checked in with the German authorities," he replied gruffly.

"Not necessary," I continued. "We will just be here a few more days."

"You said, 'We' decided to stay. Who is with you?" he asked.

"Yes I did," I replied, trying to hide my anger. I was beginning to feel uncomfortable and decided I needed to hurry and find out what I needed. His questions continued. "How did you get here? I don't see a car."

"I got a ride," I said. "Do you remember the man I was with when I stopped by a few days ago? He gave me a lift." The store keeper seemed confused. I quickly added, "I also need kerosene and matches." He walked behind the counter and returned with a box of matches and a container that held kerosene.

I said, "Better make that two boxes of matches."

Before he turned to get more matches, he commented, "Your accent is different."

"I used to live in Canada," I murmured.

Again he left and returned with a box of matches. I asked, "Do you have any tea?"

He pointed behind me. I went to the shelf and picked out a box. After everything was placed on the counter, I pulled out a wad of francs. I wasn't sure of the value of the francs but acted as if the money on the counter would be sufficient. He made a comment about German Reich marks but I pointed to the Francs. He took the money on the counter and handed me back some of it. I wasn't sure if he had taken more than he should have. I smiled, thanked him, and packed everything in the backpack. As I walked to the front door I asked him if I could have a couple of burlap sacks. He handed me two that were lying on top of a basket of cucumbers. As I opened the door to leave, he asked, "Where is your friend's car?"

"I'm going to meet him down the road."

"Which direction are you going?" he asked.

I pointed with my finger.

As I walked away he shouted, "Are you hiding out?"

"No, why would I do that? We're just getting away for a few days," I yelled.

He yelled back, "You should report your whereabouts to the authorities."

I walked away, knowing it would not be safe for me to return to the store again. I was running behind schedule, if I wanted to make it back to the cabin before sunset. I decided to make a quick stop to see if the chickens were still at my earlier hiding place. I spotted one of them near the bushes and started to chase it. The chicken weaved and darted while I attempted to grab it. It took a sharp turn to the right at the same time I lunged right, falling on top of it. I practically smashed its head. It was so stunned, I easily picked it up and dropped it in the burlap bag.

When I got back to the road, I started to jog. My jogging eventually turned into a fast walk. After a while, I started jogging again. I found the stick I had left as a marker. There were buzzards on top of the body. I yelled and ran toward them as they reluctantly flew away. I grabbed the rifle and took off running.

I didn't stop to eat or drink. The last three miles of my return trip were uphill. It was a gradual incline, but I could feel the difference in my legs. As the sun was starting to set, I saw the cabin in the distance.

No lights were on in the cabin, which wasn't a total surprise. Not having matches created a number of challenges. When the door opened, I was greeted with hugs and kisses. Joshua grinned and said, "Papa." The first thing I did was put the kerosene in the lamps located in the cabin. Immediately, the cabin became well-lit for the first time. Camille noticed the burlap bag moving and asked, "What's in the bag?"

"A chicken," I replied.

She laughed, "How in the world did you get a chicken?"

"It found me on the side of the road. After hauling it all this way, I've decided to call it Chirpy."

Joshua responded, "Chirpy?"

Camille whispered, "You should never name a chicken."

"Why?"

She whispered in my ear, "How do you feel about removing Chirpy's head?"

"I get your point," I said wryly.

"For now, we'll just put her in the tool shed," suggested Camille.

Joshua walked with me to the tool shed. When I released the chicken, it started to flap its wings and squawk. Returning to the cabin, Joshua was coughing and was short of breath.

As we sat around the table, Camille examined the supplies I had purchased. I asked her how long Joshua had been coughing.

"Sometimes I think he is doing better, but then he starts coughing and sounding congested again. I'm glad you got the tea., I'll make some right now. He needs more rest."

As we drank our tea, Camille noticed the rifle I had brought back. I told her how I had stumbled onto the dead Frenchman. I also told her about having to wait for the Germans to leave the store. She asked me about the storekeeper.

"He asked a lot of questions; wanting to know if we were hiding," I answered, not wanting to share too much information with her.

Camille had a worried look on her face, but I told her not to worry. No more visits to the store. With the supplies we now had, and the game in the woods, we could sustain ourselves at the cabin for a long time. She was noticeably relieved.

After tea, she told Joshua it was time for bed. She climbed the steps to the loft and told me not to be long. I told her I wanted to sit up for a while. She then said, "Don't wait too long, I'll be in bed naked." I didn't wait long at all.

The next day it rained all day. We enjoyed the day of rest and the convenience of having matches. Camille prepared a meal with the rice I had brought back. Our special treat was the biscuits stuffed with jam. I checked on Chirpy and decided to let her out of the tool shed. She strutted around the cabin looking for insects or anything else she could find to eat. Camille said the hen needed to be returned to the tool shed by evening or she would become dinner for a fox.

The next few days were easier than our first days at the cabin. We had an established routine and the cabin was easier to maintain since it had been thoroughly cleaned. We had venison left and I was confident that I could catch fish when needed. For the first time, I saw two rabbits in the woods close to the lake. Having enough became less of a worry. The big bonus came when we discovered Chirpy had laid an egg in the tool shed. Chirpy had literally saved her own neck.

It was our third week in the cabin, it was late July. I wondered about the invasion of Europe. I wanted to ask the storekeeper questions about the war, but knew that would only increase his suspicion. When using the rowboat, I would listen for gunshots or artillery fire. Our hope was to outlast the Germans and then to make our way back to the farm in Amiens. Each morning, when we climbed out of bed, we were one day closer.

After walking in the woods for most of the day, looking for something edible to shoot, I returned to the cabin to find Camille crying. I put my arms around her and asked, "Why are you crying?"

She pressed her face against my chest and said, "Joshua's not getting any better."

"Is he getting worse?" I asked.

"I think so, he sounds so congested, and he's having trouble breathing. I'm so worried."

"Do you want me to go and get medicine?" I asked.

"Who's going to give that to you?" she asked, wiping the tears from her cheeks. "It's just too dangerous."

"There must be a doctor in Charleville-Mezieres," I added, trying to give her hope.

"There are also Germans. Not all doctors are like Dr. Benoit," she answered.

"What do you want to do?" I asked.

"Let's sleep on it," she said. "I've got something to rub on his chest. Maybe he will be better in the morning."

The next morning, Joshua was not better. There was no doubt he was worse. He was running a temperature and was listless. Camille was beside herself; she was almost paralyzed with fear. Finally I said, "I will take him to the general store and call Dr. Benoit. It is just a three-hour drive, I know he will come."

"What about the storekeeper?" she asked with concern.

"I'll deal with him," I remarked.

She began to clear the table and commented, "I'm going with you," she declared, as she cleared the table.

"You don't have to do that," I said, trying to keep calm.

"I'm coming with you," she replied, determined to do just that.

I knew better than to argue with her. We packed something to eat and filled the canteen with water. I placed Joshua over my shoulder in a fireman's carry hold and took off down the hill.

It was cool and breezy, but at least it wasn't raining. Camille offered to help carry Joshua, but I refused the offer. Joshua never said anything. I could feel the heat from his body. We made good time and much to my relief, I didn't see any trucks or cars parked in front of the store.

When we entered the store, the storekeeper walked toward us and stared. Before he had a chance to say anything, I said, "My son is sick, I need to use your phone to call a doctor."

"Why don't you take him to the doctor in town?" he asked, in his usual gruff voice.

"Because the doctor I'm calling is a family friend. He knows the boy."

"Where is this doctor friend?" he asked.

"Out of town, but I know he will accept the call. I will give you money."

"I don't understand why you can't see a doctor here," he replied.

I lost all patience. I handed Joshua to Camille and then grabbed the storekeeper by the front of his shirt and picked him up off the ground. I yelled in his face, "Dammit, this boy is sick and I'm going to use the phone to get him help. I don't have time to put up with your shit."

I put him back down and he stumbled backwards. He had a hurt, angry expression on his face, but he didn't say anything. He walked behind the counter and I went to the phone. Since I had no idea how to make a call in France, Camille took over the call. I could only listen to half the conversation taking place on the phone. I could tell by the expression on Camille's face and the comments she was making, that Dr. Benoit would be coming.

I took a wad of francs and placed them on the countertop. The storekeeper grabbed the bills but continued to glare at me. I remembered seeing a picnic table that was beside the store. I took Joshua in my arms, and we made our way to the picnic table. Camille put Joshua's head in her lap. I took a drink from the canteen and wiped the sweat from my forehead. I knew I had been a little rough with the storekeeper. Early in life I had realized patience was not one of my better virtues.

Time passed slowly as we sat on the picnic table benches. Camille, on occasion, would have me wet a cloth to put on Joshua's forehead. After two hours of waiting, I became restless and began to pace back and forth in the driveway. While pacing I heard a loud noise coming from two motorcycles. I slowly walked back to the picnic table. Two German soldiers dismounted their motorcycles and went inside. What the storekeeper might say to the soldiers worried me. They were in the store a long time. Finally, the front door opened and the soldiers walked toward their motorcycles. One soldier passed and looked our way. In a low voice I told Camille not to look up. I continued to look at her, but I was also aware of the soldier. He seemed to be studying us. Then there was the roar of motorcycle engines and they roared away, spinning gravel as they entered the main road.

It had been four hours and I began having doubts about Dr. Benoit coming. I breathed a sigh of relief when I saw his car pull into the driveway. His wife, Mary, was on the passenger side. I waved at them as he pulled the car close to us.

Dr. Benoit did not waste any time attending to Joshua. He got out of the car carrying his black bag and walked directly to him. He told Camille to keep Joshua's head in her lap. He listened to his lungs and heart. He then took his temperature and checked his throat and ears.

When Dr. Benoit was through with his examination he said, "I think Joshua has pneumonia, this time it's worse. I'm going to give him a shot and I want to take him with me. It might be necessary to have him hospitalized."

Camille interrupted him and said, "I'm going, too."
"I don't think that is a good idea. There seems to
be renewed interest in the Vel'd'Hiv Roundup."
I asked, "What's that?"
He replied, "In 1942, the Nazis ordered the roundup
of Jews in Paris. It spread quickly to other areas.
Even with the American and British invasion, there
seems to be a renewed interest in the rounding up
Jews and sending them to concentration camps in
Germany. It's like they want to make a final purge
before they evacuate. It is incredibly dangerous for
you. I can treat Joshua without bringing any attention
to him. Even if I have to take him to the hospital, it
won't raise suspicion; trust me on this. I will take
care of him. You and John need to hide. Hopefully,
we can all be reunited soon."
      Camille was not happy, but she seemed resigned
to the situation. She added, "When Joshua gets better,
will you bring him to us?"
      "Yes, but this may take some time. I'm worried
about him. I will do whatever I need to do to get him
well."
      After a few moments of silence, I asked, "What
about the war?"
      "The Americans are pushing toward Paris. I'm
optimistic, but right now we just need to live day by
day."
      Camille, Joshua, and Mary sat in the backseat
while I moved to the passenger side of the front seat.
I rolled down the window of the car and once again
saw the storekeeper watching us. Had I known then
what was to come, the storekeeper would have met a
bad ending.
      Dr. Benoit drove on the main road, then turned onto
the bumpy road that led to the cabin. Like before, he
drove as far as he could and then stopped. It was hard
for Camille to leave Joshua, even though she knew it

was for the best. She kissed and hugged him and then the two of us waved and walked toward the cabin. We entered the dark cabin and immediately lit the lamps and started a fire in the stove. We had not eaten for a long time. Camille sat on the couch and began to cry. When I walked over to her, she stood and wrapped her arms around me. As she continued to cry, I could feel her tears touching my neck. I held her tightly, and assured her that everything would be okay.

"Joshua will get well and we will be together again," I said, trying to encourage her.

"Why do things have to be so bad?" she replied.

"I don't know, but I think they will get better. We just need to outlast the war."

I held her until the crying stopped. She then made dinner and got ready for bed. That night she held me tightly as we slept. It had been a difficult day and the future was still uncertain.

With Joshua being gone, we remained in bed for a long time. Both of us were lying on our backs staring at the ceiling. I'm sure she was thinking of Joshua. Camille was the first to get out of bed. She went down the ladder and started fixing something for us to eat. We did not always have coffee. We didn't want to run out too fast, so sometimes we would go a few days before brewing a pot. This morning, however, I could smell the coffee. It motivated me to get out of bed.

We ate a large breakfast, and I helped Camille with the dishes. I had to go outside to pump water from the well. I decided I could fix it without too much trouble. I was never too handy, but it was worth a try. As I walked back from the well, I could hear Chirpy in the tool shed. I opened the door and the hen immediately scooted out. I checked, but found no eggs in the usual places.

Before I started on my pump project, I sat at the table with Camille. She poured the rest of the coffee in our cups.

I thought I heard something, but I wasn't sure. I looked at Camille, asking her if she had heard anything.

"It sounds like a car," she answered.

"A car could never make it up the road to the cabin," I said. Suddenly, I sensed danger approaching.

We stood up and walked to the front window next to the door. The noise got louder and both of us realized it was getting closer. Camille grabbed my arm and said, "What do we do? What if it's the Germans?"

"It's too late to run. We would be shot," I answered.

Camille pointed to the cabinet in the kitchen. "What about the identification papers Dr. Benoit gave us?" she asked.

"If we used them and it was discovered they were false, he would be arrested."

"I'm so scared," she said.

Our greatest fear became reality. A jeep with a German soldier at the wheel and an SS officer on the passenger side drove in front of the cabin. They leaped out of the jeep and hurried toward the front door. The soldier had an automatic rifle with a strap hanging from his shoulder. The SS officer was tall and had a scar that ran down one side of his face.

The SS officer banged on the door. I opened it. He said something in German and then the soldier interrupted in French, "Who are you?"

I responded, "Joseph and Camille Bernhardt."

The officer spoke in German and again the other soldier interrupted. "Why are you here?"

"To get away from the city," I replied.

Immediately the SS officer had rage on his face. He grabbed Camille by the hair and forced her to her knees. He then pulled out his pistol and placed the muzzle on her temple and cocked it. He said something in German which was quickly translated by the soldier. "You have one chance to tell the truth or she will die. Are you Jews?"

"Yes," I responded, knowing that I condemned all of us with that word.

The SS officer took Camille's head and threw it towards the floor. Her face hit the floor and bounced. At the same time, the soldier took the butt end of his rifle and plunged it into my stomach. I fell to my knees. We were picked up and dragged to the jeep. We were thrown in the backseat. Camille had blood trickling from her nose and chin.

I was trying to get my breath.

As the jeep turned around and started down the hill, Camille wet her pants, and the urine rolled on the floor of the jeep. When the SS officer noticed the urine, he took the back of his hand and swung it against the side of Camille's face. He then yelled something in German, which was interpreted as "clean it up, Jew pig." Camille took the bottom of her dress and began to wipe up the urine from the floor of the jeep.

We continued to bounce down the road at a high speed. When we got to the main road, the driver accelerated. We were heading toward Charleville-Mezieres. At the speed we were going, it didn't take long to reach the general store. The driver sharply turned the wheel. We entered the parking area at a high rate of speed. He then applied the brakes, causing all of us to lunge forward. The SS officer got out of the jeep and went into the store. One minute later, he returned with the storekeeper. They stood at the front door while the SS officer pointed at us. The storekeeper nodded and the officer returned to the jeep. It was now obvious the storekeeper had reported us.

When we got closer to town, I saw more German soldiers and trucks. When we passed, the soldiers

would salute the SS officer. We kept going down side
streets until we reached a building with a large Nazi
flag draped on the entrance. The jeep turned on the
road next to the building and stopped next to a small
building with large doors. It was a garage. We were
grabbed and dragged to the front door. There were
two soldiers standing out front. A few words were
exchanged and then one of the doors opened. Camille
and I were shoved through the door. The door was
shut and locked. The building was a garage, but it
contained no cars. It was dark and it was difficult for
our eyes to adjust to the lack of light. A few seconds
later I realized there was someone sitting in the
corner. I walked closer and felt like I recognized the
man. I said, "Father Glaize?"

The man looked up and said, "Joseph, Camille."
He then stood and we all embraced.

"What are you doing here?" I asked.

"I was transporting a French fighter to safety. This
time the cigarettes didn't work." He looked at Camille
and added, "What happened to you?"

"I'm a Jew," she replied.

He then hugged Camille and patted her on the
back of her head. We all sat down. "What are they
going to do with us?" I asked.

"I don't think they know I speak and understand
German. I heard the SS officer talk about a
concentration camp. He mentioned a couple of them."

"Is that like a work farm?"

"Maybe at one time. I've heard from some priests
that they have become death camps for many people."

We sat for a long time without saying a word. We
had not received food or water. I found a cloth in the
garage and used it to wipe some of the dried blood
from Camille's face. I was holding her hand when a
thought came to my mind. I looked at Father Glaize
and said, "Will you marry us?"

"What do you mean? I thought you were married."

"No," I answered. "I'm not Jewish but Camille is. I love Camille and I want her to be my wife."

Camille looked at me and said, "I want you to be my husband."

Father Glaize responded, "But you are Jewish."

Camille responded, "We have the same God."

Father Glaize appeared to be thinking. He then stood and asked us to stand. "I will marry you. I believe God has brought you together, so who am I to question His will?"

We repeated vows and sealed them with a kiss. I didn't stop Father Glaize when he referred to me as Joseph Bernhardt, God knew who I was. I did not know what the future would hold, I just knew somehow it was better with Camille as my wife.

CHAPTER TWENTY TWO

Part III

August 7, 1945

During the night, we slept very little. We were given nothing to eat or drink. All of us worried about what tomorrow might bring. Just before dawn, Father Glaize took our hands and offered a prayer. He prayed for our safety and asked that God would have mercy on us.

At daybreak, a soldier opened the door and brought us bread and water. We scarfed it down. Then we sat and waited. Although we could hear people talking, it was impossible to hear what they were saying. When a soldier finally opened the door, Father Glaize told him we needed to use the bathroom. The soldier smiled and pointed to a corner in the garage. We took turns using the bathroom as the solder watched. He then yelled at us to get in the truck. Father Glaize helped Camille step into the back of the vehicle. Once we were in the truck, a soldier with an automatic rifle strapped over his shoulder got in.

As we rode down the streets of Charleville-Mezieres, Father Glaize, in German, asked the soldier, "Where are you taking us?"

"To the train station."

"Where will the train take us?" he inquired.

"I don't know, probably to one of the camps. That's where the Jews go."

The soldier was correct. Once we arrived at the train station, we were loaded into a train car. There were six other people in the train car with us. They were carrying suitcases. All of them looked weary, tired, and afraid. There was a married couple with a child close to Joshua's age. All of them were surprised to see Father Glaize. He was still wearing his priest collar. The door of the train car was closed. The train started to move and quickly picked up speed. Father Glaize asked the man next to the child, "Why are you here?"

"We are Jews," he replied.

"Do you know where we are going?" asked Father Glaize.

The man responded, "I could hear some of the soldiers talking about Dachau."

"Is that a concentration camp?" asked Father Glaize.

"Yes, I have heard bad things about this place."

The train never slowed down. At times, all of us would bounce and stumble. To avoid falling, we sat on the floor.

When the train finally began to slow down, Camille whispered to me that we were in Lille. I could tell that she was thinking of Joshua. We were so close, but it made no difference. We were prisoners and at the mercy of our captors.

When the train stopped, the door opened, and SS soldiers began to yell. One of the soldiers had a dog on a leash. It was barking and showing its teeth. We started to run as the soldiers yelled. We ran until we reached a series of loading docks. We saw trains filled with people. I saw arms hanging out the small windows and hear the moans of people inside. When we reached one of the loading docks, we were stopped and told to sit. Soon we were joined by more than thirty other people carrying suitcases. An SS officer approached one of the soldiers and they appeared to be arguing with one another. I could hear the soldier yell "Auschwitz" as he pointed to a train to the left of us. The SS soldier shook his head and said, "Dachau," pointing to the train in front of us. Finally, the SS officer walked next to where we were sitting. He used his arm to signify a dividing line. Pointing to one half he said, "Auschwitz." The other half would go to "Dachau." We were in the Dachau group. We were told to stand as the door to one of the train cars opened. We could see people packed so tightly they could barely move. A ramp was placed before us. A soldier screamed at us to go up the ramp. People moved and shoved as Father Glaize, Camille and I made our way to the corner. We held each other, trying to position ourselves so that we would not feel smothered. The door closed, people began to cry and scream out of fear.

As the train pulled away from the station, we began to bump into each other. It was almost impossible to fall down. We were so tightly packed that we were supporting each other. The heat became unbearable, people began to faint. When this happened, people tried to make room for the person to sit. Camille placed her head against my chest. I could feel her body jerk. She tried so hard to hold back the tears. I knew Father Glaize had worked in Munich at one time so I asked him how long the trip would take. "All day," he replied.

A couple of hours into the trip, Camille asked me about the man who was at her feet. I bent down to see if the old man was okay. I noticed he was not moving, then realized he was dead.

The moaning and tears went on throughout the day. It was hot. The train car reeked of urine. None of us had eaten or drunk anything all day. More people were falling to their knees, crushing others as they fell. I felt exhausted. I could only imagine what the older people on the train were feeling. The train began to slow. Everyone was relieved, yet terrified at what would happen when the doors opened.

I could never have been prepared for what would happen next. The large doors opened, but this time there was no ramp. As people jumped to the ground, they were immediately met with the sound of yelling and barking dogs. SS solders used whips to move the people along faster. An old man stumbled with his suitcase, falling to the ground. A guard quickly approached him. He took his club and beat the old man until he was unconscious; the SS soldier just kept hitting him. The old man's blood was slung in every direction until he was dead. People screamed, but nobody stopped walking. I continued to hold Camille's hand until we reached a point where women and children were being divided. As she got in the line, I continued to watch her, wondering if this would be the last time I would see her.

The horror continued. Small infants were removed from mothers and stacked in a pile. When the lines were divided between men and women, guards and certain prisoners took suitcases and other possessions. They started sorting through everything. Shoes were tied together and placed in piles. A man grabbed for what appeared to be a book. He was savagely struck with several blows to his head. He fell to his knees, but managed to stand and continue walking.

We were kept in lines as we stood in front of an SS soldier seated at a table. When I reached the front, I was asked my name and where I was from. I answered, "Joseph Bernhardt from Amiens, France." The soldier responded, "Jew." I quickly went with the other men who were registered.

We were herded like cattle into a room and told to remove all of our clothes. I placed my clothes and shoes on a hook. I was tattooed with a number on my left arm. Everyone had a terrified look as the first step in dehumanizing us took place. Next, we had all body hair shaved. I could hear some of the guards laughing, poking fun at the size of our penises. The shower came next, freezing water blasted our bodies. We were then disinfected with some type of powder and given a pair of striped pajamas. My top had a yellow badge on it, which I knew was the Star of David. My pants were way too big. I was able to exchange later with a man whose pants were too small. Next, we were given some type of wooden shoes, a hat, and a red bowl.

As I ran with the other prisoners, I noticed some of the women prisoners being led out of the shower area. I saw Camille with her cut hair and loose fitting striped pajamas. She saw me, and we both continued to stare at each other until a woman guard noticed and hit her on the back with a club.

I had not had anything to eat and apparently it was too late for the evening meal. Instead, I was shown to my barracks and told where I would sleep. I was then led outside with other men and told to stand at attention. As I stood there, the first thing that hit me was the smell. It was a smell of death and disease. It was as if everything here was in decay.

I stood at attention with the other new arrivals, I took in my surroundings. I realized we were standing there waiting on the prisoners to return from their meal. I slowly turned my head to view my surroundings. The fence that surrounded the camp was high and had barbed wire on top. It also appeared to have electricity running through it. At strategic locations, I could see rifle towers with soldiers in them. Around the camp was a creek. There were rows of barracks and a building that was not a barrack. In my barrack, there were rows of wooden platforms that were used as beds. We were going to be stuffed into cubicles like sardines in a can.

I was standing in some type of courtyard. I assumed it was used for roll call. After a while, I saw the men coming from their meal and standing in formation. I was shocked to see the condition of them. Some looked like skeletons, many had sores and bruises on their faces. No one said anything. It was like a group of walking zombies taking their places in line. The faces were expressionless. No one showed any emotion.

Once everyone was in rows, a roll call was conducted and reported. In front of us stood an SS guard who looked like a bulldog, so we nicknamed him accordingly. He had a short neck and a head that seemed too big for his body.

We stood for at least an hour. Some of the men in front of me were having a difficult time standing. When a man fell, he was grabbed by the Bulldog and dragged to a bench. He was then stripped of his clothes and whipped to the point of unconsciousness. Then he was pushed off the bench. The Bulldog stomped his leg. Although I was standing in the back, I could hear his bones break.

We continued to stand in formation. Although something was being broadcast over the speaker, I had no idea what was being said. As we were standing there, two other SS soldiers walked up to the Bulldog. After exchanging a few words, the Bulldog pointed to a man in the front row. The two SS soldiers walked over to the man and pulled him out of formation. The man was tall and thin and looked like skin and bones. One of the soldiers lit a cigarette and put it in the prisoner's mouth, while the other soldier reared back and punched the prisoner as hard as he could. The punch knocked him unconscious. All three of the SS guards started to laugh, giving the guard who had inflicted the punch a pat on the back. It was apparent they were having a contest. The Bulldog picked another prisoner and the other guard had a turn. The prisoner fell to the ground but he was not knocked out. The other guard started to laugh, which angered the guard who had thrown the punch. He took out his anger on the prisoner by kicking him in the head repeatedly. When we were finally dismissed, the three bodies were left in the courtyard.

In the barrack, I learned I would be sharing my sleeping space with two other men. I was sleeping in the center rack with them which meant I had people sleeping over me and under me. We were sleeping so tight it was impossible to turn over. I heard the door of the barracks lock.

All of the men were exhausted to the point of collapsing. I soon heard the sound of snoring. I also heard coughing and an occasional loud scream, probably the result of a nightmare.

In the middle of the night, I felt something dripping on my leg. I wasn't sure what it was but the smell gave it away. There was urine dripping on my leg from the man who was sleeping over me.

CHAPTER TWENTY THREE

Dachau, August – September, 1944

It seemed like the middle of the night when a person wearing a yellow armband began to scream at us to get up. Everyone jumped up, and quickly made their way to the door. When I got up, I realized that the man above me was dead. He was not the only prisoner who had died during the night, two other men had died as well. A prisoner wearing a yellow armband yelled at three men to get the bodies. They dragged the bodies across the floor, while the other prisoners ran out of the barrack. I later learned that the prisoners with yellow armbands were Kapos who were assigned by the SS guards to supervise us.

I followed the prisoners as they quickly made their way to the sanitary facility. There were only a couple of places for hundreds of men to wash. I made my way to one of the outside toilets, all placed in a row. There was no running water or plumbing. It was essentially a row of outhouses without walls. The smell took your breath away, sanitary conditions were nonexistent.

I jumped off the seat when I saw everyone scrambling to make their way to roll call. It didn't take long to realize why everyone was in such a hurry. We had assigned rows of ten. Everyone took his place and stood at attention. The dead bodies were placed in their usual place in line. Even dead people were part of the roll call.

As we stood at attention, I watched an old man who could barely move make his way to the formation. The Bulldog spotted him. He quickly grabbed him and pushed him toward the platform that was used for hanging prisoners. The man fell. A guard picked him up and hit him with a club. When they reached the platform, the rope was put around his neck, and the floor opened. The man kicked a few times until his body went limp.

Everyone in formation looked straight ahead, as if nothing had happened. Under the control of the SS guards and officers, the Kapos started counting. The one in front of us made a mistake and had to start over. I could tell he was nervous as he quickly started recounting. We stood in formation for what seemed like two hours. The guard would occasionally scream for everyone to remove his hat. Then he would scream to put it back on. When one of the men dropped his hat, he was clubbed so hard that the club splintered into pieces. The man remained on the ground. When he didn't get up, he was shot.

I could see prisoners in front of me start to sway. I knew they were exhausted from standing. Finally, we were dismissed for breakfast.

We went to the breakfast area and got in line with our tin bowl. The bowl was filled with coffee that had no taste and looked more like mud. I took my serving and walked away. I downed the coffee in just a few gulps. One of the prisoners had just received his serving when a guard intentionally bumped him, causing his serving to spill on the ground. The guard then took his club and hit the man repeatedly until he was unconscious. A whistle blew, and we hurried back to the roll call area. The man who was beaten was left on the ground. The Kapos yelled for someone to pick him up. A prisoner dragged the unconscious man back to formation.

When we returned to formation, several more guards appeared. Some of them had dogs on leashes. The guards and Kapos started to yell for the prisoners to quickly join their work teams. I had been assigned by the Kapos to the gravel detail. I assumed it would be hard labor.

As we went through the gate under heavy guard, some women prisoners were leaving. I couldn't tell for sure, but I thought I saw Camille. After we exited the gate, we walked over a mile until we reached an area that contained larger boulder-like rocks. As we got closer, some of the guards began to kick men for no apparent reason. They got pleasure from beating and harassing the men. The men were handed picks. Since I was in the back, the picks had been distributed before I reached the front of the line. The men with picks began to pick and bust rocks. I picked up rocks and piled them up. When a cart came by, I helped put the gravel in the cart. The people with the carts pulled the gravel down the road and dumped it on the sides of the road.

After several hours, some of the older men began to slow down. The guards screamed to make them speed up. Everyone tried to work as fast as possible while guards insulted and beat them. When the whistle sounded, we returned to camp for lunch. Lunch consisted of soup. When the whistle blew again, it was back to work. This time it seemed harder because I was hungry and I felt like I was losing strength. I could only imagine what it was like for the older men, especially the ones who had been here a while. One of the older men stopped and rested several times. None of the guards said anything to him. He would rest, then lift and swing the pick for a few more minutes. Another man fainted, falling at my feet. A guard walked over to him and shot him in the back of the head.

Another whistle sounded. We started our walk back to the camp. The guard yelled at me to carry the man who had been shot. I lifted the man onto my shoulder. His limp body fell against my back. I was exhausted, but knew what would happen if I stopped or rested. At afternoon roll call, I dropped the dead man in his designated spot. Again the Kapos begin to take count, making sure the dead were included. The evening roll call was another chance to brutalize prisoners. All of us were exhausted and feeling the effects of no food or water. When someone dropped, he was either killed or beaten with a club. After more than two hours of standing, one of the guards, who had accompanied my work detail, came forward and pulled a man from formation. It was the same man I had seen stop and rest while we worked. The man was grabbed and dragged to the hanging platform. Within a matter of minutes, he was hanging from a rope. The prisoners in my immediate formation were ordered to march around the hanging platform so we could see the body.

A few other prisoners were singled out for punishment. I could not comprehend the brutality that one person could inflict on another. I was especially terrorized by the fact they seemed to enjoy it.

We were dismissed for dinner and ran to get in line. I received a kind of soup that contained a few pieces of cabbage in it. This time, I also got a piece of bread.

I returned to the barracks. It had become obvious we were not going to be allowed to leave. In the barracks there was a prisoner who had a green triangle on his shirt. Although he was a prisoner, he was in charge once the door was locked. He continued to scream and harass the prisoners. Nobody said anything to him. He was a person to be feared.

Finally, men began to crawl into the bunks. It was so tight that I had to reposition myself two times before the men in the bunk with me could get into a position to sleep. We were touching and the smell of bodies made me gag. As I closed my eyes, I recounted the events of my first day at Dachau. It was just one day, but already it seemed like an eternity. I assumed every day would follow the same routine of roll call, meals, work, and brutality. I wasn't sure if I could cope with it. I had spent my first day in a constant state of fear. When I was almost asleep, I felt something bite my legs. I scratched the area, disturbing the man next to me.

I was hoping things would get better, but they didn't. The next four days were worse. The routine was the same but the brutality escalated. One prisoner, for some reason, was singled out and taken to a pole where his arms were placed behind him and tied. He was then pulled up the pole with a rope. His shoulders became dislocated. He cried out in pain. When he was dropped to the ground, he was unconscious. His body was left there until morning roll call. The Bulldog walked over to the body and put a round in the man's head. That same morning we stood in formation for more than four hours. It began to rain. I was sure there would be more dead bodies in the barracks the next day.

At evening roll call, we had a different guard in charge. He must have been gone for a while and decided to make up for lost time. An older man, who didn't seem to know what was happening, was singled out by the guard. The old man looked like death and seemed disoriented. The guard took his hat off and threw it in the no man's land, which was the ten-foot zone next to the perimeter fence. The old man didn't move but continued to stare at the guard. The guard started screaming at him to get his hat. The man seemed confused, but started to walk toward his hat. Once he crossed into the no-man's area, he was shot dead by a tower guard. The SS guards started to laugh, mocking two other prisoners by grabbing their hats and pretending to throw them.

That evening, when I returned to the barracks, it seemed quieter. I could tell the prisoner, who was called the blockfuerher, was not feeling well. There was no yelling. The other prisoners were either sitting or lying on their bunks.

A prisoner who had a lower bunk across from me waved for me to join him. I slowly walked his way. He patted the bunk, signaling for me to have a seat. When I sat down, he said in French, "I'm Otto Kohler."

I answered, "I'm John; I mean Joseph."

"John Joseph, you are new here," he replied.

"Yes, four days. How long have you been here?"

He rubbed his face with both hands and responded, "I've been at Dachau two years, but I was at Auschwitz for two."

"How have you survived this? I've only been here four days and I'm not sure if I can make it."

He replied, "Mostly, I've been lucky, but I have learned a few things. You've got to have something to live for. Do you have a reason to live?"

I answered, "Yes, at least I hope so. My wife is here."

Otto stared at the floor as we continued our conversation, "My wife and children were with me at Auschwitz. I'm not sure if they are still living. I live my life as if I will see them. Even if I don't, I live for the day I will hear music being played in Vienna. I think of the times I have sat in concerts and listened to the great masters play."

"How do you live with the constant fear of being killed?" I asked, trying to grasp the reality of what had happened to me.

"You adapt to the environment. That's why some of the men don't do well. They are not used to having their lives controlled and being told when to eat and shit."

"But even if you do adapt, that doesn't mean some guard won't decide to kill you," I asserted.

"This is true. That is why I have learned to be... I'm not sure how you say it in French. Do you speak English?"

"Yes, very well," I responded.

"Then I will speak in English. I think the word in English is zombie. I have become a zombie. I am the walking dead. I try to tune out everything around me."

"Don't you fear dying?" I asked.

"I believe I am already dead. It is just a matter of when it becomes official. You are a young man and that will help you."

I added, "I thought this was a labor camp."

He grimaced at the remark, "The idea that work will set you free is a lie. Have you heard of the final solution?"

"No, I haven't."

He continued, "This is an order from Hitler to exterminate the Jews in Europe. These are death camps, we are here to die. You will die of malnutrition, work exhaustion, disease, or murder."

"But you have stayed alive four years," I replied.

"Yes, as I said, I have been lucky. There are things that will help you. Never be in the front of the line. Always be in the middle. Never be late and never lose your shoes or bowl. The guards are looking for reasons, so don't give them one. Also, never limp or act as if you are sick. The guards want to eliminate anyone who cannot work. You also need to try and keep your body as clean as you can. This will help with lice and fleas.

"Do you ever take a shower?" I asked.

"At one time, we could shower every two or three weeks, but things have changed. We have become too crowded. If you get a chance, try to wash. The Kapos seem to like it when you are clean. I think that is why I have a better job."

"What do you do?" I asked.

Otto responded, "I work in the kitchen. It is not easy, but it is better than working hard labor. We do not eat enough to work such hard labor. This is why so many die, especially the older men."

"How do you get jobs," I inquired.

"There is a cast system. As a Jew, you are at the bottom, along with the Russian soldiers," he replied.

"There are Russian soldiers here?" I asked, surprised that any Russians would be in a concentration camp.

"Yeah, they are sometimes used for target practice on the rifle range. You can hear the shots."

"What about the women here?" I asked.

"This camp has always been for men. It just started taking women. I guess the same rules would apply. I imagine some of them may work in the factory, but that doesn't mean it is easy. The women guards appear to be just as brutal. Besides, there are always SS men wandering over to their barracks."

"Who are the people with the colored badges?" I asked, assuming they were of some importance.

He answered, "The green badge is for criminals. They are the murderers and rapists. That's why they are in charge of the barracks. The political prisoners are red."

"Would that include priests?" I asked.

"Yes."

"What about the violet and pink?" I continued.

"They are the Jehovah's Witnesses and homosexuals. I'm not sure about the other colors though, I've never been around them."

"Who are the men in the white coats? They seem very intimidating."

He continued, "They are doctors who pick prisoners to do experiments on. Sometimes people don't come back. It's not good if you get picked by them. It's also not good if you get picked for a crematory job."

"What's that?" I asked.

"Those are the people who pick up the dead bodies every day and take them to the crematory to be burned. They usually look for strong, young men to do this job. They don't seem to last long. The work is hard but maybe the Germans don't want any witnesses to the burning of bodies. There are a lot more bodies now."

"Why is that?" I inquired, I became more uneasy with his remarks.

He continued, "There are more prisoners. It is getting crowded, and I think it is going to get a lot worse. The Americans, British, and Russians must be having success. Many of the prisoners we are getting have come from other camps. That's why I think we are going to get a lot more. Dachau was the first camp and one of the biggest. There are thousands of camps so they have to send prisoners somewhere. I also think the SS will want to kill more to make room."

For the first time, there was a pause in our question-and-answer conversation. The prisoners were starting to get in their bunks, so I stood up. Otto placed his hand on my arm and said, "You are young, you must adapt and live. One day we will be rescued from this hell. Every day I pray to God not to forsake me but to deliver me from hell, you must do the same. Next time, we will talk about good things. I will tell you about my Vienna and the music I love. You can tell me the good things about where you live."

I went to my bunk, squeezing in with the two other men. Within a matter of seconds, I felt something bite me. Again, I scratched, which caused everyone to change positions. I had learned much from Otto. For some reason, he had singled me out. Most everyone I had met did not talk with anyone. This was not a place to make friends. Still, I was glad Otto chose to talk with me. The information he shared was frightening, but in some ways it gave me hope.

CHAPTER TWENTY FOUR

Dachau, Fall, 1944

The days were breezy and the early morning was much cooler. Although the striped pajamas were thick, they were no match for the cool mornings. During the early morning roll call, I found myself shaking. I could hear some of the prisoners cough, an early sign of a possible deadly illness. The shift in wind direction brought the smell of burning flesh across the courtyard. Ashes fell on us as we stood at attention. All of us knew where the ashes came from.

For the first time, I became aware that my appearance must have changed. When I first arrived, I was shocked at the appearance of prisoners. I knew that I had lost significant weight. I also had sores on my legs from flea bites and I usually had diarrhea. On certain days, I felt much weaker. It was all I could do to keep up the pace of work that was demanded. I was not getting enough nourishment.

My job had changed, which was both good and bad. I was now digging up potatoes. This job at least served a purpose. The hauling of gravel seemed like a made-up job. Harvesting the potatoes was still not easy. It was made worse by the demands of the guards to work faster. The weather was cooler, which made it better. I was now working with several older prisoners. They continued to be the ones to receive the abuse. The most difficult part of harvesting potatoes was looking at food. Every man must have had the same thought. Everyone knew, however, that being caught with a potato or having a piece in your mouth was certain death.

The wind began to pick up, which caused dirt from the field to hit against my skin. While digging, the dirt would fly in my face. The guards moved farther back from the field. They stood in a huddle to talk and smoke. As I continued to dig, I saw a prisoner with a potato in his hand. I knew he was trying to decide whether or not to take it. He laid it on the ground but kept looking back at it. As I glanced his way, I saw him put it under his hat. The potato was so small, you wouldn't notice it. I understood the hunger he felt, but couldn't understand why he would take the risk.

We marched back to the camp, fighting the dirt and sand blowing in our faces. Once in formation, I was glad the wind was at our backs. We stood longer than usual. As I stood there, I saw four carts pass in front of us filled with dead bodies. The bodies were piled so high that the prisoner pushing the cart had to stop because the bodies kept falling off. This was the first time I noticed that one of the carts was carrying the bodies of several dead women. They looked older than Camille, but it was hard to tell. Camille's barrack was at the other end of the camp. I would only see women prisoners when I was going to or from my work assignment. Once I thought I saw her, but I couldn't be sure. The woman was about her size and age. She was limping, which caused me great concern.

It was almost dark, and we continued to stand in formation. The carts carrying dead bodies must have already reached the crematory by now. Huge streams of smoke rose from the chimneys of the furnaces followed by the terrible smell. Then the ashes began to fall on us. Otto was right about things getting worse;

the daily death count had to be going up. I estimated that there were at least 100 bodies on each cart.

The guards seemed to be pre-occupied with other things. After another hour of standing, certain prisoners were signaled out for punishment. Three prisoners were whipped for working too slow. I continued to practice the advice Otto gave me about being oblivious to what was happening around me. I did notice when the prisoner who had taken the potato was pulled out of formation. The guard stood him in front of all of us. He removed the prisoner's hat, causing the small potato to fall to the ground. The guard then walked over to one of the three prisoners who had been whipped and was still lying on the ground. He put a bullet in his head. He then dragged the potato stealer over to the dead body and told him to take a bite of the man's leg. When the prisoner didn't respond, the guard threw him on the dead body and put a pistol to his head. He kept screaming at him to take a bite. The prisoner frantically reached down to take a bite of the man's leg. Blood and flesh was hanging from his mouth. The guard continued to yell at him to chew. When the guard was satisfied he had swallowed the flesh, he picked the prisoner up. He then kicked him toward the hanging platform. Within a minute, the prisoner who had taken a potato and was forced to eat human flesh, was hanging by his neck. The guard continued to scream in German. I did not understand what he was saying. He kept repeating the same phrase over and over again. As he paced back and forth, I realized what was happening. We were all being punished for what the potato stealer had done. There would be no dinner for the prisoners in my barracks. After working all day with very little to eat, the thought of going without food was hard to bear.

We were now in our fifth hour of standing in formation. The men who fell were quickly beaten with clubs and left on the ground. As dark fell and the awful smell drifted in our faces, one of the prisoners broke formation and slowly walked toward the fence line. A guard yelled but the man did not stop. When he reached the no-man's zone, he was immediately shot to death. A half hour later, another prisoner did the same thing. They both had reached the point that it was no longer worth the struggle to live. It was a feeling I was beginning to understand.

That evening in the barracks, Otto motioned for me to come over to his bunk. Because of the increased numbers in the barrack, we sat on the floor and propped our backs against the wall. We were both exhausted. The barracks was so cold it felt good to be shoulder to shoulder with him. Still looking straight ahead he said, "Let me tell you about my beautiful Vienna. In the spring, the flowers bloom and you can walk the streets and take in the beautiful sites. Although I'm Jewish, I have been many times to St. Stephens Cathedral, it is magnificent. It took hundreds of years to build. What I love most about Vienna is the music. I have been to the concert halls and listened to the masters play. When I'm there, I close my eyes and take in every note. Some people probably think I'm asleep. It is my way of letting music soothe my brain. This is how I feed my soul. The best restaurant in the world is there; it is called Griechen Geisel. It was the favorite restaurant of Beethoven and Mozart. When I eat there, I remind myself that I might be sitting at Mozart's table."

I asked, "How long did you live in Vienna?"

"I grew up on a farm outside of Vienna, but my father moved all of us to the city when he opened up his own jewelry business. That's why I ended up going to the university there."

"How did you learn to speak French?"

"My mother is part French, and I learned English at the university. I also studied for a short time at Oxford. That is how I learned to speak English."

A prisoner briefly interrupted our conversation, by coughing so loudly that we could no longer hear each other talk. Once the prisoner's coughing spasm had subsided, I continued to ask Otto more questions about his life. "What did you study?"

"Philosophy and the humanities", he responded. "I love the arts, especially classical music. Just before I graduated, my father had a stroke. As the oldest son, I took over the business. I will always enjoy my music. I lived in the best city in the world for music lovers. Do you like classical music?" he asked.

"I don't know, I haven't really listened to it. I do like jazz," I responded.

"Yes, jazz. That is very American. Have you been to America?"

"I lived there for a while."

Otto turned to look at me with great interest and said, "What was it like?"

"I was young, but I thought it was beautiful," I replied.

"Tell me the most beautiful part."

I was having difficulty thinking of what to say. Finally I said, "The river."

He asked, "Is it a big river?"

"Not necessarily, I guess I just have good memories there."

Otto patted my knee and said, "That is good, you need to hold on to good memories. What is your good memory in France?"

Without any hesitation I replied, "Being at the lake with Camille and Joshua. We would swim and then Camille and I would drink wine in our underwear."

"That is indeed a good memory. How old are you, John Joseph?" he asked.

"I'm not sure what day of the month it is, but my nineteenth birthday is very soon."

"Don't expect the Germans to bake you a cake," he chuckled.

This was the first time I had smiled since I arrived at Dachau. Otto continued by saying, "We Jews are known for our humor."

Everyone started to crawl into their bunks, so I stood up and went to mine. We squeezed in, and tried to get comfortable. The following morning, when the Kapos screamed for us to get up, I panicked when I noticed my shoes were missing. This would likely be cause for hanging. I looked below and in my bunk. I always slept with them in my hand. For some reason, I had forgotten to get them before going to bed. People were beginning to hurry out when I noticed a man still in his bunk not moving. I checked him, he was not dead. I felt, however, that death was knocking on the door. I took his shoes off his feet and put them on mine. We wore the same size.

CHAPTER TWENTY FIVE

When the first snow came, I thought it had to be around November. The white snow seemed to give the camp a clean blanket. The blanket was short-lived when the snow turned red with blood and covered with bodies.

I was allowed to take a shower for the first time. It was freezing outside so the water was beyond cold. The shock to my body was a welcomed feeling. I didn't have much time, but took every opportunity to clean the boils on my legs and to clean my head, which constantly itched from lice and flea bites. There was no soap, so we were bathed in some type of antiseptic solution. Our clothes were placed in an apparatus in which they were exposed to radio waves. I'm not sure what the purpose was, but the stink remained.

I continued to harvest potatoes and face the abusive guards hitting and yelling at me. The potatoes should have been harvested before any type of snow came, so the guards worked us at an inhuman pace and many prisoners fell from exhaustion. This resulted in more hitting and kicking. An older man was kicked so hard in his knee that I heard bones break twenty yards away and the man fell to the ground and couldn't move. He started to crawl and dig up more potatoes. When the guards went toward him, I expected him to be shot. Instead, they yelled at me to pick him up. They told me to drop him on the side of the road and to carry the body to roll call at the end of the day. I kept looking at the guards who were huddled together trying to keep warm. For the first time, I dared to grab a potato vine and place it in my mouth. I slowly chewed and swallowed it. Unlike a potato that required extensive chewing, the vine dissolved more easily. I did it again but decided not to flirt with death any longer. I was getting weaker and the work was getting harder, which was a bad combination.

When we were told to fall in, I grabbed the injured man and put him over my shoulder. He was an old man, and nothing but skin and bones; he was no heavier than a child. I thought he would be dead when I picked him up, but he wasn't. The man knew he would be killed when we returned to camp. He asked if I spoke French. I told him I did and he responded, "They are going to kill me. If you make it out alive, tell my son and daughter-in-law that I love them. Tell them to have many children."

"I will do that. What is his name?"

"It is Joseph Bernhardt," he answered. "His wife's name is Camille. They live in Amiens."

I was stunned; I was carrying Joseph's father on my shoulder. The same Joseph who saved my life. I started to ask about his wife, but decided that was not a good idea. I remembered Camille saying his parents had moved to Paris. They must have been rounded up and sent to different camps. Without any prompting, the man added, "My wife went to Auschwitz."

When we entered the camp, I placed the man in his designated spot. He could not stand so he sat on the ground which was still partially covered with snow. He lived in a different barracks so he was under the command of a different guard. When the guard saw him sitting there, he walked over, pulled out his pistol, and put a bullet through the back of his head. His body went limp, and the snow beneath him turned red.

That evening I told Otto what happened. He told me that many families would no longer exist after the war, it was all part of the final solution. How ironical that I was carrying Joseph's father on my shoulders. The irony was even greater now that I had become Joseph Bernhardt.

With the potatoes harvested, I hauled manure while doing latrine duty. It was unsanitary and the likelihood of disease had increased. Every chance I could find I took snow and cleaned my hands and clothes. The cold was almost unbearable, but I had to stay as clean as possible.

When I took the buckets to the dump, I heard rifle shots. It sounded like I was on the rifle range. There was a pause and then the shots resumed. The next targets were probably being set up. When the range came into view, I discovered the targets were prisoners. Otto had said that Russian prisoners were sometimes used for target practice. I kept my head down and never looked again. Perhaps, I would have a chance to be close to the women's barracks at some point.

That evening at roll call, we stood in the cold as our bodies shook and our teeth chattered. The wind chill made it even colder. Two SS guards approached the Bulldog, he pointed toward us. The guards had been drinking and they were here for sport. It had been a while but I had remembered seeing the one guard, he was the one who could knock a prisoner unconscious with one punch. The two guards staggered toward our formation. A prisoner in the second row was pulled from ranks and told to stand at attention. One of the guards removed his jacket and hat and started rotating his right arm as if he were warming up. He then stood in front of the prisoner, reared back, and with all his force, punched the prisoner in the face. The prisoner fell backwards. The guard had swung with such force that he fell on top of him. The guard got up, checking to see if the prisoner was unconscious. He then jumped up and placed his arms over his head just like a prize fighter who had knocked an opponent to the canvas. The other guard looked up and down the formation and appeared to have his eyes locked on me. I remembered Otto saying sometimes it was a matter of luck. This was not going to be my lucky day. The guard pulled me out and took me to the same place where the prisoner had been punched. He threw down his cigarette and removed his coat and hat. The guard and I were about the same height, but he was much heavier and seemed to have some difficulty keeping his balance. He planted his feet and threw a roundhouse punch that caught me on the chin. I slumped to the ground and feigned unconsciousness, the pain was intense. The guard was yelling and bouncing near me. Then someone grabbed my balls and my eyes popped open. The guard who had knocked his man out started laughing and mocking the other guard.

The second guard started kicking me. He pointed to a small building and kept kicking me to go in that direction. We were going to the standing cells that resembled tall lockers. I was shoved inside the standing cell and the door was locked. It was impossible to sit or kneel, and I was forced to stand straight up and to remain on my feet.

I had no idea how long I would be here, I tried to block that out of my mind. I was already exhausted and I would get no food. The left side of my face had no feeling from the blow I had received.

After two hours, my legs started to shake. I felt like the walls would crush me. I forced myself to think of other things; like a picnic on the lake, or the smile on Camille's face when she was teaching me to milk a cow. I thought about the river. As the night dragged on, I began repeating what Otto had told me, "Oh God, do not forsake me. Deliver me from this hell."

CHAPTER TWENTY SIX

Dachau, January-March, 1945

Winter arrived and everything that Otto had predicted came true. We were more overcrowded each day. The people arriving were prisoners from other camps. Otto had said there were thousands of camps and that when the Americans, British, and Russians started to squeeze Germany, Germany would transport the prisoners to central camps. The prisoners who arrived in the train cars were mostly dead upon arrival. The ones who had survived the trip looked diseased and close to death. Our barrack was designed to hold 250, and now had over 1,000 prisoners crammed into the same space. Disease easily spread so it was not unusual for several bodies to be hauled to formation every morning. The latrine area was a pigsty, unsanitary, foul smelling, and diseased. Because of the increased numbers, showers were eliminated. The guards increased their brutality. It was as if they needed to reduce numbers to keep pace with all the arrivals.

The weather was bitterly cold. We had no heat in the barrack so, on occasion, a prisoner would freeze to death. The guards kept us in formation for hours. Prisoners shook so badly they looked like they were dancing. When this happened, they were stripped of their clothes and given lashes. After being whipped, they were forced to stand naked in the cold wind and snow. If they didn't die by the end of roll call, they would be dead by morning.

One evening, while standing in formation, three SS guards approached our area dragging hoses. When they reached us, the guards hooked up the hoses. They walked through the ranks, randomly picking out prisoners. I remembered how Otto had said that sometimes it is a matter of luck. Ten prisoners were chosen and told to strip. They were than sprayed with water. The prisoners tried to avoid the spray but couldn't. After they had been drenched, they were told to remain standing. When we broke for dinner, they were left behind. That evening, they did not return to the barrack. At the morning formation, we found them lying on the ground frozen to death.

I tried to do what Otto had suggested and stay somewhere in the middle. The day I was pulled out of ranks and used as a punching bag was probably the result of looking younger. The guard was looking for more of a challenge in the sport of knocking someone unconscious. The next morning, after standing all night in the cell, I was released and allowed to return to the barrack to retrieve my bowl. I could hardly walk and my legs felt like Jell-O.

Standing in ranks became a time of fear. Although I tried to keep my eyes looking forward, all around me prisoners were either killed or abused. Carts rolled in front of us with bodies twisted in every position. One guard enjoyed the fear he could produce by letting his dog attack one of us. When the prisoner attempted to push the dog away, it made matters worse. A prisoner was cut so badly that blood dripped down his legs and arms. He was left bleeding until he collapsed.

Today was no different from any other morning roll call. We stood as the Kapos counted everyone, including the dead bodies. The Bulldog seemed preoccupied with other things so he was not in punishment mode. A car drove near us and four men wearing white doctor's coats got out of the car. I had witnessed the doctors taking twenty to thirty prisoners on occasion, but it had been some time since they had been this far down in the line of barracks. Now it was a roll of the dice for all of us. Prisoners never returned after the doctors took them away.

The doctors walked up and down the rows of men selecting prisoners randomly. It appeared the healthier prisoners were being selected, I tried to look sickly. The doctor walking down my row stopped directly in front of me, examining me from the top of my head to my feet. He then grabbed me by the front of my shirt and pulled me out of line. I stood with the other prisoners who had been selected. When the rest of the unlucky ones had been chosen, the doctors got back in their car and drove off. A guard had us to form two lines, then we were marched toward the hospital.

At the hospital, we were split into groups and escorted to different parts of the building. For the first time since I could remember, I felt warm. The building was heated, and I could feel my fingers tingle as they got warm.

With three other men, I was led down a hallway. As we passed various rooms, I saw a tank of what appeared to be ice water with a man submerged in the tank. I tried not to stare, but I could not pull my eyes away. To them, I was considered no different from a rat or monkey. Down the hallway, I saw a woman who was nude and strapped to a bed with her legs positioned far apart. At the end of the hall, the four of us were told to have a seat in a small room that contained an examining table and jars filled with some type of liquid on the table next to a wall.

We sat there saying nothing for more than an hour. I had closed my eyes when the door opened and a man with a white coat appeared. He walked over to the table and poured the contents from one of the large containers into four small glasses. He then took a glass and gave it to each of us. Without any other explanation, he told us to drink it. The liquid was thick and had a bitter, salty taste to it. We gagged, but we were told to keep drinking. After drinking the liquid, we continued to sit while the doctor looked at us. I could feel my stomach churning as a feeling of nausea came over me. The man across from me started to vomit. He was handed a bucket. Within a minute, all of us were holding buckets. One man fell to the floor; his body started twitching. Another man fell to his knees; his body began to lurch as he tried to vomit but couldn't.

I kept throwing up until there was nothing left. I felt dizzy and lightheaded and still felt sick to my stomach. The doctor pulled out his clipboard and made notes. He then examined us by using the stethoscope and taking our temperature. Two of the men continued to lie on the floor while the other remained in his seat with his eyes closed. I was so sick I could hardly move, I forced myself to stand. The doctor looked at me. I asked, "Can I go?" He looked puzzled. Again I repeated, "Can I go?" I wasn't sure if he comprehended what I had said so I spoke the word "go" in German. The doctor called for one of the workers. He escorted me to an area outside the building and told me to stand at attention, I stood for more than an hour. I was so sick I felt I might die. I was joined by five woman prisoners who all looked like they were in shock and were breathing deeply. I wanted to ask about Camille but knew that was a bad idea.

They marched us back to the camp. Although I felt like death, remaining at the hospital meant death. I silently said a prayer, "God, do not forsake me but deliver me from this hell."

I arrived back in time for the evening roll call. As I passed through the ranks, I saw Otto and he gave me a nod. I felt as if I were going to have the dry heaves. I had the urge to throw up, but nothing was there. Despite the freezing cold, I could feel sweat forming on my forehead. I fought the urge to bend over, I wanted no attention drawn to me. I hoped whatever foul stuff I had been forced to drink at the hospital would quickly pass through my body.

The clouds were moving and snow looked eminent. The sweat on my forehead was beginning to cool and I was shivering. The Bulldog had singled out a prisoner to humiliate and terrorize. He had the man strip off his clothes and stand naked. Then he had another guard bring his dog with him. When the dog handler shouted something, the dog began to growl and made attempts to bite the prisoner. The guard held tightly to the leash but the dog was strong enough to bite the prisoner on the leg. The Bulldog wanted him to bite the prisoner's testicles. He pushed the prisoner in the back and the dog bit his penis. Blood poured onto the ground. I could see that the dog had destroyed part of the man's penis; both the Bulldog and the dog handler began to laugh. The dog was pulled away, and the prisoner was allowed to put on his clothes. The blood had stained the front of his pants. He was punched in the back and told to get in formation, he had great difficulty trying to walk. When he was pushed a second time, he fell to his knees. Bulldog took his club and started hitting him repeatedly on the head. Blood splattered on Bulldog's face. After the second blow, the prisoner was without a doubt dead. Bulldog, however, continued to strike him. Nothing was left of the man's head but pieces of brain and skull. When he was finished, he turned to us and started screaming. The rage he showed was not new, but was becoming more frequent and more random.

After witnessing the bloodbath, we were dismissed for the evening meal. I was not sure if I would be able to eat, but I knew I had to try. The soup was mainly water but the piece of bread was what I wanted. I put my red bowl to my lips and slowly started sipping the soup. When nothing happened, I drank some more. It was a few minutes before I began to feel the soup coming back up. When it did, I held my mouth tightly shut, I did not want to vomit. This would be considered wasting food and could result in being hit or something worse. The soup started coming through my nose. I held my bowl up to catch it. I waited a few minutes and then dipped the bread in the bowl and continued to eat in small bites. This time the food stayed down. Once I had finished, my stomach began to cramp. The cramps were so bad I started to walk in circles to get some relief, but then diarrhea set in. I felt the warmth of liquid running down my leg. I continued to walk with the hope no one would notice the liquid dripping out of my pants.

Back in the barrack, I sat next to Otto's bunk. The barrack had become so overcrowded that we hardly fit in the space without being in a sleeping position. The cramping and diarrhea had mercifully stopped.

Otto came over to where I was sitting and sat next to me. I explained everything that had happened and told him I was not sure what the liquid I had drunk would do to me. I then said, "I'm not sure how long I can do this."

He whispered, "You made it through today. The liquid will leave your body and you will feel better."

"It's not just the liquid," I continued. " I try to block things out, but it has become almost impossible."

"Remember what I said about having a reason to live?" asked Otto.

I lifted my head and replied, "Yes, but I'm not sure if I have that reason anymore."

"What if I could find out?" Otto interjected.

"You mean if Camille is still alive," I responded.

"Yes," he continued.

"You can do that?" I asked, overcome with hope.

"I think so, I work in the kitchen area and often talk to a Kapos who works in the factory. He might be able to find out."

"I don't want you to get in trouble."

Otto smiled and whispered, "I won't, I know this man. He will be cautious. I think he likes me because I tell jokes."

"That would be wonderful, it would give me hope."

Otto slapped my knee and started to stand. As he looked down at me he said, "I will see what I can do tomorrow, but there is no guarantee."

"I know," I pointed to a man who was coughing so loud and hard that he was spitting up blood.

Otto remarked, "He has tuberculosis."

"Is that contagious?" I asked.

"Yes," Otto responded. "Especially in crowded, enclosed spaces."

The next day I felt better. When I went to the latrine, I did my best to clean up. These days, it was almost impossible to have access to water. Maybe I had been lucky after all and survived my ordeal with the doctors.

At the morning roll call, it started to snow. Snow always had a cleansing effect but there was nothing clean about this place or the people in it. The doctors returned much sooner than I would have expected. They walked the ranks and selected around thirty people. My body tensed up as they walked by me. As they passed, I was infuriated knowing they were going to use these men as lab rats.

I was picked as a replacement to haul coal in wheelbarrows. It was better than hauling manure. My strength had returned, and I felt I could keep pace with the screaming demands to work faster. One thing I noticed was the guards were running out of tasks for prisoners. There were too many of us. The answer to the problem was to have workers engage in meaningless work, like moving a rock pile, only to move it again the next day. It was also a license for increased abuse. No matter what the work, it was never performed fast enough. More prisoners were being killed and more bodies were hauled to the crematory.

That evening in the barrack, just after the door was locked, Otto motioned for me to come over to his bunk. In a soft whisper, he said, "She is alive."

I grabbed his shoulder and blurted, "Camille is alive?"

"Yes, she works in the factory."

"Is he sure it's Camille?" I asked.

"Short, French girl named Camille?"

We both took a seat on the floor. I slapped his knee and said, "That is great news. Is she okay?"

"Are any of us okay?" he responded.

I asked, "Does she look healthy?"

"I'm sure she looks like the rest of us. So, John Joseph, you must keep living."

That night, as I laid with four other men pressing against me and the sound of coughing running through the barrack, I felt a sense of optimism for the first time since arriving at Dachau.

The days and months just ran together; I guessed it was toward the end of February. The days and nights were still cold and there was no sign of spring. More and more prisoners rolled in. Otto pointed out the men that had typhus, they ran high temperatures and were unable to get off their bunks. It wouldn't take long until someone would carry them roll call, where they would be shot and piled on a cart. It was an assembly line of death.

I overheard a guard say something about March while I was hauling coal. I had been in hell for almost seven months. So far, I was a survivor but so many things worked against the chances of leaving here alive. To endure, I needed to block out the negativity and just get through each day and think of my future with Camille.

I thought about her all the time; I could see her face when I closed my eyes, especially her smile. I remembered the first time she told me she loved me and how I asked her to repeat it. I worried about her constantly. She was strong and spirited, but nothing could stop disease or the random luck of being singled out.

The snow turned to mud, making walking difficult in certain areas of the camp. At roll call that evening, the Bulldog took delight in hitting prisoners and then pushing their faces in the mud so they couldn't breathe. As we stood for three hours, two guards who were from a different part of the camp approached the Bulldog with a prisoner marching in front of them. The prisoner was tall and skinny, and looked like a skeleton. He stood there with his head bowed toward the ground. The two guards talked with the Bulldog while the prisoner stood there. Suddenly the two guards threw the prisoner to the ground and stripped him of his clothes. They pushed him toward the hanging platform. When they reached the platform, they put him on the ground. I couldn't see what was happening but I could see the prisoner resisting as they were doing something with a rope. The next thing I knew, I was watching a man dangling by a rope that was tied to his testicles. His head was pointed toward the ground and the entire weight of his body was held by a rope that was attached to his testicles. At first he tried to move, but the pain was too great. One of the guards ran to get other guards so they could see their handiwork. They pointed and laughed. I closed my eyes and again prayed, "God, do not forsake me, but deliver me from this hell."

CHAPTER TWENTY SEVEN

Dachau, Spring, 1945

The change of weather and comments made by the guards meant we had made it to spring. The transports continued arriving daily with prisoners from other camps. Many were dead on arrival. The barrack was beyond crowded. I was sure we had at least 1,500 living in the barrack. Many of the new arrivals were too sick to work. Diseases were spreading so quickly that the daily death toll had to be over 200. The crematory was working nonstop with a constant smell of burnt flesh and ashes filling the air.

Otto had told me that the stock pile of food was diminishing at a rapid pace, and it wasn't being replenished. There were times when we had nothing to eat, but no one seemed concerned about this. Each day people collapsed and died in front of me, primarily of starvation. I watched a man pick up sawdust and eat it. When no one was looking, I picked up a handful and put it in my mouth.

What made matters worse was the increased brutality of the guards. Everyone seemed on edge. I lived in a constant state of tension and fear.

I thought it couldn't get any worse, but it did. The next three weeks were more chaotic. The structure of routine was breaking down. The SS guards, sensing the chaos, took out every bit of frustration on any prisoner who happened to be standing near. I tried to stay "in the middle," I tried to be invisible.

During morning roll call, three carts full of dead bodies rolled in front of us. One cart was being pushed by a prisoner whose strength gave way. He kept digging his feet in but couldn't get enough traction to move the cart. Bulldog walked over and struck him with his club until the man was unconscious. He then looked for a replacement and his eyes locked on me. I stared straight ahead, hoping he would look elsewhere. Instead, he walked over and grabbed me by the shirt and told me to push it.

I was able to move the cart, but quickly became out of breath after twenty yards of pushing. I couldn't stop, so I kept breathing though my mouth in short bursts of air. I sounded like a train coming down the tracks. After a few feet a body fell off. The man had blood all over his shirt and his face was unrecognizable. I was able to lift the body but it took three tries before I could get it to land on top of the pile. As I continued pushing the cart, I remembered Otto saying, "You never want the job of hauling bodies, prisoners who have that job don't last long."

Instead of taking the bodies directly to the crematory, I was told to stack them in an old barrack. I became nauseous when I saw the number of bodies stacked in the barracks. The smell was overpowering, but the visual imagery of the twisted, stacked bodies reaching seven feet high made me turn around and walk outside. The guard started screaming at me to stack the bodies. After removing all the bodies from the cart and stacking them, I was so weak my arms felt limp. I walked to the side of the building and began to vomit until there was nothing left in my stomach. I couldn't stop the lurching sensation in my throat.

I took the empty cart and returned to the other end of the camp. As I passed the barrack, the women were standing in formation. I looked for Camille but it was impossible to pick her out. Everyone, except for height, looked the same. Some of the women's hair had grown out. As I glanced toward them a second time, I saw one of the guards beating a prisoner. The woman fell to her knees as she was struck again and again. Since the woman was not very tall, I felt my heart starting to race. I looked away and kept pushing the cart.

The next morning at roll call, I wasn't sure if I had the permanent duty of hauling bodies. This was part of the confusion that seemed to be taking place. As we stood in formation, most of us noticed that some SS officers were getting in cars. Some of the valuables that had been taken from prisoners when they arrived at Dachau were being loaded on a truck. I glanced to my left at Otto, he gave me a nod. Both of us knew this was a good sign. I felt a sense of hope and some excitement. This, however, was quickly replaced by worry when I saw guards marching a group of prisoners to be hanged.

The Bulldog yelled at the Kapos, who were counting the number of prisoners in formation. Because of the number of dead bodies that had been dragged to formation, it almost seemed like we had more people lying on the ground than standing. I was distraught when the work groups were formed and I was back pushing the death cart.

Later that same day, after soup had been poured into my bowl, Otto motioned for me to join him. Because of the large number of prisoners and fewer guards present, Otto appeared comfortable talking with me in a low whisper. As I drank the soup, he said, "We are going to meet next to the latrine."

"What are you talking about?" I asked.

He whispered, "I've asked some of the prisoners who are leaders to meet."

"Why?"

"I'll explain then."

I slowly walked away. At the appropriate time, I headed toward the latrine. Otto and six other men were standing next to the building. As I walked toward them, I kept glancing to my left and right to see if anyone was watching. When I stood next to Otto, he said, "I haven't got long, I asked you to meet because I think you are leaders who can be trusted. I believe Americans are getting close. We can see people leaving and the new prisoners have said that's why they were moved to Dachau. We've got to be smart to ensure our survival."

One of the prisoners standing with us whispered. "What do you mean ensure our survival?"

Otto answered, "It's been rumored they have orders to kill all prisoners before they leave."

Another prisoner added, "What can we do?"

Otto replied. "There will be times when we can disrupt and even resist. We need to buy time. We will meet here at this time every day unless something comes up. Tell no one else."

Later that evening in the barrack, I asked Otto, "Do you really think the Americans are coming?"

"Yes, I've seen the guards packing things up. The Americans have to be close. Soon we should hear planes and artillery."

I was energized. Liberation had been a dream, but I never wanted to get my hopes up. To be this close gave me a sense of optimism I didn't think existed. Otto touched my arm and whispered, "They will try to kill us."

I murmured, "We can't be so close and not make it."

"We have to be smart and work together."

CHAPTER TWENTY EIGHT

A few days later, we heard planes and then we saw them - American planes flying directly overhead. There was excitement throughout the camp at the sight of the planes. The rumors started, which diminished the excitement. Everyone I spoke with said the same thing. "They are going to kill us."

Nobody slept, the uncertainty of our future caused most of us to feel frustrated and depressed. My thoughts also turned to Camille. Was she alive and if so, would we come so close only to never be reunited?

That evening I heard bombs exploding; I heard the sound of the railroad being strafed by the low flying planes. We were ordered out of the barrack and into the open area used for roll call. Only the Jews were ordered to go to the open area. We became shields for the camp. Although I stood as a potential target, I didn't care. I was happy to see the planes. I saw the worried look on the faces of guards, and experienced a sense of joy in seeing them afraid.

The next morning at roll call, there were fewer Germans. I did not see one SS officer. As we stood there, trucks full of supplies were pulling out. Next, the people from the hospital started to leave. We continued to watch as the trucks pulled away. The prisoners kept turning and looking at each other. Everyone was in fear of what would happen next. We stood and waited. An announcement came over the loudspeaker that there was going to be a total evacuation of the camp.

Nothing happened after the announcement, the guards were confused, but the day went on. Although we had nothing for breakfast, there was soup served at lunch. As we held our bowls of soup, the men who made up the underground camp committee found each other. Otto, in a low whisper said, "The evacuation will be a death march. We have to do everything we can to delay and resist. You do not want to go on the march."

Another member of the committee said, "There are not many guards left. They will have trouble rounding us up and keeping us together."

Otto added, "That's right; I think the guards are afraid the Americans will show up at any time. Tell everyone to resist when they can."

In the evening, we stood at roll call for hours. Finally an announcement came to return to the barrack and bring any possessions back to formation. The order implied we were going to be leaving. The only real possessions people had were bowls and hats. As we entered the barrack, prisoners began to talk and mumble. Otto told the men in the barrack to remain where they were as long as possible. Everyone was squeezed in the barrack so tight it was difficult to stand.

It was now dark and the lights in the camp had been turned on. The loudspeaker kept repeating the order to return to formation. Next, we heard gunshots and guards screaming. As the prisoners slowly exited the barrack, the guards made an example out of some of the prisoners by shooting them in the head.

While waiting and not sure what would happen next, the gates of the camp were opened. Over 100 barefoot women from Auschwitz walked through the gate. The women had walked a great distance and appeared to be close to death. Their arrival seemed to cause even more confusion for the guards. Another order came over the speaker, telling prisoners to return to the barrack. I felt like the delay and the confusion of the women arriving had bought us another day.

The next morning, the guards attempted to round up prisoners for a march. It was not going well; there was confusion because prisoners were not following directions.

I stayed close to Otto as the guards continued to scream and make threats. The only thought that stayed in my mind was, "I am so close."

Although there was an attempt at a meager breakfast, it was obvious there was no food to be served. It was midday and the guards again were trying to get prisoners rounded up. Since the number of guards was less than in the past, it was more difficult for them to keep order.

The guards were again distracted when a transport from Buchenwald arrived. The men who were marched into the camp were half-naked, walking skeletons. The number and sight of them caused confusion and further delays.

The guards were becoming frustrated and angry. The Bulldog took out his pistol and shot two prisoners. Another guard fired an automatic rifle into the air. With pushing, shoving, and intimidation, the guards began to move around 7,000 prisoners toward the gate entrance. The Bulldog dropped back to keep forcing prisoners in line. He apparently was not going with the guards who were in charge of the march.

As we turned near a barrack, I slipped out of line and went behind the barrack. I peeked around the corner of the building and watched as Otto was moving between the prisoners who were being marched. He was attempting to get to the far right side so he could also slip away. One of the guards spotted him and grabbed him, he then pulled out his pistol and held it to Otto's head. Otto quickly stepped back in with the large number of prisoners who were approaching the gate. I thought he might have one additional chance to slip out. I saw a few other prisoners escape the march, but Otto was not one of them. He was now with the death march. As I watched them walking with guards on all sides, I could only pray that Otto would find a way to escape. He had survived five years of hell only to be this close to being free. I grieved for him as I saw the column of prisoners disappear out of sight. I knew in my heart I would not be alive if it were not for Otto.

After the prisoners left, there were even fewer guards to control the still large number of prisoners. In addition, the sound of artillery fire in close proximity meant the Americans were getting closer. Excitement and fear were emotions that kept battling within me. I walked closer to the women's barrack, but I could not see Camille.

Before we were forced into the barrack, the underground committee met near the latrine.

In the absence of Otto, a Czech took the lead and told us that we should spread the word that everyone should remain in quarters and refrain from any guard contact. The word spread quickly, no one slept during the night. We continued to hear artillery and some fire. I found myself looking over to Otto's bunk, wishing he were here.

At day break I saw the Czech and two other members of the underground committee walking toward the commandant's office. Two men wearing Red Cross armbands entered the same building.

A while later, two SS men emerged to remove the SS insignia and decorations from the gate. The prisoners who were watching started running toward the gate, I started running, too. Before we got to the gate, we saw American soldiers standing there. I looked toward the sky and said, "Thank you, God, for not forsaking me and for delivering me from this hell."

.

CHAPTER TWENTY NINE

As soon as I saw the American soldiers appear, I heard gunfire. I was not sure who had fired but in a matter of seconds about forty guards were dead. During the confusion of gunfire, prisoners took matters into their own hands. As additional prisoners came toward the gate and saw the bodies of guards lying on the ground, they could not resist the opportunity to kick the bodies. I was glad to see that Bulldog was among the dead guards. The resentment and hatred I carried for months was released when I too kicked what was left of his face.

As I stepped back and viewed my surrounding, I fell to the ground and began to cry. I had not shed one tear since arriving at Dachau. I had been terrified, and lived in a constant state of fear. Now at this moment, I could let out the pent-up emotion I had successfully bottled for almost nine months. I was not alone in the release of emotion, I saw many prisoners with tears rolling down their faces. As I looked around, I saw prisoners who were so sick that this feeling just might be their last.

Prisoners were beginning to move closer to the gate, which was now opened. When they saw the soldiers from the 42nd and 45th Infantry Division, they walked up and touched them. I saw one prisoner fall to his knees and kiss the boots of a soldier. The soldiers appeared stunned at what they saw; they moved slowly with eyes wide open. I heard one soldier yell for men to join him at the train cars. In the train cars, there were hundreds of dead bodies, most of which looked like skeletons. As the soldiers continued to examine the camp, I turned and ran toward the women's barrack. The barrack was at the other end of the camp. My run quickly became more like a shuffle as I became weak from expending energy. I saw women standing in front of the barrack. Like everyone else, they seemed joyous but confused as to what would happen next. I walked through the women, looking for Camille. When I didn't see her, I yelled, "Camille." A woman standing a few feet from me pointed toward the barrack. When I entered the barrack, I did not see her. I noticed some women lying in the bunks, so I went from bunk to bunk. The first woman I saw on the bunk was dead, the second was also dead. When I got to the third bunk, I saw Camille. I felt a huge lump in my throat and a pain in my chest. I put my hand on her forehead and found she was burning up with a fever, her eyes were closed. She moaned when I shook her. I had seen this look before, and knew she was seriously ill. I also knew she was alive and time was against her.

I picked Camille up in my arms; I felt like I was picking up a child. She could not have weighed more than seventy pounds. I carried her out of the barrack and walked with her in my arms as fast as I could.

When I reached the gate, a soldier with a red cross on his helmet who I recognized as a medic approached me. He was surprised when I spoke in English, "This is my wife; she needs help. I think she has typhus fever." He took Camille from me and walked toward a large medical tent that was being erected. I followed as he placed her on a cot and began to shout to others for assistance. He turned to me and said,

"You cannot stay here, this will become a quarantined area."

I backed away slowly. With tears falling down my cheeks, I said, "Please don't let her die."

Other sick prisoners were being taken to the tent also, I was in the way. A corporal who was standing close by came to me and asked, "Is she your wife?"

"Yes."

"Tomorrow you may come here and ask for me, I'm Corporal Barton. I will let you know how she is doing. We are a little overwhelmed right now, we just have one doctor. We have some nurses and other medics coming. We have to start with the most ill first, but we will get to everyone."

I said, "Thank you, I will come tomorrow."

The corporal was right; they were overwhelmed with what they found at Dachau. I'm sure troops had discovered the barrack with stacked bodies. They had to deal with the dead, the almost dead, and the sick and confused.

Soldiers quickly began addressing the needs of prisoners, particularly regarding food and sanitation. There was also the problem with identification and deportation of people back to their various countries. Many of the people at the camp had nothing to return to.

The loudspeaker was used to share information and to give commands. The people in the camp were not pleased with the idea of being told to return to their quarters. Everyone, however, understood the tremendous task that was in store for the American soldiers. As I walked toward my barrack, I overheard soldiers talking about the bodies that had been found along the road leading out of Dachau, I immediately thought of Otto. He was on the march that went down the road.

By evening, we had a meal prepared for us. It was again soup but this time there was actually something in it. I knew that certain foods would be introduced slowly; we were not used to a lot of solid food. We did have some decent bread, and for the first time in months, I did not have to use the red bowl that was handed to me the day I arrived at Dachau. This was the same bowl I occasionally had to urinate in. We had no one yelling at us or hitting us. I could see a steady stream of sick prisoners being carried on stretchers. They were loaded into ambulances and transported to the medical treatment area. I was blessed to have found Camille when I did. She was one of the first to receive any type of treatment. I could only imagine how the nonstop flow of sick people entering the medical tent was impacting the medical personnel.

Although I wanted to sleep, I knew that I couldn't. I did nothing but think and worry about Camille. I had thought for months that our chances of survival were not good. Now we were close. I didn't want to think about it, but the more I tried to push it out of my mind, the more I contemplated what I would do if Camille did not live. After tossing and turning, trying to avoid the idea, I reached the conclusion that I would turn myself in to the commanding officer. I did not know what would happen after that. It was hard to imagine I would be considered a deserter, after being in hell for ten months.

The next morning, after having bread and warm coffee, I made my way toward the medical tent. I was stopped and questioned twice. I was allowed to continue and I had no trouble locating Corporal Barton. I found him at the front of the tent behind a makeshift desk. His job was to log people in and to take down information. At first, he did not recognize me; I reminded him of our conversation. He told me to have a seat on the ground while he went to see what he could find out.

After about fifteen minutes, he returned. I immediately stood. "I talked with a nurse about your wife. She told me she had responded well to the medication and that her temperature was down. The signs were promising, but it is still too early to say if she is out of the woods."

I asked, "When can I see her?"

He placed his clipboard on the small temporary desk and said, "That's a problem, you can't see her until you're checked out."

"When can I get checked out?" I asked.

"We're working on everybody as quickly as we can," the Corporal responded.

He could see the disappointment on my face. He looked at his clipboard and said, "Just have a seat and I will do what I can."

After sitting for about two hours I asked, "What day is it?"

"It's April 30," he replied.

I had lost track of time, but knew that it must be spring. The weather was pleasant, which made waiting tolerable. The warm sun felt good as it struck my face. I recalled the days when people were left to freeze to death.

Corporal Barton was working nonstop, ensuring the non-ambulatory were being processed as quickly as possible. He looked down again at his clipboard and said, "I need some information." He took my name and where I lived. When he asked for a birth date, I calculated the approximate age of Joseph and gave him a date and year.

I was then taken to a large tent where men were seated in rows and told to wait. Minutes later, a private escorted me to the receiving area. I saw other former prisoners being carried in on stretchers. Once my paperwork was examined, I went from one station to the next. My filthy clothes were removed and taken to be burned. I was scrubbed with soap and water and shaved, including my scalp. The best part was when I was given clean U.S. Army pajamas, I had almost forgotten what something clean smelled like. I was dusted with some type of powder and then sent for a chest X-ray. Finally, I was placed in a ward and given a clean bed to sleep in.

Sleep finally came, I wasn't visited by nightmares nor did I wake up to the sounds of screaming. When I awoke, I sought out one of the nurses and told her about my wife. She told me she would do what she could. After breakfast, she returned and said, "You can see your wife." I was elated. I followed her out of the mess area and she said, "You sound like an American."

"I lived in America for a while."

She asked, "Where did you live?"

"Allentown, Pennsylvania."

She added, "I'm from Philadelphia."

Camille had been moved to a different area, which could be a good sign. I entered a tent with long rows of beds and spotted her immediately. She looked beautiful.

I thanked the nurse and walked over to the hospital bed. Camille had her eyes closed. She looked more like a child than an adult. Her scalp had been shaved, and she looked pale. Her left arm was hooked to an IV, she had sores on both arms. The covers were pulled up, and she looked warm and peaceful.

I bent over and whispered her name. When she didn't respond, I said it louder. She opened her eyes and was confused at first, but then I saw her smile. When I saw the smile, I lost it; I began to cry. She reached her hand out and I took it in mine. When I regained my composure, I whispered in French, "Je t'aime."

In a whisper, barely audible, she responded, "Je t'aime." I had waited so long to say those words to her again, I never thought I would get the chance. I continued holding her hand and looking at her. Her eyes would occasionally start to close and then suddenly pop wide open again. She started to say something, but I couldn't understand what she was saying. I leaned closer and she asked, "Am I going to live?"

"Never a doubt. It will take a little time for you to get stronger, but you'll be as good as new."

She smiled as her eyes closed. I continued to hold her hand and look at her while she rested. A nurse came by to check on her, she listened to her heart and checked her temperature. The nurse said she needed rest. I slowly dropped her hand by her side. When I did, she whispered, "Kiss me." I gave her a kiss on her lips. When I stood up, she smiled and closed her eyes.

As I started to leave, I caught up with the nurse just before she began to check another patient. "Is she going to be OK?"

The nurse seemed overwhelmed, but paused and said, "She is improving, but we are also battling malnourishment. I will feel a lot better when she begins to eat."

"Can I see her every day?" I asked.

"You can see her until you leave," the nurse said.

Defiantly, I shouted, "I'm not leaving her! I will never leave her again!"

The nurse didn't answer, I returned to my ward. After seeing Camille, I had renewed hope. I was, however, keenly aware that hope can be smashed within a matter of seconds.

The next two weeks I followed a routine of sleeping, eating, and visiting with Camille. The camp exploded with excitement when the news spread that Germany had surrendered. I felt stronger every day. I especially enjoyed eating food that wasn't floating in hot water. Camille had turned the corner, too. She was improving each day, she was eating solid food, and color was returning to her face. She was still weak and could only get out of bed to visit the restroom or to take a short walk on the ward. When we talked about Joshua, her spirits improved even more.

Both Army and the Red Cross were in the process of relocating patients. When someone came to talk with me, I reiterated that I was not leaving without my wife.

One day, I had a chance to talk with the doctor who was in charge. First, he assured me that I could stay until my wife could leave, he then asked several questions about life in the camp. Since I spoke English, he found it easy to ask follow up questions without turning to an interpreter. During our conversation, he shared that his staff had treated at least 20,000 sick patients. He also told me that perhaps as many as 30,000 people had died at Dachau. I asked him about the prisoners who had been marched out of camp the day before liberation. He said most had been killed.

On May 21, Camille and I were dressed in our new traveling clothes and told to wait for the next truck. We carried only a Red Cross package with toiletry items in it.

Camille was able to make a telephone call to Dr. Benoit. She learned of the good health of Joshua and made arrangements for us to be picked up at the Lille airport. After the call, she had a newfound energy and optimism. Both of us looked remarkably better; we still didn't need a comb or brush, but we had put on weight and our skin wasn't as ghostly pale.

Finally, a truck pulled up and thirty people, most of whom were in their twenties or thirties, loaded into the back. As the truck drove away from Dachau, all of us saw the front gate with its sign "Work will make you free." No one said a word. We had been delivered from hell.

CHAPTER THIRTY
Part IV

Lille, France, 1945

The military plane was full of displaced camp survivors. We were all wearing Red Cross clothes. There was very little talking except for an occasional question about the camp where someone was held.

Camille was excited and anxious, Dr. Benoit told her he would bring Joshua to the airport. We had not seen Joshua for ten months. He would now be three and a half. Camille worried that he wouldn't remember her. A nurse gave her a straw hat to wear. Although our hair was starting to grow back, she was concerned that her appearance might scare him. She held the hat in her hand. She would decide whether or not to wear it when the plane landed in Lille.

The plane would be making three stops in France. Lille was the first stop.

As the plane taxied on the runway, Camille placed the hat on her head. Although she had put on some weight, she still looked thin. The hat gave her an almost childish appearance. I held her hand and assured her that everything would be all right.

When it was our turn to exit the plane, both of us paused and looked at people who were waiting for arrivals from the plane. It was easy to spot Dr. Benoit; he was tall, and his curly hair made him stand out from the rest of the crowd. Next to him was his wife and standing in front of them was a little boy dressed with a shirt and tie.

When we got close, Camille bent down to hug Joshua. At first, he held onto the pants leg of Dr. Benoit. Camille said, "Joshua, it's Mama." He then slowly moved toward her. She took him in her arms with tears rolling down her cheeks. As she continued to hold him, the hat seemed to get in her way so she removed it. At first, Joshua looked startled but Camille continued to hold him and whisper softly in his ear. Then to my surprise Joshua said, "Papa." He held his arms, up gesturing for me to take him. I picked him up, and he gave me a big hug and held me tightly. Tears streamed from my eyes, they were a combination of relief and joy.

We all began hugging each other and within a matter of minutes, we were crying and kissing one another. Dr. Benoit said we could talk later. We walked to the car, leaving behind the horrid pain of the last months.

The city had seen some destruction. It was wonderful not to see soldiers, trucks, and Nazi flags. I wasn't sure what my future was going to be, but at least I now had one.

At Dr. Benoit's home, his wife insisted that we sit and rest while she prepared something for us to eat. Camille went with Joshua to see his toys, I sat in one of the comfortable chairs with an ottoman. Dr. Benoit brought me a glass of wine. I sipped the wine, and cherished being in a comfortable chair, drinking French wine.

When Camille returned, Dr. Benoit handed her a glass of wine; we talked and talked. The conversation centered on the things Joshua was able to do. After Dr. Benoit poured more wine, I asked, "When did you know something was wrong?"

"Joshua had some difficult days when I brought him home, he needed hospitalization. Since he was my patient, no one said a thing. He had pneumonia and later complications with asthma. When I got him home, he recovered quickly. The Germans had withdrawn from Lille, and I thought it was a good time to return him to you at the cabin. I drove up the hill as far as possible and walked the rest of the way with Joshua. When I entered the cabin, I knew immediately something was wrong. Everything was left in place, including dishes on the table and food on the counter. I looked everywhere; I walked toward the lake and woods, the only thing I found was a chicken wandering around. Back at the cabin, I noticed a bloodstain on the floor close to the door. I drove back toward town and stopped at the general store to inquire about you. When I asked the owner if he had seen you, he didn't answer me, so I asked him a second time. He then told me that the Jews had been captured, I pressed him for answers. That's when I realized you had been sent to a camp. I tried to get information from the French authorities, but nobody knew anything. It was a prayer answered when I got your call."

Anger bubbled up inside me at the mention of the store owner. He had changed our lives forever, and for what? In another two weeks, it wouldn't have made any difference. The Germans would have been gone.

Dr. Benoit turned toward Camille and asked, "What was the camp like?" She kept shaking her head no.

I then added, "We can talk later, it was very painful."

Dr. Benoit understood and suggested that we eat. When we went to the table, Joshua insisted he sit next to his mama.

We had not had a home-cooked meal in almost a year. Mrs. Benoit kept serving us additional helpings. She told us she was going to put some meat on our bones. We were, however, not used to eating that much and kept insisting that we were full. Mrs. Benoit brought us coffee, and Joshua left the table to play with his toys in the living room.

Dr. Benoit said, "I want you to know that you can stay with us as long as you want. You need to get your health back. I want you to rest and eat good meals. You also need to have time with Joshua. Don't worry about getting work and paying for anything, that will come later. I know you will want a place of your own and that you will need to have jobs. I can help with that. I'm your doctor and that's what I'm telling you to do."

I had never said anything about being married to Camille. He had already assumed that we would be staying together. I guess, after what we had been through, he assumed we had an inseparable bond.

After an awkward pause, Camille said, "Thank you, Dr. Benoit. I have always known that I could call upon you at any time. I can never repay you for all you have done."

He replied, "It's because I want to do it, you are like our second daughter. I don't want you to worry about your future. Let's let it unfold a little at a time." Both of us thanked him. We stood and hugged.

Camille took great joy in giving Joshua a bath and getting him ready for bed. Mrs. Benoit moved a twin bed into our bedroom for Joshua. After he was asleep, Camille told us she was tired and that she was going to bed.

After Mrs. Benoit went to bed, Dr. Benoit opened another bottle of wine. We went into the family room and sat in the big comfortable chairs. I took my first sip of wine and said, "Dr. Benoit, I want you to know I married Camille."

Looking startled he asked, "How is that possible?"

"Just before we were sent to Dachau, a Catholic priest married us."

"I see. Are you Catholic?"

"No," I said.

Dr. Benoit propped his feet on the coffee table as he leaned back in his chair. "So a Catholic priest married a Protestant and a Jewish girl?"

"Yes," I answered.

"Well, I'll drink to that." He took his wine glass and held it up, I did the same. He then followed up by saying, "I think God has brought you two together. That is the only plausible explanation I can think of. I'm happy for both of you."

I took another sip of wine and added, "I can't imagine living without her."

As we continued to sip wine, Dr. Benoit appeared to be in deep thought. He set his glass down. Leaning forward, he looked directly at me and said, "I've got an idea; I think you need to become Joseph Bernhardt. Now that you're back in France, you have an identity problem. Nobody really knows about Joseph's death, so you can become Joseph. That will make you about seven years older. Hell, you even look like him! Nobody around here really knew him. His parents moved to Paris. The problem would be his parents."

I replied, "I don't think that is a problem, his father is dead. He died in Dachau. I'm almost certain his mother died in Auschwitz."

"I'm sorry to hear that. Does Camille know?"

I answered, "Not yet, I'm waiting for the right time to tell her."

"If you take his identity, I can get the documentation you need. A friend who is a lawyer owes me a favor. We could get his transcript from college. I think Joseph went for one year."

"Do you really think it will work?"

He responded, "Why not? Your French is good enough, but you need to be able to read and write in French, also. My wife can tutor you. Also, the farm in Amiens is under Joseph's name. Sell it and use the money to get a place here. I'm positive Joseph had a mortgage, but you would get some money."

Feeling relief I said, "It just might work. When we got married, the priest thought my name was Joseph. But Camille will need to be comfortable with this."

As Dr. Benoit poured some more wine he commented, "Talk with her."

For the next two hours, I shared my experiences at Dachau. Dr. Benoit listened with great interest, occasionally shaking his head. It helped me to talk about it, this was my way of healing. When there was a pause in the conversation, he asked, "What about Camille?"

I answered, "Her experiences were similar but she chooses not to talk about them. I think this is her way of coping. For Camille, the past is the past. Her focus is on the future."

CHAPTER THIRTY ONE

The next two weeks involved resting, eating, and shopping for clothes. Mrs. Benoit insisted on taking us shopping. I reminded her that we would gain our weight back and these clothes wouldn't fit but she was undeterred. We were going to have a new wardrobe.

As we shopped, I could see heads turn. Even though we had put on weight, we were both thin and had buzz haircuts. Camille was wearing makeup and her new slimmer fitting clothes helped her self-image. At the insistence of Mrs. Benoit, we purchased clothes that were big on us. She reminded us more than once that she was going to put some meat on our bones.

The generosity of the Benoit family was unbelievable, they wanted to help us get our feet on the ground. In a few weeks, their daughter and her husband were coming to visit and Camille looked forward to seeing them, but was worried that we might be too cramped with so many in the house. I was getting stronger every day. We made trips to the park with Joshua which was the highlight of our day. We would sit on the bench as he played with other children. I realized as I watched him play that I would never take for granted these opportunities to be together. There were many days at Dachau when I thought I would never see children laughing and playing again.

Dr. Benoit, on two occasions, slipped me some money and encouraged me to get out of the house. I was reluctant to spend his money. I was anxious to move forward and look for work. On many days I would sit for hours as Mrs. Benoit helped me with reading and writing French.

One day I asked Camille if she would like to get coffee at the nearby café. Mrs. Benoit was more than happy to watch Joshua. After the confinement we had felt for so long, we enjoyed the idea of having leisure time together.

It was a beautiful summer day, and we sat at one of the outdoor tables. Camille wore a stylish hat that made her look very feminine. She had more color in her face and her wonderful smile was returning. The waiter brought us coffee and pastry. It was so rich I didn't finish mine. When Camille noticed she reached over to get mine. "It certainly wouldn't take much time to put on weight with this diet," she said.

When the waiter came back, we both asked for a second cup of coffee. When he returned with the small espresso cups, I looked at Camille and said, "I want to talk with you about something."

Excitedly she said, "Let me go first."

"Okay, you go first."

"We have gone through so much together. I never realized that first day when I saw you standing in front of the farmhouse wearing Joseph's clothes that we would be together today."

"We are married."

"Just let me finish," she said. "If you decide to leave and return to America, I will understand. I don't want you to feel any obligation."

I leaned across the table and replied boldly, "I love you and you are my wife."

She placed her hand on mine. Looking directly into my eyes she asked, "What about your life in America, your family, or a girlfriend you left behind?"

"Camille, you are my life; I have left my life in America behind. You told me not to look back. I want to look forward, but I can only look forward if it is with you."

She leaned over the table and kissed me. "I prayed you felt this way, I just needed to hear it. You have gone through hell for me. I never thought I could love someone the way I love you."

We didn't say anything for a while. Camille looked over at me and asked, "What did you want to talk about?"

It took a minute to gather my thoughts. "The first night after Dr. Benoit picked us up at the airport, we stayed up and talked for hours. He told me that I would have difficulty establishing an identity in Lille. He told me the easiest and best thing I could do would be to become Joseph. He knows that only three people know of Joseph's death - you, me, and William. He told me he had a lawyer friend who could establish a new identity. I would have papers and everything I needed to start a life."

"What about Joseph's parents and family?" she asked.

"Joseph's father died at Dachau," I answered. "I'm sure his wife also died; she was at Auschwitz. Didn't you say that his family originally came from Germany?"

"Yes."

I continued, "Then there is a good chance they didn't make it. Dr. Benoit also thought it would be possible to sell the farm in Amiens. He said the farm was under Joseph's name, I would need to go with the lawyer to make the sale. The money could be used to get us started. I told him you needed to be okay with me becoming Joseph Bernhardt."

Camille looked thoughtful. She shrugged her shoulders and said, "Joshua thinks you are his father."

"I know."

Camille took her right hand and tapped the table. "Then it is done," she said. "Some people will know, but they can be trusted."

"Then I am Joseph Bernhardt," I replied with conviction.

"You will always be John, to me, the American who saved me. When would you go to Amiens?"

"As soon as Dr. Benoit and the lawyer can set it up. They didn't think we would have any trouble finding a buyer. First, the lawyer would need to get the paperwork done. Would you like to go?"

"Do I have to be there?" she asked.

"I don't think so," I responded.

Relief came over her face and she replied, "Then I don't want to go."

We continued to sip coffee and watch as people walked in front of us. Camille put her hand on mine and said, "It's very hard for me to look back. I don't want to talk about the past, especially Dachau. It is the only way I can retain my sanity. Do you understand?"

"Yes, we'll leave the past in the past."

She squeezed my hand and said, "Thank you! I want to bring Joshua up in the Jewish faith. Now, more than ever, this is important to me."

Smiling, I replied, "That is as it should be. What do I need to do?"

"You need to familiarize yourself with our traditions and practices. I don't expect you to attend Temple; Joshua will just think you don't practice your faith much. You can also attend church if you like."

I added, "I'll cross that bridge when I get to it."

She continued, "I'm also thinking about going to the bakery my parents used to own. I know everything there is to know about baking and running the shop. Maybe they are looking for help?"

I brushed my hand over my head as if I had hair and said, "Maybe they need a good-looking Frenchman who has a slight accent."

"The good-looking is certainly true. Your accent is getting better, I'm amazed at how well you have done."

"Not well enough," I added.

"I'll help you. Maybe you could teach me English."

Our café visit was perfect, both of us needed to get things on the table for discussion. At first, I was hurt that she would even think I wanted to leave, but I then realized she was right. We needed to reevaluate where we were now and where we wanted to go. It was true that I sometimes thought about the child I left in America; I wondered what the child looked like, was it a boy or girl? What Diane had told our child about me?

Later that night when people were going to bed, I started to pick Joshua up from the couch. He had fallen asleep and I was going to take him to bed. Camille lowered my arm and said, "Leave him on the couch, we could use some privacy tonight."

CHAPTER THIRTY TWO

Over the next month, I found it difficult to be patient. I wanted so much to start a new life with Camille in a place of our own. However, I needed an identity which couldn't be rushed. I read the newspaper each day to hone my reading skills. I also followed the war in the Pacific with great interest. My brother was there and each time I read about the terrible loss of life, I wondered if my brother was still alive. One morning I read the account of the atomic bomb being dropped on Hiroshima. Shortly after that, the paper was full of articles and pictures of the unconditional surrender of Japan. The war was officially over. I became more like Camille, I would rather not think about it.

One afternoon, Camille came home excited about her visit with the owners of the bakery that her parents once owned. She wanted to talk and suggested we return to the small café down the street for coffee. Mrs. Benoit said she would watch Joshua.

Camille was so excited she had trouble containing her enthusiasm. After our coffee was served, she placed both hands on the small café table, and said, "Guess what?"

"What?" I asked, enjoying the excitement in her face.

Beaming, she replied, "We have jobs."

"What kind of jobs?" I asked.

"Let me start at the beginning." I loved watching her excitement. Her hair had grown out so much that she looked like a roaring twenties flapper. With her contagious smile, now combined with her excitement and zest for life, I was truly lucky to be married to this incredible woman.

She continued, "I wanted to go by the bakery to see if they might need some help. Boy, do they need help! Business has been terrible; the shop no longer has the reputation it enjoyed when my parents owned it. Everything has gone downhill. The owners remembered me and wondered what had happened after my parents died. I gave them the short version and then we began to talk. The problems started when they couldn't keep a baker longer than a month. Benard Collin, that's the owner's name, said there were many times when the baker didn't show up. They never had the right inventory, so they were constantly running out of things. He and his wife are getting older and they really don't have the energy to do everything the shop needs. I told them I knew everything about baking, and I didn't need recipes. They were in my head. Guess what they said?"

"They want to hire you," I presume.

"Even better than that, they want to hire both of us."

Shrugging my shoulders, I said, "What would I do?"

"You'll be my assistant, I am going to teach you to be a baker. Actually, I'm going to teach you to be a world class French baker. Once you get the hang of it, you'll become chief baker. I plan to be home with Joshua. If Mrs. Benoit will watch him part of the time, I can also help. Mr. Collin suggested that if it works out, you would become the manager. If sales go up, he would be willing to share the profit. Isn't that great?"

"Wow! Me, a baker. Could I really learn to be a baker?"

She laughed and added, "If you can milk a cow, you can be a baker."

"Then I'll be a world class one. Do I get one of those chef hats?"

"If you earn it," she replied with satisfaction.

Again, I received a passionate kiss in a café. I was becoming more comfortable with this, as it was not unusual to see couples embracing and kissing in public.

What great news! I had other marketable skills other than making mortar and hauling block. I was excited about this adventure. In the back of Camille's mind, she was hoping that one day we could own the bakery, the same bakery her parents had started and developed into a successful business. The Benoits shared in our excitement. Dr. Benoit celebrated by opening one of his prize bottles of wine.

The work was harder than I had expected, I had to learn to use a different measuring system. We both arose early each morning and took the long walk to the bakery. Mrs. Benoit watched Joshua until noon when Camille returned. I liked working the counter and interacting with customers. My French had improved to the point I was very comfortable talking. My unusual accent was disappearing. Mr. Collin was impressed the day I spoke to a customer in English.

The big hit at the bakery was the chocolate-filled pastry; Camille had perfected the recipe. On occasion, we would be sold out of them by nine o'clock in the morning. Although my baking skills were improving, I was not totally comfortable baking by myself. Camille, being a good teacher, encouraged me to do more and more on my own.

As fall came and the weather was beginning to get cooler, our sales began to increase. Mr. Collin agreed to my suggestion to serve coffee and to add a few tables in the front of the bakery.

Finally, the day I had been waiting for arrived. Dr. Benoit had received paperwork that included my birth certificate and school records, including the college transcript. I could now prove I was Joseph Bernhardt. Now, I could sell the farm in Amiens.

Dr. Benoit had found a buyer. He said it would be quicker and easier if I accompanied him and the lawyer to sign the necessary paperwork. His lawyer would read over everything in advance so that we would only need to meet and sign the bill of sale and a few other papers. I was worried about putting his lawyer in such an awkward position, but Dr. Benoit said not to worry. I was excited. Although we did not have a lot of money, we could now find a home of our own.

The following week, Dr. Benoit picked up the lawyer and the three of us were on our way to Amiens. His lawyer was a young man just out of school and the son of an old friend. I hoped he was not jeopardizing his career.

It did not take long for us to reach Amiens. The traffic was light and the weather was good. As we drove into town, it brought back many memories, like trading and selling goods and being harassed by the German soldiers. There was the nearby field where I parachuted down, it was in that field where my life began to change. I also thought of the farmhouse. I remembered, most of all, how terrified I was after I shot the SS officer.

Before we went to the law office, we stopped for lunch. The young lawyer went over the paperwork, reading parts of it to me. The price was better than I had expected. Although there were many things that would need to be paid off, I could afford a down payment on a house. The lawyer was surprised the buyer did not try to drive a harder bargain.

At the office building, we were shown to a conference room adjacent to the attorney's office. After a few minutes, a man dressed in a suit walked through the door. Behind him was William Williams. William was the man originally from Wales who helped me sell and trade goods at the market. More importantly, he was a friend who helped save our lives.

I never dreamed he would be the buyer, he was a small farmer who was barely making a living. Maybe he had saved money and saw this as an investment? Maybe he knew that when he saw the seller was Joseph Bernhardt, this would be another way he could help. Either way, it was another blessing.

William and I acted as if we had just met for the first time. As the lawyers were passing papers back and forth, I glanced at William and he smiled. After ten months in Dachau, my belief in the goodness of people was severely damaged. Looking at William, with the smile on his face, gave me hope that were still a lot of good, compassionate people in the world.

As the lawyers discussed the value of the property, I learned that the house had been burned to the ground. When I heard this, I glanced at William; he was busy signing papers and did not look up.

With the papers signed, we all stood and shook hands. Joseph Bernhardt had just sold his farm to William Williams.

As the lawyers continued to talk, I told them I wanted to share a few things about the farm with the new owner. The two of us walked out of the building and around the corner. William turned toward me and grabbed me in a hug. After an extra pat on my back, he said, "I thought you and Camille were probably dead."

I answered, "We were close to being dead." I told him about Dachau and my new life in Lille.

He motioned for us to sit on a nearby bench and said, "When I heard that Joseph Bernhardt was selling the farm, I knew it had to be you."

"How can you afford to buy the farm?" I asked.

"The wife and I don't spend a lot of money, I've been saving for years. The Nazis didn't help my savings plan, but I had enough to buy it. I don't need the house, just the land."

"What happened to the house?"

He continued, "When the SS found the major dead, they burned the house to the ground and killed the remaining animals. It was good that you turned the cows loose through the broken fence, or they would have killed them too. If everything goes according to plan, I'm going to buy the farm next to yours. The lady is getting old and can't keep up with it. Then I will have the land I need to really become a big time farmer like Andre Bellamy."

"How are the Bellamys?" I asked.

"They're fine. The German soldiers who were looking for you tried to scare them, but they didn't flinch. Spreading that fertilizer in the old barn was smart, the dogs did nothing but sneeze. They couldn't pick up a scent. The following week, everything changed. When the prison was bombed, the Germans spent their time looking for the French fighters. Not long after that, they had to be worried about the Americans. It was a great day when they packed up and moved out."

I looked directly at William and said, "William, would you do something for Camille?"

"Just name it," he said.

I continued, "There is a body buried at the farm that will never have a marker on it. Can you put flowers on it or something?"

"Yes." He laughed and said, "Your French is getting pretty good. In fact, it is better than mine. I've got another surprise for you."

"What kind of surprise?" I wondered.

"Your truck. The Germans left it alone so I took it, It runs great."

"That is great news," I said. "We really need something to drive."

We spent a few minutes catching up on each other's family. He then handed me the keys to the truck, it was parked in front of the office building. When I asked how he would get home, he told me his high-priced lawyer would give him a ride. We embraced again. Both of us promised to keep in touch, knowing that we probably wouldn't see each other again.

I told Dr. Benoit and my lawyer that I would be driving my truck home. When they looked confused, I told them the new owner said he didn't have need of it. I didn't think it was necessary to say anything else. I also told Dr. Benoit I might be a little late getting home because I had a stop I wanted to make.

Although it was out of the way, I wanted to go by Cambrai on my way back to Lille. I knew Father Glaize had survived Dachau, but I wasn't sure if he was still the priest there. I came from a home where my mother could easily pass guilt to me for even simple things, like not cleaning my room. My brother, however, never seemed to be bothered with guilt. For me, lying to a priest was at the top of the guilt scale.

The drive went quickly as I passed some familiar roads. I remembered the road we crossed after leaving the gypsy camp, I wondered if the Gypsies had fared any better after the war.

I entered through the main gate of the beautiful cathedral and walked down the hallway to the church office. As I turned the corner, I saw Father Glaize talking to a worker. Once he saw me, he stopped his conversation and ran toward me. He gave me a hug and said, "Joseph, I have often thought of you. What are you doing here?"

I replied, "I had some business in Amiens and wanted to come by the church on my way back to Lille."

"I'm so glad you did. Come in my office and we'll talk in private."

He asked the lady in the office to bring us coffee. I followed him to his office and took a seat. I thought he looked very good; he had put on the weight he had lost and his hair had grown back. He cleaned his glasses and put them back on. He smiled and said, "I saw you briefly when Dachau was liberated. I think things got pretty confusing. How is Camille?"

"She is doing great, she was very sick when the camp was liberated. I stayed with her until she was well enough to travel."

Before I finished answering he asked, "And how is your son? What was his name?"

I replied, "Joshua. He is also doing well."

"Are you living in Lille?"

"Yes, I'm learning to be a baker."

He patted me on the back and said, "That's wonderful."

The lady from his office brought in a pot of coffee and poured it in our cups. On her way out, she closed the door. Father Glaize said, "These are the things I will never take for granted the rest of my life. Every morning, I take a walk and then sit in my comfortable chair. I have truly learned to appreciate the simple things in life."

I added, "I know exactly what you mean. May I ask you a question?"

"Sure."

"Were there times your faith was challenged?"

He removed his glasses and stared at the table. After a short pause he replied, "Yes, when I saw all the evil around me; it was hard to understand how God could let this happen. I do believe God does not want bad things to happen to His people. This is part of living in a world that has evil in it. I continue to pray for more understanding in these matters."

After a brief pause I said, "I have something I would like to confess."

There was a slight pause and then Father Glaize said, "Go on."

"Do you remember when you married Camille and me?"

Nodding he replied, "Yes, in the shed after you were captured."

I continued, "I know you were surprised that we were not already married. That's because when we came here for help, I led you to believe we were both Jews. That was not true."

I went on to explain everything about myself, including being an American that was dropped behind enemy lines. He listened intently, taking in every word. I told him that I loved Camille, and I wanted her to be my wife that day in the shed. I wasn't sure of our future or even if we would be allowed to live. I told him that I was a protestant from America and Camille was Jewish.

When I was finished, he said to me, "I knew things were not exactly right that day. I did, however, feel that God had brought you together. I do appreciate you telling me everything. Unlike some priests, or rabbis, for that matter, I'm not going to pass judgement on the people God has chosen to bring together. That's how I see it. You also need to know that what you have told me stays in this office."

Relieved I said, "I cannot tell you how much better I feel. I could not live with the fact I had lied to a priest, especially a priest who had done so much to help me."

Father Glaize added, "I will continue to pray for you and Camille. I hope you will come to visit me, it is not a coincidence that our lives continue to cross."

As I drove back to Lille, I thought about everything Father Glaize had said. I wanted to believe that everything that was happening in my life was being directed by an unseen hand.

CHAPTER THIRTY THREE

My father always said if you work your ass off, good things will happen. He was a man with a great work ethic who, despite his drinking, was a good role model when it came to work. Though he drank too much in the evening, he always made it to work the next day.

Camille and I were working hard, and it was beginning to pay off. With the check we received from selling the farm and a signature from Dr. Benoit, we were able to buy a flat that was close to the bakery. We didn't have a lot to put in our new home, but it didn't matter. Camille began to decorate every room with what little we had, including the bathroom. We saved our money, slowly purchasing furniture and other necessities. Camille fell in love with a quilt she had seen in a store and once she purchased the quilt and placed it on our bed, she constantly walked past the room to admire it.

The work was hard because of our early morning hours. I had learned enough about baking to be the early morning baker. At midday, I would walk home to watch Joshua. Camille would then go to the bakery and prepare things for the next day. In the afternoon, I would return to the bakery and work until closing. This routine was followed every day but Saturday. Saturday was the Sabbath. On Saturday, Camille left everything up to me. For the first time, we could purchase clothes and the things we needed to be on our own. Dr. Benoit and his wife would still occasionally watch Joshua. They loved being a part of his life and keeping his room filled with toys.

Father Glaize had said the hardship he had endured made him appreciate the simple things in life, this was also true for Camille and me. In the evening the three of us would snuggle on the couch under a warm blanket. Every morning, despite the early hour, I always took time to prop my feet up on our coffee table to enjoy a cup of coffee before heading to work. Otto had said classical music soothed his brain. When I had saved enough money, I bought a record player and two albums of music by Beethoven and Mozart. In the evening, I would pour a glass of wine and play one of the records. I would lean back in the big chair and close my eyes. After a while, Camille would join me. Sometimes Joshua would fall asleep listening to the music. Otto was right about the music, Otto was right about a lot of things and I thought about him often.

The next ten months went quickly. The bakery shop was busy and profits were up. Mr. Collin was true to his word and increased my pay. Orders were backing up in the morning and we hired an additional person. At Camille's insistence, we hired a woman who was a Holocaust survivor who frequented the bakery. Lucille was a great addition and we hoped we could do our small part in helping her heal.

One afternoon in late June, Mr. Collin pulled me aside and told me that Camille and I should take a vacation. He felt like it would do us good to get away. He was confident Lucille could keep things running while we were gone. Although he suggested two weeks, we agreed on a one-week vacation in July.

Camille wasn't sure where we should go. She wanted to relax, but not leave France. Dr. Benoit generously offered his cabin near Charleville-

Mezieres. He had paid a man to grade part of the road to make it easier to reach the cabin.

I was unsure how Camille would feel about returning to the cabin. While we had many wonderful memories of the cabin, we also had a traumatic one. Camille never spoke of that time. When I mentioned it to her at dinner, she smiled and said it was a great idea.

Camille went shopping to purchase three bathing suits. When she got home, we all modeled our new suits. After my comments about her revealing suit, she reminded me that I was the only man who would be looking at her. It was hard to imagine what we looked like a little more than a year ago. Camille's hair was now shoulder length. She didn't have any trouble filling out her new suit. When I made a comment about her hair, she told me that she might not ever cut it again.

The truck was packed with things for the week. We stopped at the store to purchase items for the refrigerator. Things would be a lot easier now that the cabin had electricity.

We left early Monday morning before the traffic became congested. Working in a bakery had its advantages when it came to getting up early. It was fun to see Joshua's excitement about the trip. The morning was cool for a summer day. It felt good to be doing something different.

There was no comparison to our last trip to Charleville-Mezieres. There were no Nazi trucks or soldiers carrying weapons, and I wasn't afraid of being stopped and arrested.

When we passed through town, I saw the garage where we had been held with Father Glaize. Camille noticed the building, but neither of us said anything. As we left town and turned on the road that would lead us to the cabin, we saw the general store. There were no cars parked out front but, it appeared open. I was sure Camille was thinking the same thing.

Since we were on our official summer holiday, Camille and Joshua were wearing shorts. I had on comfortable slacks and a shirt that was opened at the top. We looked the part of people on vacation. The general store had not changed, including the owner. He looked the same.

I wasn't sure if he recognized us. He watched as Camille went down the aisles picking out grocery items. I kept looking at him. When he noticed my stares, he turned and began to move a few items on the shelf in front of him. The more I looked at him the angrier I became. When Camille put the items she had selected on the counter, I stepped next to her and asked, "Do you remember us?"

The owner said, "No."

Angrily I said, "Sure you do, you asshole. We're the family you sold out to the SS."

"I was only doing what the law required," he replied, as he stepped back from the counter.

"That's bullshit. Do you know the hell you put us through? Did you read about the concentration camps? It was worse than that. You signed our death certificates."

He lost all eye contact with us, quickly putting the grocery items in a box and totaling our bill. Camille, being much calmer, said in a soft tone of voice, "My husband has a right to be angry. What he said about Dachau is true. But I know I have a clear conscience about the war. I am French and I stood by my countrymen. That means all countrymen. Those who did not will have to live with that the rest of their lives, especially those who worked with the Nazis to bring harm and death to their countrymen." She took the two cartons of eggs and placed them gently on the top of the box that contained the other grocery items. I looked at the owner. His head was bowed. He would not meet our eyes. Camille had hit him between the eyes with shame. It was a more powerful hit then my choice of curse words. I walked behind Camille as we left the store. Her strength and poise were amazing and made me proud.

Dr. Benoit was right about the road improvement. We didn't have any trouble driving to the front of the cabin. As we unpacked, I could see the excitement in Joshua's face. When we entered, I ignored the blood stain on the floor near the door and immediately went to the kitchen. There was a stove and a refrigerator. We no longer had to use the hand pump, which never worked anyway. I followed Camille to the bathroom which had indoor plumbing. Joshua found his old wooden train and took it with him on the back porch. When we joined him, we heard him say "Chirpy." There were at least five chickens in the backyard pecking on the ground. I looked at Camille and said, "I'll be damned."

"I can't believe a fox has not eaten all of them," she replied.

Camille started to prepare dinner and Joshua kept asking to go swimming. Camille said, "You've got time."

Joshua quickly put on his suit and waited for me. We splashed in the water, and I roughhoused with him. He loved to be tossed high so he could make a big splash. Camille walked down to the water, carrying two glasses of wine. We sat on the wooden deck watching Joshua chase minnows. I took a sip of wine and said, "This is a good memory."

Tears formed in her eyes. "It was really our beginning," she said softly.

"Maybe one day I'll buy this place."

After Joshua fell asleep, we slipped out onto the back porch, listening to the crickets and watching the moon's reflection on the still water. We held hands. Both of us thought, w*hat a difference a year can make.*

The next day was spent with an early morning walk in the woods, followed by a huge breakfast. Joshua and I fished off the dock and caught enough fish for dinner. This time, however, I did not have the pressure of knowing that we would not eat if we didn't catch anything.

In the afternoon, a breeze blew across the lake, and the sun was partially covered by clouds. Camille suggested that we row across the lake to enjoy the sunset. Joshua and I still had on our bathing suits, while Camille was wearing one of her new silk blouses and shorts with a large straw hat and big sunglasses. To me, she looked like a Hollywood movie star. She was carrying a basket containing sandwiches, wine, and two glasses. I rowed to the middle of the lake and stopped. Camille opened the basket and gave a sandwich to Joshua. I opened the bottle of wine and filled our glasses. We continued to sit in the boat, admiring the beauty of the setting sun while Joshua played with the water. Camille poured the next round of wine and moved over closer to me. She took a sip of wine and placed her head on my shoulder.

Sitting quietly, she whispered, "I want us to have a baby and I want to start tonight."

I took my wine glass and touched her glass. "I'm willing to work overtime on this," I said.

The week went by quickly and I was true to my word about the overtime.

When Camille asked Joshua if he wanted a brother or sister, he was excited and was quick to answer, "A brother."

Mr. Collin was right about getting away. We both loved working at the bakery, but it was good for us to have the time together with Joshua.

As we drove back, I started to think about the bakery and what we could do to improve it. I think Camille was thinking about a baby.

CHAPTER THIRTY FOUR

As it turned out, we didn't need a lot of practice when it came to getting pregnant. A few weeks after returning from our lake vacation, we learned Camille was expecting. Camille immediately began to decorate Joshua's room. Joshua would be sharing a room with a brother or sister.

As the months went by, Camille got larger, and her time at the bakery decreased. With the addition of Lucille, everything ran smoothly. Camille still managed to be creative and introduced two new baking ideas that became big hits.

One afternoon, when I was helping with cleanup, Mr. Collin came into the bakery. This was an unusual visit, as the bakery had begun to turn a good profit, I had seen less of Mr. and Mrs. Collin. I just assumed they were pleased with the way things were going and didn't feel a need to be looking over my shoulder. I joined Mr. Collin at a small table and offered him a cup of coffee. Although I usually cut my coffee with cream or hot water, Mr. Collin preferred the strong taste of an espresso. He took two sips, then placed his cup on the saucer. He had a worried look on his face so I immediately stopped my small talk and prepared to listen.

He heaved a deep sigh and said, "Joseph, my wife is very sick."

"I'm sorry to hear that, Mr. Collin."

Mr. Collin seemed to have difficulty maintaining his composure. I continued to wait as I slowly stirred my coffee.

He cleared his throat and said, "I just got back from the doctor's office. My wife has had a minor stroke and is going to need lots of care. I have decided that I am going to be the person who will care for her."

"Is there anything Camille and I can do to help?"

"Yes," he nodded. "You can buy the bakery."

I replied, "I really don't have that kind of money."

Again, he cleared his throat, and then continued. "I have spoken with the bank and they are willing to work with you on a loan that will make it possible. I'm really not interested in making a big profit, which will make it easier on you. The bakery would have gone under had it not been for you and Camille."

"Thank you," I said.

"I mean it," he continued. "Camille's parents made the bakery a success. Camille brought it back to life. I want you two to be the owners. The people next door are looking to sell their place. They are leaving France and want to sell it quickly. They offered it to me at a reasonable price. You have always said we could be a bakery and a café. This could be the opportunity to do so. When I mentioned it to the people at the bank, they liked the idea. I think they will work with you. If you do expand, I would change the name. It doesn't make sense to name a café and a bakery after a street. I would call it Camille's Café and Bakery. How does that sound?"

I had difficulty holding back my enthusiasm. In a calm voice I replied, "It sounds wonderful. I'll talk to Camille tonight."

"If you don't want to buy it, I will have to sell it to someone else. But I would rather sell it to you."

As he stood I said, "Mr. Collin, I can't thank you enough. You have been wonderful to us. If it were not for you, I don't know what we would have done."

"I would say the same. If it were not for you and Camille, I don't know what I would have done. Talk it over with Camille and let me know what you decide."

I could barely control my excitement on the way home. I hurried along, not even stopping to buy my daily newspaper. Camille was in the kitchen, and Joshua was playing with toy cars in the hallway. I went to the pantry and grabbed a bottle of red wine. Then I moved to the cabinet for two wine glasses. Gingerly, I poured the wine and handed a glass to Camille.

She looked confused when I held my glass in the air and said, "A toast to the new owners of Camille's Café and Bakery."

Puzzled, she gasped, "What are you talking about?"

"Mr. Collin is selling the bakery to us," I said, lifting up my wine glass.

"Why now?" she asked.

"His wife had a minor stroke. He feels like she will recover, but he wants to stay home with her. He brought up the sale of the bakery. It was his suggestion that it be named Camille's Café and Bakery."

"But he doesn't have a café," Camille added in confusion.

"That's the other news," I said. "The people next to the bakery are interested in selling."

Smiling and taking a wine glass from my hand Camille said, "That would be incredible. But how would we afford this?"

"Mr. Collin told me he had spoken to someone at his bank about selling it to us. They will work with us."

She took a sip of wine and gave me a big hug.

From that point, everything happened quickly. Within a matter of weeks, we were the new owners.

Renovation of the building next door took place immediately after the papers were signed. The café had room for plenty of seating. In addition, we added outdoor tables and chairs. While I was working on renovations, Camille worked on developing a new menu and the hiring of additional staff.

The grand opening took place in April. Shortly after that, on May 16, 1947, our daughter, Michelle, was born. Two major events in less than two months had changed our lives for the better. The café was a dream come true. The first week we exceeded all expectations of sales. We had great products and were located in the perfect spot. The café and bakery quickly became a primary gathering place for people. Customers were usually waiting in line for a seat.

The arrival of Michelle far outweighed the purchase of the bakery. She brought so much joy to our lives. She was a constant source of affection, laughter, and pride.

Joshua, as he got older, became more studious and serious. His mother was delighted about his interest in the Jewish faith. He continued to make high grades. For such a young boy, he seemed to already have a plan for his life.

Michelle, on the other hand, was in constant motion. She had a zest for life and never stopped asking questions. We sat for many tea parties and were often the targets of practical jokes. It was hard to imagine that children could be so different. Camille was quick to remind me that Michelle had me wrapped around her finger. Although I would never admit it, she was right. Michelle was Daddy's little girl.

CHAPTER THIRTY FIVE

Lille, France, 1960

"Joseph, hurry up or we will be late. Be sure to wear a tie."

With a slight moan I said, "A tie?"

"Yes. You need to wear a tie. The Opera de Lille is a fancy place. You don't want to embarrass Michelle."

I only owned one suit and three ties so it wasn't hard to pick out what I was going to wear. Camille was right. I didn't want to embarrass my daughter. This was her big night and I wouldn't do anything to spoil it.

Michelle was just thirteen, but she had been selected to perform with the Youth Symphony Orchestra in Lille. From age four, it was obvious she was gifted playing the violin. More importantly, she loved to play. She never needed reminding to practice. Her talent had been recognized early on by her teacher. He encouraged us to seek the best instructors for her. Performing with the Youth Symphony was a great honor.

Michelle had already left with her friend's family. Since she had to be there early, it allowed us extra time to get ready.

It still seemed odd to not have Joshua in the house. He had left to attend the University in Paris to study law. That was always part of his plan, the only addition to the plan was Cindi. He had grown up attending the temple with her. They were always close friends, and Joshua spent a considerable amount of time at her parents' home. I was surprised when she decided to study medicine in Paris. I was beginning to think things were more serious between them than I had thought. Joshua always kept things to himself.

Michelle did have a room to herself. I mentioned on several occasions to Camille that we needed to find a bigger house. She would not hear of it. She reminded me how blessed we were. She felt that so many material things were luxuries that were not needed. For this reason, we were one of the last families to own a television, and we never bought a new car.

After three attempts at tying an appropriate knot, I straightened my tie and went downstairs to wait. I put a record on the record player and sat in my favorite chair. A few minutes later, I heard Camille come down the stairs. She was wearing a red dress that was cut low in the front. Her hair flowed halfway down her back, and the front was pulled to one side and held by a clip with a flower on it. She was stunning and, based on my expression; she knew the dress had the desired effect.

The Opera de Lille was seldom used for a concert. The Youth Symphony was an allowed exception to the rule. On the way, I decided to stop at a small flower shop on the corner. Camille was pleased I remembered to get flowers for our star performer.

It was nice to be dressed up and to attend such a special event in a magnificent building. Our lives were centered on more mundane events. Camille never complained.

After Joshua left to attend the university, Camille pointed out that Michelle would also be leaving in a few years. I could not imagine Michelle being gone. She was the center of life in our house. Camille was right, though. Her music teachers had already told us she should study in Paris.

I could not keep my eyes off the first chair violinist. She was a somewhat taller version of her mother. She looked so grown up in her black dress. It was easy to see how much she loved playing. Her head would move and her eyes would open wide when she played.

At the completion of the concert, parents were allowed to go backstage to meet our children. Michelle was in the middle of the group of young people. They were hugging each other and laughing. When she saw us, she sprinted towards us and gave us a hug. I handed her the bouquet of flowers and she gave me a kiss on both cheeks.

I told Camille and Michelle that we needed to celebrate by going out to dinner. When I suggested the restaurant, Michelle grabbed my arm and Camille shot a worried look. The restaurant I wanted to take them to was eloquent and expensive. I reminded both of them I didn't get many opportunities to take two beautiful women to dinner. Camille, I think, was even more impressed when I told her I had made reservations.

Everything about the restaurant was classy. The paintings on the wall were original art, and all the waiters wore tuxes. The chandeliers looked like they cost a small fortune. Michelle was taking in everything about our dining experience. It brought me such joy to see her and Camille enjoying everything. After looking at the menu prices, I mentally counted the cash I was carrying. Even with dessert, I had it covered.

After the entrée was served, I proposed a toast honoring the first chair violinist. Michelle looked at me and asked, "What did you enjoy the most?"

I thought for a moment and replied, "I liked everything. I once had a person tell me that classical music fed his soul. When I took my eyes off the first chair violinist, I closed them and let the music flow through my soul."

"Who was it that told you that?" Michelle asked.

"The man who helped save my life in Dachau."

Michelle asked, "What was his name?"

"Otto. I don't think I ever knew his last name. He was from Vienna."

She rolled her eyes and said, "That figures. Vienna has always been the place for classical music. All the great composers were there at one time. The city is all about great music. You should visit him."

"I don't know if he is alive."

Michelle looked at both of us, "There's one way to find out. I'll go with you."

I started to dismiss the conversation when Camille added, "She's right. We should all go to Vienna. For years, I have heard talk of Otto. Maybe he is alive. We should go. Besides, Vienna would be a perfect place for Michelle to visit."

Michelle quickly responded saying, "That's right, Dad. It would be an amazing experience for me."

"I'm outnumbered here. Vienna it will be, ladies."

• • •

With the Soviet Union's occupation of Eastern European countries, I was surprised Camille was willing to travel. Although it was never discussed, Camille had a fear of traveling outside of France because of Dachau. Michelle's desire to go gave Camille the courage she needed to travel.

The train ride through the countryside was beautiful. It was fun to watch Michelle's excitement as we traveled through West Germany and Austria. We arrived in Vienna late in the evening and had difficulty finding a cab to take us to our hotel. After walking down a side street next to the train station, I was able to locate a taxi. The driver only spoke German, which presented a challenge. When I pointed to the name of the hotel on a paper I had in my pocket, he nodded his head. The hotel was located near the outer ring of the old city. It was more luxurious than I had expected. We dropped off our baggage in the room and headed down the street next to the hotel to find a café that was still open. We were starving. Each of us ordered a bowl of potato soup. Camille and I shared a bottle of wine.

After a good night's sleep and breakfast the next morning, we started on our mission to find Otto. I remembered Otto mentioning that he was in the jewelry business. I found a phone directory and looked up every jewelry shop I could find. After making a few calls, I decided it would be easier to visit the shops. Communication on the phone was difficult. Since Otto was Jewish, it made sense that we should start with the shops located near the Juden Platz.

The first shop was located on the corner of two busy streets. The owner had never heard of a man named Otto who owned a jewelry shop. He reminded me that the Jews who had been rounded up and fortunate enough to live through the Holocaust returned to find nothing. Most of their businesses were gone. He asked me if Otto had another occupation. The only thing I could think of was his love of the arts, especially music.

We left the shop and visited every shop that might sell some type of jewelry. We left the Jewish quarter and walked down the side streets in the old city. Everyone we talked with was courteous and tried to help. At the end of the day, we were exhausted and still had no leads concerning Otto.

On the way back to the hotel to rest, we were stopped by a gentleman dressed like Mozart. He told us about the concert that was scheduled that night at the Halls of the Imperial Palace. Michelle looked at her mother with excitement, and thirty seconds later I had purchased three tickets to the concert.

We cut our rest short so we would have time to eat and get to the concert. Michelle and Camille wore the dresses they had worn the night Michelle performed in Lille. Since we didn't want to be late for the concert, we ate at the same café where we had enjoyed the potato soup. The concert hall was harder to find than we had realized. It seemed like everyone we asked gave us different directions.

We reached the Hall just before the concert started. We had seats in the middle of the concert hall, which was perfect for taking in the beauty of the magnificent Hall. Camille told Michelle that the concert program said Mozart had played in this Hall on numerous occasions.

The orchestra played the music of many of the great composers. Halfway through the concert, four opera singers came on stage to perform with the orchestra. I found myself looking at Michelle, I could tell she was ecstatic about the concert. Even if I didn't locate Otto, the trip was worth it.

At the conclusion of the concert, Michelle wanted to walk to the front to get a better look. We stood for several minutes in our row, letting people pass so we could make our way to the front. When it was clear, Michelle took the lead. There were members of the audience talking with members of the orchestra while they packed up their instruments. Michelle walked closer to the violinist to get a better look.

A gentleman with gray, curly hair, who walked with a slight limp, approached a woman who was placing her violin in its case. I found myself studying the man as he kissed the woman and picked up the violin case.

Camille asked, "What's wrong? Why are you staring at the man?"

"I think it may be Otto."

"Go find out!" Michelle yelled with excitement.

I quickly walked toward the man before he got away. I touched him on the shoulder and in English said, "Excuse me. Is your name Otto?"

He turned and looked at me. A smile came over his face. "John Joseph!"

Otto grabbed me in a tight bear hug. We embraced and patted each other on the back. He then repeated, "John Joseph. I can't believe it's you."

"I'm so glad to see you. I was afraid you were dead."

Otto introduced his wife Esther. I introduced Camille and Michelle. Esther told Otto that she was going to meet with a few friends from the orchestra and suggested that he take us for dessert to catch up on things. Camille nodded her approval.

The small café was located a half block from the concert hall. After we ordered dessert and coffee was poured, Otto asked if he should speak in English. I suggested French, so he easily switched to French.

"I'm a little rusty with French," Otto admitted; "But if I mispronounce something, just let me know. How long are you going to be in Vienna?"

"We have two more days," I replied. "I came here to see if I could find you. We also came so that Michelle could attend a concert and see some of the sites. She is a very talented violinist."

Otto looked at Michelle and asked, "Is that right? Maybe Michelle could attend a rehearsal while you are here. My wife could arrange that."

"That would be great," she replied.

Otto continued, "You know, I'm so glad you came to Vienna to look me up. I have thought of you often. I feared you and Camille never made it out of Dachau."

I added, "It got pretty bad at the end. When you marched out with the other prisoners, I didn't think you had a chance."

Otto looked at Camille and said, "Is it all right to talk about this?"

She gave a half smile and said, "Yes, it's all right. Michelle has heard a few things from her father."

Otto continued, "I didn't have a choice about the march from Dachau. When I saw you escape, I kept looking for an opportunity. There was a guard standing beside me as we walked through the gate. I realized early that this was going to be a death march. If someone didn't walk fast enough, he was shot. We had walked at least five miles before I saw my chance to escape. We had stopped at a bend in the road because a guard had to chase a prisoner. There were shots fired and everybody was looking the other way. The road was next to the woods so when no one was looking, I dove into the trees. There was a lot of confusion and the guard didn't notice I was missing. I lay in the same place until evening. Later, I walked to a nearby farm and ate some vegetables out of the garden. I stayed there a second day until the farmer told me to leave. I was walking down the main road when a truck pulled up beside me. I was frightened at first, but it was an American truck. I was taken to a temporary hospital. After a week, I was able to get a ride to Vienna. When I got back, I had lost everything...my family and business."

"I'm so sorry," I replied, not really knowing what to say.

"It was hard at first. But one day I woke up and told myself I needed to get on with living. I had a few temporary jobs until I found a job with the Arts Council. I'm now the Assistant Director. That's how I met Esther, she was also a survivor who lost most of her family. I try very hard not to think of the past. I just try to look ahead. Sometimes, however, I have nightmares which cause me to not be able to sleep."

There was a pause in the conversation and I added, "We try not to think about the past. Camille is better at that than me. We have a good life in Lille, we own a café and bakery. Our son is studying law in Paris, Michelle is our talented musician."

Otto patted Camille on the arm and said, "You are beautiful."

She blushed and said, "Thank you. You are very kind. Sometimes I don't feel so pretty."

"Take my word. You are young and beautiful and so is your daughter. It is good that she took after you and not her father."

We all laughed and Camille added, "So true."

Otto asked, "Have you seen many of the sites in Vienna?"

I responded, "We've walked through the streets but we haven't really seen a lot."

"Well then, tomorrow I will be your guide. I will also make dinner plans for us."

The next morning, Otto picked us up at the hotel. He felt it would be easier to walk from the hotel than trying to drive close to St. Stephen's Cathedral. Since arriving in Vienna, we kept getting glimpses of the cathedral. It is the Gothic centerpiece of the city. As we walked through the cathedral, I stopped and knelt near the altar. I was saying a quick prayer before I realized everyone in my party was looking at me. I didn't say anything. I rose and continued my walk.

Later, back at the hotel, Michelle asked, "Why did you stop and pray? It is a Catholic church."

"I know, but it is still the same God."

Michelle added, "My friend Julie said she saw you praying in a Catholic church in Lille. I told her she must have been mistaken."

"No, it's true. I sometimes go there to pray."

"I don't understand," said Michelle.

I hated not being truthful with my own daughter. I always thought there might be a day when I could tell her the complete story. This, however, was not that day.

I answered, "I just like the solitude and quiet of the Catholic church."

Michelle asked, "Why did Otto call you John Joseph?"

"It's just a little joke we had between us while we were in Dachau."

I quickly changed the topic by reminding Camille and Michelle that they had one hour to get ready for dinner. We met Otto and Esther at his favorite restaurant, Greichenbeisl. The restaurant had vaulted ceilings and many small rooms. Otto took Michelle to the one room where Ludwig Von Beethoven and Wolfgang Mozart had written their names on the wall. Michelle was impressed and asked me to take a picture of it.

The next day, Michelle was able to attend rehearsal with Esther while Camille and I walked the streets and ate outdoors at a café that was near the St. Stephen's Cathedral. When we had finished our lunch and continued our walk, we saw the signs for the Juden Platz. As we walked through the Jewish quarter, we were reminded that 65,000 Jews from Vienna had died at the hands of the Nazis.

The next morning, Otto joined us at our hotel for breakfast. He wanted to take us to the train station, knowing it would be an opportunity to visit one last time. Our conversation centered on the future and the need to stay in touch with each other.

The trip to Vienna was everything I had hoped it would be. I was excited to know that the man who had saved my life was alive himself.

CHAPTER THIRTY SIX

Lille, France, 1967

Joshua completed law school and married his childhood sweetheart. The wedding was a mixture of joy and sadness. The sadness was the result of so many missing Jewish family members who had died in concentration camps. Camille cherished the excitement of a new daughter. We loved Joshua's wife and knew they were perfect for each other.

After the wedding, the big surprise came when they informed us they would be moving to Israel. Both of them had found jobs in Tel Aviv. Although disappointed, I was not surprised. Joshua had deep faith and had mentioned on several occasions the need to go back to his roots. Within a year, we had a grandson. I was both moved and sad when Joshua told me they had named their son Joseph. They were naming their son after me. Even though he was being named after me, in reality they were naming their son after the real Joseph, the father of Joshua. I still carried some shame knowing that Camille and I should have talked to Joshua years ago about his real father. We both harbored mistrust when it came to the government. We always had fear that my true identity, were it to be discovered, would cause the life we loved to unravel.

At the insistence of Dr. Benoit, I bought the cabin on the lake. It was something we had talked about doing but never wanted to approach Dr. Benoit about. To our surprise, it was his idea, getting older had made it difficult for him to go there.

I built a fire pit in the back. This became the place where we sat each evening sipping wine. Michelle would sometimes bring her violin and play while we sat and enjoyed the view and solitude.

As expected, Michelle had lots of offers to attend various universities. Her talent at playing the violin was well known. Camille and I were proud every time someone expressed interest in having her attend their university. We were sometimes selfish in our desire to have her stay in Lille, because the greatest opportunity was in Paris. Michelle was reluctant when it came to leaving us, but we convinced her it would be foolish not to take the opportunity.

After she left, the house, which had always been filled with her laughter and music, now seemed quiet. Although it was an adjustment for both of us, we slowly made the transition.

It was made easier because we truly loved each other and enjoyed the simple things in life. We went for walks in the park, occasionally stopping by a café to share a bottle of wine. In the evenings, I watched the news on television and listened to music. One evening I found a record album that Michelle had left at home. The album was in English, which surprised me. I remembered Michelle talking about the Beatles, but I had never heard any of their music. I found the music to be quite enjoyable and relayed some of the words to Camille in French.

The first year Michelle went to the university, she would come home every chance she could. The second year was different. Although she continued to write and call, her trips home were rare. She had many friends at school and Camille and I began to think she might have a serious boyfriend. She constantly talked about a boy named Bernard. It seemed like everything she talked about involved him. All that we really knew about him was that he was older. Apparently, he had recently graduated and was on some type of fellowship in the music department. When I talked with her on the phone, I was tempted to ask questions about Bernard, but decided against it. Michelle never liked it when I pried into her personal life. She found it easier to talk with her mother about boys.

It was a beautiful spring day in Lille. I convinced Camille that we should leave the café in the hands of the new manger we had hired. The manager was highly skilled, and the business practically ran itself. I took Camille to our favorite restaurant and ordered a top-of-the-line bottle of wine. Camille seemed surprised.

She asked, "What is the special occasion?"

I replied, "Twenty-four years ago today was the first time I ever saw you."

Camille sighed, "Has it really been that long?"

"Yes," I said. "But it is a day I will never forget."

She rolled her eyes and whispered, "Do you realize that makes me forty-two?"

"You look twenty-two," I said.

"Thank you. I can see a few wrinkles."

"I don't see any," I said, causing her to blush.

She said with a smile. "You may need glasses! I just can't believe it has been that long."

We finished dinner and slowly strolled back to our home. As we walked, Camille placed her arm around me and placed her head on my shoulder.

When we reached the house, Camille suggested that we have a cup of coffee. She wanted to change into something a little more comfortable, too. She had to notice the big smile on my face.

As we enjoyed our coffee with our feet propped up on the coffee table, the phone rang. Camille answered it.

"It's Michelle," she whispered.

We were always excited to get a call from Michelle. As I continued to sip my coffee I noticed that the expression on Camille's face had turned more serious. The only thing I could hear Camille say was, "Talk about what?"

When she hung up, Camille returned to the sofa, I asked, "What was that about?"

She answered, "I'm not sure."

"What do you mean 'not sure'?"

Camille continued, "I could tell she was upset. She had a very serious tone. She was doing her best to hold it together. She told me she would be home tomorrow and that she had something important to talk with us about. When I asked her what it was about, she responded, "We can talk tomorrow."

I asked, "She didn't give you any hint?"

"No. It was very strange. She just kept repeating that she needed to talk with us face to face."

The phone call definitely put a damper on the evening and most of the night. Both of us began to speculate what could be so important that she had to come home to tell us. My thoughts unfortunately turned to the possibility she could be pregnant. I remembered what that feeling was like and as a result, tried to block it from my mind.

As in times past, we picked Michelle up at the train station. She was wearing jeans and a long sleeve blouse, which was pretty casual dress for her. When she saw us, she smiled and ran to give us hugs. She didn't appear upset, but she wasn't her usual laughing, joking self either. When I attempted to ask what she wanted to talk about, she smiled and told us we could talk at home.

After I parked the car and walked in the front door, I joined Camille and Michelle in our living room. They were both sitting on the couch.

Michelle sighed, "It is so nice to be home."

We didn't say anything instead we continued to look directly at her. She readjusted how she was sitting on the couch so she could look at both of us.

She then said, "I want to get married."

Camille responded, "To Bernard?"

"Yes, but it's complicated. I don't want you to be mad at me or disappointed in me. Bernard is Catholic."

Camille looked at me. I said, "Why do you think we would be mad?"

"Because he is not Jewish. I know that marrying in the faith is important to both of you. I know you think marrying someone out of the faith would never work. That's why I wanted to come home and talk about it. I truly love him and he loves me. I cannot imagine living without him. I know we can work it out. We've talked about it and I know it will work."

There was silence until Camille asked, "Why the rush to get married?"

Michelle replied, "Bernard is two years older and works at the university. He has his own place. There is no reason for us to wait."

Camille continued, "What about his parents? What do they think?"

"I think they were shocked at first, but I know they really like me and they want Bernard to be happy."

"Are you looking for our blessing?" I asked. "You don't need our permission."

"I'm looking for your blessing and your help."

I glanced at Camille and she gave me a nod. "If you truly love him and you are both committed to one another, you have our blessing," I replied.

Michelle added, "You are not disappointed that he's not Jewish?"

Camille responded, "I always thought you would marry someone who is Jewish but maybe God also has a different plan for you."

"What do you mean by a different plan?" Michelle asked.

"I'm just saying there are people in this world who, for some reason, God has decided to bring together as husband and wife."

Again Camille glanced at me, and this time she had to notice the smile on my face. Michelle must have been surprised that we were not angry or shouting. She had grown up in a home where Jewish traditions were practiced. She also knew how important maintaining the faith was to Camille.

Both of us continued to ask questions about Bernard. We tried not to have Michelle feel like she was being interrogated. We had met Bernard once when we had visited Michelle in Paris. We really didn't know much about him, which worried us. Michelle calmly answered our questions and shared additional information about his future plans. I was convinced the more we talked that both of them had spent a lot of time talking about marriage. It was not impulsive.

After our question-and-answer period had ended, I said, "You said something about needing our help."

She responded, "Yes. Bernard's priest said he would not marry us because I'm not Catholic. I'm not ready to become Catholic, but I know I want to marry Bernard. He checked with other priests, but none were willing to help us. I thought of the rabbi, but knew that would be a dead end. We would like to get married in a church because we feel God has brought us together. Do you know a priest who might marry us?"

Trying not to smile I said, "I just might. I'll make a call. I know that before he would consider marrying you, he would want to talk with both of you."

"That's not a problem," replied Michelle. "We could come to Lille most any time."

"It would not be in Lille. It would be in Cambrai."

Before Michelle returned to Paris, I called Father Glaize. I know I caught him off guard with my request. At first he didn't even respond. There was complete silence. He said he would like to meet and talk with Michelle and Bernard before he made a decision. This was not an easy thing for him to do. I knew, however, that Father Glaize didn't always follow the book of rules when it came to what he considered God's work.

It was three weeks before all the schedules could be coordinated to have Bernard and Michelle meet with Father Glaize. Camille and I met Bernard and Michelle at the train station in Lille. I could tell that Camille instantly liked Bernard. He was mature for a person his age and it was obvious to both of us he loved our daughter. I thought it would be stiff and awkward having him at our house but the opposite was true. He fit in immediately, Bernard put all of us at ease, it was not an act. We went out for dinner that night to our favorite restaurant.

On the drive to Cambrai, I shared some information about Father Glaize. I told Michelle and Bernard that he had been sent to Dachau because he supported French resistance fighters. I also told them he had helped Camille and myself on two occasions. When Michelle asked for specifics, I simply added he was a good friend.

When we arrived at the church, I wasn't sure what role I would have in the meeting that had been planned. I quickly learned I had no role. After introductions and a few hugs, Father Glaize had Bernard and Michelle follow him to his office. He met with them for over two hours. During that time, Camille and I walked through the church grounds.

We eventually returned to the church and sat in the back pew.

Finally, we saw Father Glaize leading the way down the hallway. Everyone was smiling; Michelle was carrying a pamphlet and a book in her hand. We stood to greet them.

As Father Glaize got closer he said, "We are going to have a wedding."

Everyone hugged and Camille began to cry. Although I was very curious about the meeting that had taken place, it really wasn't any of my business. The important thing was that Father Glaize was satisfied and my daughter was happy.

Three months later, in June, we had a wedding. Like Bernard, we also liked his parents. I could tell they were anxious about meeting us. We felt the same way. We were all proud of our children. I knew they loved our daughter by the kindness and affection they showed her. Religion was never a topic we discussed. Father Glaize stressed the part about God bringing two people together. When he said that, Camille reached over and grabbed my hand, squeezing it softly.

After the wedding, Camille and I knew our lives would be very different. Our children left home and they were both now married. They would be raising their own families. Camille reminded me that children are meant to leave and have their own lives. She also was quick to point out that being grandparents was another gift from God that we would get to enjoy.

CHAPTER THIRTY SEVEN

Lille, France, 1988

Our children and grandchildren continued to be a major part of our lives. Michelle and Bernard's three girls often stayed with us on weekends and we continued to have wonderful weekends at the cabin. It is a central part of our lives and as well as theirs. We made trips to Paris when one of our granddaughters sang in the school choir.

Although we did see our grandson, it was as if we were strangers each time we visited. We visited Israel twice, trying to develop a better relationship with him. As our children got older, they naturally became more involved with their busy lives as well as the lives of their children. Joshua's wife was good about writing letters and sending us pictures of our grandson.

Camille and I spent more time with each other. Although I was still the owner of the café, I had a manager who kept up with the day-to-day operation of the business.

Camille had taken a painting class and enjoyed her new hobby. I was always reading and listening to music. In our early sixties, life had become very different. On numerous occasions, one of us would comment how blessed we were. Camille was the champion of enjoying the simple things in life. A walk in the park, followed by a dessert at a small vendor stand, could be the highlight of the day. We were both content with our lives.

One afternoon, after a walk in the neighborhood, Camille told me she was tired and wanted to go to bed. The next morning, she woke up late. When she entered the kitchen, I had already made coffee and was reading the paper at the table.

As she picked up a cup for coffee, I teased her and remarked, "What a sleepyhead."

She walked over and sat in her favorite chair. After taking a sip of coffee she said, "I'm not sure why I'm so tired. I feel like I could go right back to sleep."

"Why don't you? Your body must be telling you something."

"Yes, like the pain in my lower back," she added.

I asked, "Did you pick up something heavy?"

"No. It's not that kind of pain."

I took off my reading glasses and suggested, "If it doesn't get better, you should see Dr. Benoit."

Although Dr. Benoit was in his eighties, he still practiced medicine part-time. He did not look his age and still had plenty of energy, seeing patients kept him busy.

Another week went by, and Camille still felt tired and complained about the ache in her back. After my constant nagging, she got an appointment with Dr. Benoit. After her examination, he told her he wanted to do some blood work and have a scan done at the hospital. He would also be consulting with an internal specialist at the hospital. He assured Camille this was standard procedure to assist him in determining a cause for her tiredness and pain.

At the hospital, I waited with Camille in the waiting area of the specialist Dr. Benoit had recommended. He called both of us in, and we took a seat in the two chairs facing his large cherry desk. He continued looking at the folder in front of him. His reading glasses were perched on the tip of his nose. We sat there in silence waiting for him to say something; He took off his reading glasses.

In a solemn voice he said, "The scan shows a large mass on your liver. I'm also concerned with your blood test results. I don't want you to panic. There are a number of factors that could be contributing to this. I am recommending that I do exploratory surgery. I'm not really going to know what I'm dealing with until I see it. The surgery is not that involved and it will tell us what we need to know."

With little expression in her voice Camille asked, "Do you think I have cancer?"

"I'm not sure. That's why I want to do the surgery."

Camille didn't show any emotion. She calmly asked, "When would you like to do this?"

"In the morning," he replied.

We both must have looked surprised. The doctor calmly said, "The sooner the better."

That afternoon, we went through our normal routine of dinner, coffee, and watching T.V. Neither one of us said anything about the upcoming surgery. That night, I don't think either one of us slept.

After the surgical procedure, Camille was recovering from the anesthesia in the recovery room. The doctor found me in the waiting room and asked me to follow him to his office. Before I sat down, I knew it was bad news. The doctor was solemn. He seemed to have difficulty finding the right words to say.

Finally, he said, "I don't have good news. Your wife has liver cancer. It has also spread to other parts of her body."

"What kind of treatment will she have?" I asked.

"You will need to talk with your wife about that."

I was surprised by his comment. I stood and said, "What do you mean?"

"Your wife is going to die from this cancer. We can give her treatment that might extend her life a few months, but the treatment will make the quality of her remaining life worse."

Tears began to form in my eyes. "How long does she have?" I asked.

"Months. Somewhere between two to six."

I had difficulty catching my breath, tears streamed down my face. Within a minute, I was sobbing. The doctor left the room to give me some privacy. The more I tried to pull myself together, the more I seemed to lose it. It was over twenty minutes before the doctor returned. I gradually gained control.

The doctor sat next to me. "Do you want me to talk with your wife?" he asked.

"No," I responded. "I will tell her once she returns to her room."

I walked outside and took a brisk walk down two streets in front of the hospital. By the time I got back to the hospital, I had regained my composure.

When I reached her room, she was still asleep. There was not another patient in the bed beside hers. I pulled up a chair and found myself staring at her. Camille had always looked younger than her age. At sixty-two, she could still pass for a woman in her late forties. Her long hair was now a combination of brown and gray. As I continued to study her face, I felt my throat tighten. I could not imagine living without her.

An hour passed before she awoke. She was still trying to come out of the fog from the anesthesia. The nurse came in and asked her if she was hungry. Although she said yes, she never touched the food in front of her.

She closed her eyes a few times and then looked directly at me and asked, "What did the doctor say?"

I went through everything, including the decision about whether or not to receive treatment. As I spoke, tears began to roll down her cheeks. We both cried. She lifted up her arms, as I sat on the bed so I could hold her. I held her close for a long time.

Camille took hold of my hand. She asked me when she could go home.

I replied, "I think in a couple of days."

Wiping the tears from her face she said, "I want to go home. I don't want the treatment. I want to enjoy the little time I have."

"Do you want me to call the children?" I asked.

"Not right now. I want you to take me to Venice. I want to ride in a gondola and have an Italian man sing love songs to us. Then I want to visit the cabin."

I pulled her close to me, "Okay, that's what we will do."

After a week of recovering at home, Camille was ready to go. She knew there was a clock running and she didn't have time to waste. The train ride to Venice was comfortable. I purchased first class tickets to ensure it. During the trip, we spoke about our children and nothing else. When Camille got tired, she rested her head on my shoulder. When she slept, I closed my eyes and tried not to think of anything but Venice.

At the train station in Venice, I decided to spend more money to ease things for Camille. We took a water taxi from the train station to the dock close to St. Mark's Square. When we got to the hotel, I suggested that we rest before going to the square. The trip had been tiring and she welcomed the opportunity to rest.

We both slept for over three hours. When we awoke, I asked Camille if she wanted to shower. She told me she could shower later, I knew she was anxious to make the best of our trip. She knew better than I did the importance of pacing herself. As we walked toward St. Mark's Square, we crossed two canal bridges. When we crossed the second bridge, I saw the gondolas lined up. It was late in the evening, we had not eaten dinner and I wasn't certain if this would be the best time for our boat ride. Camille surprised me when she suggested we go on our boat ride. The man's French was not very good and his English was worse. I took him aside to explain that Camille was ill and that I wanted our boat ride to be special. I pulled out a wad of paper currency and asked him how much this would get me. He glanced and told me one hour. When I acted disappointed, he looked at Camille and then said two hours.

I asked him about singing Italian love songs but he just shrugged. I told him we had to have singing and he left us and walked over to another man who was standing next to his boat. The other man looking over, waved for us to come to his boat. The first man told me that Andrea had the best voice in Venice and he gave him my money.

We boarded the gondola. The gondolier, Andrea, quickly demonstrated his great voice. As he steered us down the narrow canals, he sang so loudly the sound bounced off the buildings. The songs were definitely love songs. Camille took the blanket that was given to us and placed it over our legs. She then placed her head on my shoulder. I noticed occasionally that she closed her eyes as she listened to the songs being sung.

We went up and down canals. When we went underneath a bridge, people on the bridge would stop and listen. The boat ride was everything I had hoped it would be. As we headed back to our starting point, Camille thanked me and told me how much she loved me. This made everything perfect, we were still so much in love.

The next day we slept in and had breakfast at the hotel. Camille surprised me when she told me she would like to visit the Doge Palace. I knew the excursion would entail a lot of walking. We would need to take our time and stop to rest whenever we needed to.

In the afternoon we rested at our hotel. When it was almost dark, we walked toward St. Mark's Square. We stopped to eat at a small Italian restaurant near the canal. Camille ate very little. I encouraged her to eat some bread. She reminded me that she had never been a big eater. She did enjoy the wine however. We did not hesitate when the waiter poured us our second glass.

The evening was topped off by listening to the different orchestras as we moved around the square, we sat at a table enjoying a cup of expensive coffee. It was the perfect way to end our extraordinary day.

The next morning Camille told me she was a little tired, but that she really wanted to visit the Jewish Ghetto. At the Jewish Ghetto, we visited the site where Jews in Venice were rounded up to be sent to concentration camps. As we walked around the area where this took place, Camille placed her hands on the walls and closed her eyes. I knew she was feeling the fear and terror of the people who had been held behind these very walls.

The ride home from Venice was spent reminiscing about our trip. It saddened me to think that we should have taken the trip years earlier.

As soon as we returned home, Camille wanted to go to the cabin on the lake. She reminded me that time was precious. The next day, I packed the car and we headed to the cabin. I stopped along the way so Camille could take pills for pain. Instead of taking an occasional pill, she was now taking the pills on a set schedule.

The cabin had always been our refuge and the place where we had created so many memories. So it was not a surprise that Camille wanted to spend some of her remaining days there.

The cabin had become a second home to us. We had family photographs displayed throughout the house. We had made numerous changes to the cabin. The most recent change was screening in the back porch. This allowed us to sit out in the evening without being attacked by bugs.

Although I tried to get Camille to rest, she insisted on doing things in the cabin. The biggest surprise came when she started baking. She prepared a pastry that was loaded with chocolate. I suggested a picnic of wine and pastry by the lake. It was a beautiful spring day with a light breeze coming off the lake. After drinking our second glass of wine, Camille laid her head on my lap. I brushed the hair from her face and told her that I loved her very much.

She said, "I love you, too. Promise me you will keep our family together."

"I promise. Camille, I don't know how I can live without you."

She raised her head and looked directly at me saying, "The one thing we learned at Dachau is you must go on living."

"Yes, but I will miss you so much. You are not just my wife. You are also my best friend."

Camille sat up and took my hand. After a minute of silence she said, "John, I'm the luckiest person on earth. I have had a good life. There were times when death would have been welcomed, but God had other plans."

"I feel the same way. I plan to see you on the other side."

Camille wanted to sleep on the porch so I brought the mattress from the bed and placed it on the floor. We wrapped up in the covers, holding onto each other.

During the night, I could hear her moan. I knew the pain was getting worse.

The next morning, she did not feel like making breakfast so I prepared eggs and toast. Again, she ate very little, but asked for her pills. After both of us had drunk a second cup of coffee, she said, "John, it is time to go home. We need to let the children know."

"I'll pack the car."

CHAPTER THIRTY EIGHT

Everything seemed to be happening more quickly than expected. Although the doctor had told us two to six months, I now thought it might be sooner rather than later. I called Joshua and Michelle as soon as we arrived home. Both of them seemed angry that I had not contacted them earlier. Although I tried to explain, they still were upset. Finally, I just told them to come home quickly.

Camille was comfortable in our bed and seemed to be sleeping a lot. She did not want to return to the hospital. Dr. Benoit gave me instructions on administering morphine. I knew that Camille wanted to be coherent when the children and grandchildren came so I administered the minimum amount.

When the kids arrived, they immediately went in to see her. It was difficult for Michelle to see her mother so weak and frail. When it became too hard, she would excuse herself to attend to one of her children. When the room became too crowded, it was Michelle who suggested we take turns visiting with Camille. On several occasions, Camille closed her eyes and fell asleep. When this happened, everyone left the room except for me.

A woman from the synagogue came to the house to see me. She was there to ensure that everything regarding the death, funeral, and burial would go according to Jewish laws and customs. I was relieved to have her there, I didn't have a clue what to do and

I knew this would be important to Camille. We planned who to call and where the body would lie and how to notify people within 24 hours and all other religious traditions.

As darkness approached, Joshua's wife and Michelle's husband took their children to the nearby hotel. Our house only had one additional bedroom and one bathroom. I remember asking Camille if she would like to move to a larger home. She seemed surprised whenever I brought it up. For her, the house was more than adequate.

I was aware that Camille was no longer eating and had not gone to the bathroom in hours. I remember Dr. Benoit talking about the body shutting down in the end.

I continued to sit next to her bed and hold her hand. She was awake and surprisingly alert. Her voice became a whisper, and it became necessary to lean over the bed to hear her. I knew she was aware the end was near. She asked first to speak to Joshua. He took my place by the bed and Camille told him how proud she was of him and his family. She asked that he make sure our grandson would remember her. Joshua was too choked up to answer. He just kept nodding. Next, Michelle took the seat next to the bed. Camille told her what a joy she had been and that she should continue playing the violin.

As Michelle stood up, Camille said something. Michelle did not understand so she bent over so her mother could whisper it to her again. Michelle then stood up and told us that Camille wanted her to play the violin. In her old room, we still had the first violin Michelle had ever played. It was small and had not been played in years. Michelle returned and began to play. The music from the old violin was still beautiful to the ear. More importantly, it brought a smile to Camille's face.

When Michelle had finished playing, Camille asked for more morphine. I went to the kitchen and returned with a glass of water so she could take the pill. She now had difficulty swallowing, which was painful to watch. Her eyes shut. In a few minutes, she opened them again. She said something, but I wasn't sure what she had said. I got so close my ear touched her lips. She was asking for me to hold her. I leaned over the bed, placing her arms around my neck. Bent at the waist, my back began to ache. I did not move. I held her in that position for over an hour. I could hear her breathing becoming more labored. Her eyes opened.

She whispered, "John, I love you."

I held her tight and whispered, "I love you, too."

In a louder voice she said, "John, I love you."

I responded, "I love you."

Camille placed her face next to my neck and said, "John, you have been my life."

"You are my life. I will miss you so much."

Another twenty minutes passed, and I noticed Joshua and Michelle had returned to the room. Then, in a faint voice Camille said, "John, I love you."

I continued to hold her in the same position. I no longer could hear her breathing. The arms that had once draped around my neck became limp and fell to the bed. I knew she had passed but didn't want to let her go. Joshua gave me a pat on the back, and I stood up. The three of us hugged and cried.

We walked to the living room and took a seat. I kept taking deep breaths followed by long sighs. Michelle got out of her seat and walked over to me, placing her arm around my shoulder.

We stayed in that position until Joshua spoke. "Papa, why did Mom call you John?"

I responded, "It must have been the morphine."

Michelle added, "Yes, but I remember Otto calling you that when we went to Vienna."

I added, "That was just a joke between us."

Michelle continued, "Papa, one day I want you to share more about your life with us."

"Someday. Right now we need to bury your mother."

I could not get over the number of people who attended the funeral. You get to know a lot of people when you own a café and bakery for forty years. Although I expected to see Dr. Benoit and his wife, I was really surprised to see Otto, Father Glaize, and William Williams. I was reminded how many lives Camille had touched and how many people had impacted our lives. I had planned to give a eulogy but got so choked up that my son had to finish for me.

I was pleased that Michelle decided to stay for a week after the burial. I really didn't want to be alone. She was a big help going through her mother's belongings. She kept asking me if I wanted to keep something personal. I told her that I had a lifetime of personal memories stored in my head and my heart.

A few days after Michelle left, I felt so alone. I found myself walking through the house, looking at pictures and things we had purchased. I was constantly making enough coffee for two people. On more than one occasion, I would set the table for two. I began to feel there was a ghost in the house. Everywhere I looked, I could see Camille.

In the evenings, I would drink too much wine, which helped bring about a period of continuous crying. Sometimes it hurt so much I felt my chest tighten. I wasn't sure if you could really die of a broken heart, but I was beginning to think that might be my fate.

As the weeks passed, I did better. It helped when I went to the café to drink coffee with friends. Michelle called me often to check on me, which also helped. Once I found that walking seemed to help, I wore out a pair of shoes. In the evening, I would sometimes think of my conversations with Otto in Dachau. You have to have something to live for. I thought of my children, grandchildren, and the simple things in life that Camille felt were so important. I never realized how much Camille and I did together. Although I could do them by myself, it just wasn't the same. I particularly missed talking with Camille. She was my best friend and there wasn't anything we couldn't talk about.

On two occasions, I returned to the cabin. I found myself walking around the cabin touching things that Camille had purchased with so much excitement. I sat in her favorite chair. Most of the time, I sat on the back porch staring at the lake while crying. It wasn't the same anymore.

One evening I sat on the grass next to the lake. As I watched the water hit against the bank my thoughts returned to the river. For the first time in years I wondered what happened to Diane, and more importantly I wondered what our child was like.

I sent a letter to Michelle asking if she would like to have the cabin. I received an immediate reply stating she would love to have the cabin. It brought a smile to my face when she stated it was her hope that her children would have the same wonderful memories of the cabin that she had had as a child.

I was told by many people that time is the great healer. I did find this to be true. Before I knew it, the weeks had become years.

CHAPTER THIRTY NINE
Part V

Lille, France — Allentown, Pennsylvania, 1990

On August 1st, I had a wakeup call regarding my own mortality. After morning coffee, I began to experience tightness in my chest. In addition, I had shortness of breath. I kept waiting for the symptoms to go away but they didn't. I walked next door and asked my neighbor to take me to the hospital.

The hospital ran lots of tests to determine a diagnosis. My doctor said I had experienced a minor heart attack. I wasn't certain how to interpret the word minor. I did know that it got my attention. He gave me a list of do's and don'ts, which I promised to follow.

The following week, I visited Dr. Benoit. He no longer practiced medicine, but he was certainly a person whose opinion I valued. He told me he was tired of being so closed up inside the house and would prefer to meet me at Camille's Café. I was reminded that Camille's name would live on for many years to come.

I had not seen Dr. Benoit since the funeral, but we had talked on the phone a few times. He was always good to check up on me. Over the years, I had learned to regard him more like a father. He was my role model when it came to compassion and being a good father.

I took a table in the corner of the café. Since I was the owner, I continually had to tell the waitress I didn't need anything. She was determined to make me feel like a valued customer.

I saw Dr. Benoit from a distance, walking down the street. He looked frailer than I ever remembered. Instead of a brisk walk, he took small, slow steps. When he walked by the window, he saw me and waved.

He met me at the table. We both ordered coffee and pastry. I told him, "It is so good to see you. You look great."

His hand shook as he raised his coffee cup. He smiled and replied, "I wouldn't necessarily say great. As I get older, I often wonder who the man is looking at me in the mirror."

"Let me rephrase. You look great for someone your age."

He laughed and said, "Well, since I'm eighty-four, I'll take that as a compliment, speaking of which, how old are you?"

I responded, "Joseph Bernhardt is seventy-one, but John Thomas is just sixty-four."

He laughed, "You know, I almost forgot the John Thomas part. You always looked much older than Camille, so I assumed you were the age of Joseph. Camille always did look younger than her age."

"That's true. When I first met her, she looked like a child more than a wife and mother."

Dr. Benoit leaned forward in his seat and said, "So, Joseph, how are you doing?"

"Since Camille died, it has been a day-to-day existence. I haven't adjusted to life without her. I can't begin to tell you how much I miss her. My physical health has not been good. Not too long ago, I had a heart attack."

"I never heard about that," Dr. Benoit responded.

I added, "I was told it was minor but it certainly got my attention."

"How are they treating it?"

Before I had a chance to answer, the waitress placed a pastry in front of us. After she left I replied,

"I've changed my diet and I take medication. I'm also walking more."

"You need to listen to your doctor," Dr. Benoit insisted. "There is no reason you can't have a good recovery."

I placed my coffee cup on the saucer and said, "There is one thing I wanted to ask you."

"What is it?"

"Do you think there is any problem with me taking a long trip on an airplane?"

Dr. Benoit smiled and replied, "Would this trip be a trip to America?"

"Yes."

"Are you asking medically or psychologically?" Dr. Benoit asked, as he patted my arm.

"I guess both."

"If you take your medication and pace yourself, I don't see any problem with such a long trip. I really think it might be good for you to take this trip."

"Why do you say that?" I asked.

"Because I have learned as I have gotten older, that it is good to have closure. Of course, you are the only one who can make that decision."

I nodded in agreement, "I guess there is a part of me that wants to know what happened to my first life."

"Are you prepared for disappointment?" he asked.

"I guess I'm prepared for just about anything. I've had a wonderful life."

"Then I think you should go," Dr. Benoit said with approval.

• • •

One week later, I was on a Delta flight to New York City with a connector flight to Philadelphia. The closer we got to New York City the more anxious I became. I kept telling myself it was silly to be nervous about returning to the United States. It had been forty-seven years and, as far as anyone in the United States was concerned, I was dead. At the age of sixty-four, I no longer looked anything like the young man who had gone to war. My children jokingly referred to me as Einstein. Since Camille's death, I had let my white hair grow wild. I had always had trouble controlling my hair when it got longer. Now I kind of enjoyed my new look. In addition, I had grown a beard. Unlike my hair, it was neatly trimmed. After living in France most of my life, I now had a French accent when I spoke English.

When the man in customs looked at my passport, I held my breath until he signaled me to go. I quickly retrieved my baggage and headed to my connector flight to Philadelphia. When I landed in Philadelphia, I felt excitement about being in America. I watched as people walked by me. Everyone seemed to be in a hurry. I stopped to watch one of the T.V.s in the terminal. The sportscasters were talking about the upcoming college football season. It seemed odd to be listening about American football.

It took longer than expected at the Avis car rental booth. There was more paperwork involved because I was French. Finally, the woman at the desk shared options with me. I could have a compact or I could upgrade to a larger car. Having driven a Fiat for many years, the compact seemed plenty big. When I asked if it was a stick shift, she looked confused. She said the cars were automatic.

As I drove out of Philadelphia, everything seemed so strange. Everywhere I looked there was a place to get fast food or a place to buy gas.

As I pulled into Allentown, I felt something but wasn't sure what it was. I decided it must be nostalgia.

Although so much had changed, I could still see familiar sites. I became excited when I saw my old high school. It had been converted to a middle school. Before driving to the Holiday Inn, I drove down the street where I had grown up. The neighborhood had changed a lot. Many of the houses looked like they had been taken care of. There were some, however, that were in bad shape. I suspected some of them had been condemned. I felt like a kid as I turned down my old street. My house was one of the houses that had been maintained. As I slowed down to get a better look, the house looked better than I had remembered. A porch had been added, along with a closed-in garage. I noticed bikes in the front yard so I knew whoever lived there now had children. After sitting in the car a few minutes, I pulled away and proceeded down the street.

As I passed a few houses, I noticed a woman in the front yard playing with small children. She looked like she could be their grandmother. She was tall and had gray hair. As I slowed down, I realized the house was where Shannon O'Riley had lived. Shannon was tall and had red hair when I knew her. I wasn't sure, but I had a strong hunch that this grandmother might be Shannon O'Riley. I thought to myself, *I'll be damned.*

Since it was beginning to get dark, I wanted to get to the hotel. Tomorrow would be a busy day. I wasn't sure exactly what my plan would be, but I thought I might start off with a visit to the local newspaper. Before I arrived at the hotel, I stopped for dinner. No matter what I mentioned on the menu, the young lady behind the counter asked if I wanted to supersize it. I settled on a hamburger and fries, not supersized.

CHAPTER
FOURTY

For me, the logical starting point would be the newspaper. I realized my real purpose for coming to Allentown was to learn what had happened to certain people, especially my child. I couldn't exactly start knocking on doors. I certainly did not want people to know my identity. In some cases, it was also likely that some of the people no longer lived here.

Although getting to the newspaper building and finding a parking place was easy, it seemed almost impossible to get someone to help me. The person at the desk kept apologizing for my long wait. She was quick to point out that the newspaper had cut many positions. Finally, a young man who told me he was doing an internship took me to the archives room. He apologized for the old microfiche readers that were in the room. I assured him it was not a problem. He showed me the files that contained the microfiche. When I started to look through the files, he asked if it would be all right if he left. I assured him I would not have any problem going through the files and using the microfiche reader.

After he left, I tried to make sense of how things were organized. Starting in 1960, there appeared to be a pattern of organization for the microfiche. Before that time, it was difficult to find the microfiche organized in years. I stacked the microfiche in piles that I felt reflected the appropriate year.

I was almost to the point of frustration and giving up, when I saw the year 1943 clipped together. I immediately placed the first microfiche in the reader. After going through a few papers, it was easy to identify where the articles would be and where the obituaries were located.

I was getting pretty fast in scan reading, removing, and reloading the reader. I was going so fast I almost skipped over the obituary for a day in April. I backed up and there it was.

Local Serviceman John Thomas
Dies in France

The obituary went on to say that Private John Thomas had died in the service of his country in France. It mentioned a memorial service and a list of people who would be attending in loving memory of Private Thomas. The list included Diane Clark Thomas, his wife. There was no mention of a son or daughter. It seemed particularly strange to read about Diane's parents as people who would lovingly remember Private Thomas.

It is not every day you get to read your own obituary. Overall, I thought it read well. There was no mention of a secret drop behind enemy lines. The death notice itself was listed a month after the dog tag were lifted from John's body.

After reading my own obituary, I took a break and got a cup of coffee. When I returned to the archive room, .I got into the rhythm of loading and unloading microfiche into the reader. After I moved through 1944, I looked at a stack marked 1945. Although the microfiche files were not necessarily in order by month, they all were in the correct year. I was reading the papers from February when I stopped and dropped my head. It read:

Cpl. James Thomas USMC
Dies at Iwo Jima

It stated that Mr. and Mrs. Thomas had lost both
of their sons to the war. I felt remorse for my mother.
How difficult this must have been for her. She was a
loving, kind person who poured her life into her two
sons. Neither one of us could do wrong in her eyes.
She would have made such a wonderful grandmother.

After thinking about my mother as a grandmother,
I went back to 1944 to see if I had missed a birth
announcement for Diane Thomas. I never found any
mention of a birth under Diane's name. It would not
have surprised me if her father had made
arrangements so no notice appeared in the paper.

It was almost noon. I had learned of my death and
the death of my brother. I thought about taking a
break for lunch but decided against it. I began to feel
like a detective who was in hot pursuit to solve a
mystery. In this case, the mystery was the first stage
of my life.

It didn't take long before I stopped again. This time
I didn't stop on the obituary section. It was a wedding
announcement. Diane Thomas was going to marry
Douglas Bender. The announcement went on to say
that Douglas was the assistant pastor at the Baptist
Church where Diane's father was senior pastor. I
realized she had remarried within a year of my death.
I assumed that Douglas Bender was probably older
and certainly someone favored by Diane's father. My
feelings were mixed. Although surprised to see how
quickly she had remarried, I also felt good that she
had found someone who hopefully would make her
and her parents happy. There was no mention of a
child in the wedding notice.

After reading the wedding announcement, I did take a break to get crackers from a machine. When I returned, I continued on my mission. I found a few articles that mention Douglas Bender, stories concerning the church's mission.

I continued my review year by year. I knew that I was now in search of the death of my parents. Although they could have moved, it was unlikely. In 1964, I found the obituary for my mother. She was my current age, 64. Six months later, I found the notice for my father. The cause of death for my mother was listed as natural causes. I couldn't help but think she just wore out from living with my father and dealing with the death of two sons. My father had complications attributed to pneumonia. Alcohol was probably involved.

I learned much in my first day of research. Although I was hoping for closure, I found myself feeling sad at the end of the day. Over dinner at a small Italian restaurant, I reread the notes I had taken that day. As I sipped a second glass of wine, I thought, *What if Douglas Bender is the current pastor of the Baptist Church?*

The next day I drove to Diane's old house. I stopped in front and observed as two small black children played in the front yard. I then drove to the Baptist church. The church was in need of a paint job but basically looked like I remembered. The sign out front listed Reverend Douglas Bender just below the words "First Baptist Church." I wasn't sure what to do next.

I couldn't just walk in and say I was looking for Mrs. Bender. What would I say if Reverend Bender asked who I was? As I sat there wondering what to do, I noticed there were signs in the parking lot on the side of the church. I put the car in reverse and backed up enough to pull into the parking lot. The signs were for reserved parking for Reverend Bender and Reverend Wilson. Both of the parking spots were empty.

I parked my car and entered the building next to the church. I walked down a long hallway and came to an open space where a lady with blond hair that almost looked white was sitting at a desk. I slowly walked toward her desk. She asked, "May I help you?"

I replied, "I used to attend this church years ago. I was in town and thought I would come by."

"Reverend Bender is not here right now."

I responded, "I wasn't coming to see Reverend Bender. He wasn't here when I attended the church. I think his wife was a member."

She added, "I'm sure she was. Her father was the minister."

Sounding surprised I said, "Yes. That's right. If it's OK with you, I would like to walk around."

"Sure. Take your time. I'll open up the door to the church if you like."

"That would be great."

The secretary stood and remarked, "You speak with an accent."

"I've lived in France for many years."

"I would love to go to Paris," she said.

"You should do that. It is beautiful," I replied.

As the church secretary opened the door that would allow me to enter the church, I casually asked, "Does Mrs. Bender work at the church?"

She thought for a moment and then said, "I think she did at one time. She does a lot of volunteer work, especially at the public library."

When I had completed my walk through, I stopped at the desk to thank the secretary. She continued to talk about traveling and asked me questions about France and the snobbish French people. I assured her that was not true and that she would enjoy interacting with the French people. I thanked her for her wonderful hospitality, which brought a smile to her face.

Unless it had changed locations, I knew exactly where the public library was located. As I drove down a few side streets, it occurred to me there might be a few branch libraries, too. I continued toward the main library. It was the middle of the week and there were only a few cars in the library parking lot.

I entered through the main door and slowly walked up and down the various aisles. At the end of the main fiction aisle, there was a lady with gray hair placing books on the shelves. I casually walked around her and glanced back to get a better look. She was definitely in the right age group to be Diane. Her hair was pulled up on top of her head. She was wearing glasses that were strategically placed on the end of her nose. The lady looked a little overweight. The dress she was wearing reminded me of something an older person might wear. I also noticed she had a boot-like cast on her right foot. The more I looked at her, the more I realized she looked like the stereotypical librarian. I acted as if I was looking for a particular book as I slowly made my way down the aisle behind where she was stacking books. Her face reminded me of Diane's, but I wasn't sure. I didn't really know what to do next. She noticed I was looking for a book and asked if she could help me find anything.

"I'm just browsing," I responded.

"Let me know if I can help."

I casually turned back and said, "I was wondering if you knew Mrs. Bender."

"I'm Mrs. Bender. Who are you?"

I had to clear my throat before I could say another word, "Mrs. Bender, I was a friend of your husband's in the war. We served together."

Diane stared at me, as if she did not know what to say. She removed her glasses and spoke, "Do you mean John Thomas?"

"Yes. We were both stationed at Milton Hall in England."

She dropped her arms at her side and sighed, "I can't believe this. Give me a minute and we will talk."

With the large medical boot on her right foot, she slowly made her way to the counter. She said something to the lady who was standing there. She then went over to a desk and opened the bottom drawer. She pulled out her purse and hobbled toward the front door. She then turned and motioned for me to follow her. Once outside, she said, "We can sit on the bench out front. It's not good to talk in the library."

I added, "If this is a bad time, I can come back.

"I'm a volunteer. Besides, I will be leaving shortly."

We made our way to the bench that was located beneath a huge shade tree. After she sat down, I took a seat next to her and turned so we could talk. Before I could say anything, she touched me on the arm and said, "You don't sound like you are from here. Why are you in Allentown?"

I answered, "I'm French, but I'm visiting family in Philadelphia and decided to look up John's wife."

She smiled and said, "That's very thoughtful. I was only his wife for such a short time. We were very young."

Smiling, I said, "I remember him saying that."

She asked, "Why would someone French be serving with John?"

"We were a special team made up of Americans, British and French. We were dropped behind enemy lines."

"How well did you know John?"

I replied, "I think I knew him pretty well. We lived and trained together for months. In the evening, we would sit and talk about home."

"Did he ever mention me?" she asked; her voice getting softer as she spoke.

"Yes," I said, "many times."

She rolled her eyes and said, "I'm surprised."

"Why do you say that?" I asked.

"Before he left, I wasn't very good to him. We were just so young."

"He never mentioned anything like that."

"Did he say anything nice?" she asked.

"He mentioned the river."

Diane turned red, lifting her hands to her face. "I can't believe he would mention that," she said.

I added, "He just said there were wonderful times at the river."

Lifting her eyebrows Diane commented, "It was a summer I will never forget."

"I think he said the same thing."

Diane continued, "I still don't understand why you would go out of your way to come and see me."

"When you get older," I said, "you think of a lot of things. I just felt a need."

She asked, "Were you with John when he died?"

"No. I was on a different mission."

A few seconds passed and Diane added, "You will need to meet my son. He is coming to pick me up. I can't drive with this boot on."

"What happened to your foot?" I asked.

"I fell off a ladder. Sometimes I feel so old."

Without sounding too eager, I asked, "You mentioned your son was picking you up. How many children do you have?"

"I have three grown children and too many grandchildren to count."

"Boys or girls?"

She replied, "Two boys and a girl. My daughter is the youngest."

I asked, "Who's picking you up?"

"My oldest son. He's the one I can count on to take care of his mother."

"What does he do?"

"He's a teacher at the high school."

There was so much more I wanted to ask. This had to be our son she was talking about. Then again, maybe there was something wrong with the pregnancy. There was never a mention of a child in the papers I read.

As I was thinking of something to say, Diane patted me on the arm and said, "Edward is John's son. He never saw his father. Douglas adopted Edward when we got married. He is the only father Edward has known. When he was in high school, I decided to tell him. My father didn't want me to, but I felt it was the right thing to do. I was going to name him John when he was born, but my father talked me out of it."

My chest tightened. I felt a huge lump in my throat. I was hoping my eyes would not tear up. I took a deep breath and smiled.

Diane looked up and said, "Here he is. His youngest daughter is with him, I want you to meet them."

Edward parked the car and walked to the bench where we were sitting. He looked like his mother. His skin complexion and facial features were like Diane's. He was taller than both of us and looked fit, like someone who worked out on a regular basis. His daughter got out of the car, jogging to catch up with her father.

I could not believe what I was seeing. His daughter looked like Diane when I knew her. She had the same wavy brown hair and light skin complexion. She was wearing cutoff jeans and a short T-shirt, which reminded me of Diane when she would wear her midriff blouse to the river. The resemblance was uncanny. I kept staring at her as they got closer.

When they reached the bench, Diane stood up and said, "I want you to meet somebody. I'm sorry; what was your name?"

"Joseph Bernhardt."

Looking at me Diane said, "Edward and Missi, this is Joseph Bernhardt. He knew your father in the war."

Edward clarified Diane's introduction by saying, "You knew John Thomas?"

I replied, "Yes, I trained with him in England. We became friends."

"What are you doing in Allentown?" he asked.

"I was visiting people in Philadelphia and decided to make the drive to Allentown. I remembered John lived here. I was able to locate your mother because I remembered John saying his wife's father was a Baptist minister."

"I'm glad you did. I don't know many people who knew my father. It's very nice of you to look us up. This is my daughter, Missi."

At the same time, both of us said, "Pleased to meet you."

Missi laughed and then asked, "Are you French?"

"Yes. I guess my accent gave me away."

She giggled and said, "Just a little bit. Can I ask you a question?"

"Certainly," I replied.

"What was my grandfather like?"

This question caught me off guard. It hit me hard that I was talking to my granddaughter about myself. Edward sensed that I was having difficulty getting my words out and said, "Missi, that was a long time ago."

I responded, "That's OK, I just needed to think a moment. Your grandfather was fun to be around. He had a good sense of humor. I think he was a good man who tried to do the right thing."

Edward commented, "Maybe that's the best all of us can hope for. I do appreciate you sharing that."

I replied, "You're welcome. I think John would be proud of all of you."

Edward asked, "Are you going to be able to stay a few days?"

"I leave tomorrow."

Edward replied, "It was a pleasure meeting you. I've got to get Mom home so I can get back to school. We have an open house tonight."

Edward shook my hand. I was surprised to get a hug from Missi.

Diane looked at me and said, "Give me a hug." We hugged for longer than I had expected.

While her head was next to mine she said, "Thanks for coming."

After they left the parking lot, I sat back on the bench. I never dreamed I would be able to see Diane, my son, and one of my granddaughters. I felt good about their lives. There was a moment I wanted them to know the truth. I realized, however, that their lives and mine were better left as is. I was reluctant to make this trip. Now, I felt very much at peace. Dr. Benoit was right when he told me I needed closure.

CHAPTER FOURTY ONE

The following day was my last day in Allentown. My flight from Philadelphia was in the late evening so I planned to use the morning hours for a few last visits. My first stop was Dunkin' Donuts. At Camille's café in Lille, I was constantly having customers ask for American coffee. After stopping at Dunkin' Donuts for coffee, I was beginning to understand why customers asked for American coffee. I purchased a large cup for myself, and three bags of coffee to take back home. I decided it might be interesting to test the Dunkin Donut coffee at the café.

I made sure the lid was tight on my coffee and returned to my car. At first, I didn't see any need to visit the river, but after seeing Diane, I decided I wanted to at least drive by. I placed the coffee cup in the carrier next to the dash and turned on the main highway. Although it was a short drive to where I wanted to go, I had difficulty locating roads. Everything looked so different. After going down the wrong road and having to turn around, I found the road I was looking for. Most of the area was now used for businesses. I saw several large warehouses and trucks that were used for shipping. I was beginning to think the park area I was looking for no longer existed. I kept driving until I reached an area that looked like a small park.

I parked the car and grabbed my cup of coffee. There was a small path behind a row of swing sets that I followed to an opening where there was a picnic table next to the river. I wasn't sure if this was the exact place I had taken Diane, but it had to be very close.

I sat on the bench next to the picnic table and opened my coffee. As I took sips from the cup, I tried to remember the summer of 1943. I could visualize Diane in the water without any clothes. I could also see us wrapped up in a blanket on the riverbank. We were kids full of passion and desire. We really didn't care about consequences or how our actions might change our lives forever.

I continued to drink my coffee and enjoy the breeze that was hitting my face. I thought of how Diane blushed when I told her John had mentioned the river. She said it was a summer she would never forget. The tone of her voice and her facial expression led me to believe she was remembering the passion and the tenderness. When I finished my coffee, I stood and walked down next to the water. I placed my hands behind my back and watched the water flow over the rocks close to shore. A smile came to my face and I thought, *I will always remember the river.*

I knew the cemetery where my grandparents were buried and I assumed this was where my parents were buried also. The drive was across town and I still needed to check out of the hotel. Even if I could only stop for a few minutes, I felt going to the cemetery was the right thing to do. When they died, they did not have children to attend their funerals and burials. It seemed odd, but I felt obligated to show my final respects. As the years passed, I began to view my father differently. I think he did the best he knew how to do. Alcohol brought the worst out in him. For the sake of my mother, I hoped he had changed and that their last years had been better.

The cemetery was large. I couldn't remember exactly where the burial plots were located. I drove the car to where I thought my grandparents were buried. When I got out of the car, I noticed that a burial service was taking place close to where I wanted to look.

I started walking through the cemetery, reading headstones as I went. I stayed away from the burial ceremony by walking close to the road. I went up and down rows, I thought maybe I was in the wrong section. I went a little farther and I saw the names of my grandfather and grandmother on headstones. My parents had to be in the same area. I saw the headstone of my father, followed by my mother's. When I walked closer to their graves, I noticed two other headstones. One belonged to my brother James and one was mine. Immediately, I had tightness in my chest and felt my heart racing. I did not expect to see this. I was overwhelmed with emotion and began to cry. My crying became sobs as I fell to my knees. My breathing returned to normal, but the tears flowed as they fell on my own grave.

I could not hold back the tears. Finally, I put my hands on my face trying to muffle the sound of my crying. I felt a pat on my shoulder. When I stood up, there was a young priest who must have been part of the burial ceremony, standing in front of me.

He said, "Sir, are you OK?"

I answered, "Yes, I will be fine."

He said, "I'm sorry for your loss."

"Thank you. I grieve for my father, mother, and brother but I do not grieve for the other man because God granted him a wonderful second life."

The priest had a puzzled look on his face and squeezed my shoulder with his right hand and smiled. He then walked toward the people who were leaving the gravesite of the recent burial.

I returned to my car and sat in the driver's seat, staring out the window. Dr. Benoit was right about closure. I realized that I would be leaving with no regrets because God had not only granted me a second life, but he had also granted Diane a second life too.

About the Author

    Dr. Bob Williams is retired faculty in the College of Education at the University of Central Florida. He has worked as a teacher, school psychologist, principal, and superintendent of schools.

    Dr. Williams has published articles and coauthored a leadership book for educators. In addition, he has been a keynote speaker at several different conferences and workshops. In 2014 he wrote a coming of age novel, *The Eastside of Town*. He and his wife, Linda, live in Orlando, Florida.